MW01234393

Para Jeanette,
Con mucho cariño
Ricardo Aponte

A TRUE FRIENDSHIP

This book is a must read that teases you with the Introduction and leaves you wanting more right up to the end. It is not a book that is easy to put down; you want to find out what happens next and keep turning the pages. Ricardo Aponte delivers, he has a writing style that is easy to follow and he has drawn on his military background to get the facts rights then blends in action, intrigue and just a touch of romance.

Despite being geographically close to the United States events is Central and South America seldom gets much coverage in the U.S. media. This novel takes you on an adventure that features several memorable characters involved in the American support of the Colombian government in the ongoing war against the rebels and drug traffickers in that country.

Just when you think you have it figured out the author introduces another sub plot or twist that only heightens your need to turn the page to see the outcome. The author has obviously encountered situations similar to those in the novel and intrinsically incorporates these into every chapter. He introduces insights that many of us would never have considered concerning the inner workings of the rebels groups while highlighting the complicated and fragile relationships that hold them together.

It is easy to say this novel makes you "root for the good guys and ladies" as for me I am rooting for this author to publish his next book. It has been a long time since I found a book that hooked me so quickly and left me wanting more from the author.

Brigadier General Leon Johnson, Retired

A TRUE FRIENDSHIP

A HOSTAGE DRAMA

RICO APONTE

To order additional copies of this book, contact:
Xlibris Corporation
1-888-795-4274
www.Xlibris.com
Orders@Xlibris.com
48131

CONTENTS

A NOTE FROM THE AUTHOR

As I write this the situation for the many hostages kept for political and monetary benefit by various illegal armed groups in Colombia has improved somewhat. Yet there are simply too many hostages still kept in subhuman conditions by these forces. In particular, the Fuerzas Armadas de Revolución Colombiana (FARC) keeps around fifty high value hostages. Their most famous captive is female. Her name is Ingrid Betancourt a one time candidate for the presidency in Colombia.

Her plight has come to the world's attention in recent months when the government of Venezuela interceded with the FARC and obtained the release of half a dozen of these high value captives. In another development photos and home movies of Betancourt and three American hostages surfaced after a raid of a FARC hideout in Colombia's capital Bogotá.

Marc Gonsalves, Keith Stansell, and Thomas Howes were contractors working in support of the U.S. and Colombian governments when their aircraft crashed in the high terrain of the Andes Mountains. Taken prisoner by the FARC they just marked the fifth year anniversary of their capture. Yet the world community seems in no hurry to force the FARC into releasing them nor their many hostages.

This book is a work of fiction centered about the capture of a high ranking U. S. Air Force officer by the FARC. I hope the story line helps bring to the forefront of the American conscience the plight of Marc, Keith and Tom. All characters except for the hostages named above are fictitious and any similarities with living persons is purely coincidental.

On 2 July 2008, Colombian military forces like the ones described in this book rescued Ingrid Betancourt and fourteen other hostages including the three American hostages. Congratulations go out to them on their success and the joy the families of the hostages must feel. This book is still dedicated to the three Americans now that they start a period of adjustment after rescue.

Of course I would like to thank the personnel of XLibris that made the transition to self-publishing author so simple and to my family that supported my many months of work in this novel.

FOR MARC, TOM AND KEITH

PROLOGUE

Impossible, this never happens to me! He had previously spied a beautiful woman at the airport boarding gate, and she was now preparing to sit next to him in the airplane cabin and, to his surprise, was extending her long slender arm to introduce herself.

"Hi, I am Rosario. I suppose you are going to Madrid on business." *Wow, and direct too!* He fumbled for a moment and replied in total honesty, "Hello, I am Carlos Cortes. You are mistaken, I am traveling through on business and going much farther."

She was ravishing, ash blonde, blue eyes, about five feet ten, and sported an astonishing figure that her business suit accented perfectly. She spoke perfect English with a slight Castilian accent. Her movements in the cabin were efficient, no fumbling about while putting away the carry-on bags and sitting down quietly next to him. She took a moment to place the last bag in the area underneath the seat in front and continued, "I was in Washington DC on business, but now am going home for a well-deserved rest."

At that point, they were interrupted by one of the highly unnecessary flight attendant announcements made during the boarding process, one that was probably conceived either by the Federal Aviation Administration or by corporate lawyers fearing a lawsuit of some kind. Finally, after what seemed an inordinate amount of time, the announcer ended with "And have a pleasant flight."

The good news is that he had not lost her. Instantly she turned to him and continued her thought. "My, you Washingtonians surely have some wicked traffic. No one seems to know where they are going, and those that do normally are speeding by blatantly over the posted limits."

Carlos replied, "Now that's where you are wrong again."

"Why? Are you of the opinion that traffic in Madrid is worse. At least people there know where they are going," she said quickly.

"No," continued Carlos, "I was born and bred in Los Angeles where I work happily for the Los Angeles Police Department."

She blushed instantly. Nobody could blame her; they were boarding their international flight at Dulles International Airport, Virginia, and Carlos was dressed in an immaculate business suit. He looked the part of a Washington businessman. He was in his late twenties, six feet two, and obviously in good shape. He had volunteered to work in Kuwait in support of our nation's efforts to reconstitute the police department of Kuwait just after coalition forces forced Iraqi troops out during Operation Desert Storm.

It was early May 1991, and Carlos was facing six hard months of volunteer duty. A duty that he sought out eagerly, he wanted to do something in support of his nation. Carlos had never been in the military, and he felt this duty would pay back in part his lack of previous service.

The conversation proceeded along into different aspects of Rosario's and Carlos' life. They talked about the fears all young adults face, and surprisingly, they were very similar even though their countries were so distant from each other. *Maybe it was because both of us came from Hispanic families,* thought Carlos.

Rosario was an export business apprentice. She was on company business in the USA. Carlos thought it was funny for an apprentice to go on an overseas trip, and she had let it slip that part of her business was at the Spanish embassy in Washington. But then, she was obviously very competent and would rise very fast in her line of work.

After a couple of hours, Carlos became aware that it was not her beauty that kept him enthralled with their conversation. The woman was extremely intelligent and well read. Her mind was as beautiful as her face. Carlos was smitten.

If the same was true of Rosario's feelings, it was not possible to read it in her expression. Carlos too was accomplished; he had graduated from UCLA with a degree in criminology and was presently working on a master's degree when the volunteer assignment to Kuwait put his studies and career with the LAPD on hold. Still a patrolman, he was hoping to get a promotion to detective as soon a he returned from the Middle East.

Soon, the seven-and-a-half-hour flight went by in a flash. It was on descent that Rosario surprised him again. Without prompting, she passed a piece of paper to him and said, "When you finish your tour in six months, why don't you come to Madrid and visit my great city. I will be your guide if you let me."

Carlos said to himself, *I've died and gone to heaven.*

"Of course you can be my guide, I will be honored," Carlos quickly replied. "Is this your telephone number?"

"No, by the time you come back from the desert, I will have moved. This is the telephone number of my office, they will be able to get a hold of me if I am not there when you call. Similarly, the address is my work address. Write to me soon and let me know how you are doing please."

He said, "Your wish is my command."

After they had parted at the airport, Carlos to the Transfer line and Rosario to Arrivals, Carlos could have kicked himself twice. Once because he could not believe his luck, carefully stowing Rosario's note in his wallet; and second, when he realized that he had never asked for her last name. *I hope that she is the only Rosario that works there,* he thought.

CHAPTER ONE

C ongressman Dan Smolen, (D) Florida, asked his question not knowing the answer. "Tell me, General, of all the money we have spent supporting Colombia in the last ten years, where was the money best spent?"

Brigadier General Jose "Pepe" Ramirez, a career air force officer, command pilot, and now serving as the director of operations for the U.S. Southern Command replied, "Sir, undoubtedly it is the money that supports the training and professional development of the noncommissioned officer of the Colombian armed forces. And that is the very same money that your staffers are trying to cut for the next fiscal year."

"Noncommissioned, you mean sergeants, don't you?"

"Yes, sir, in fact, the premier project was the Senior NCO Academy that we helped set up." Pepe was getting grilled; the questions were getting into the meat of his biggest mission, which was the support of the Colombian government's fight against insurgents and drug traffickers ruining their country. Any funding lost to budget slashers was going to impact negatively on the overall program. So he was answering the questions posed by the subcommittee's ranking member with his charismatic determination.

What Pepe did not know was that secretly Congressman Smolen supported his mission fully. In 1981, he had lost a family member to a drug overdose; one of approximately twenty thousand American lives lost to drugs per year. Since then, the ten-term Democrat never voted against the drug war funding. For appearances however, and constituent support, he never gave in easily to Pentagon budgeters.

"And may I add, sir," Pepe said. "It is this kind of training that is needed the most all over the hemisphere. In Latin America, the caste system is alive and well. Poor people have no hope to improve their lot. It is in the military or in the guerrilla movement where they enjoy the best chance of improving their chances in life. We are merely trying to shift the balance of popular support in the democratically elected government's favor."

Jose Luis was his given name; Pepe was the popular nickname for those so named. When he entered the air force at the tender age of twenty-one, Pepe kept his nickname as his nom de guerre. Every pilot needed one, usually assigned by his squadron's mates; but in Pepe's favor, his usual nickname stuck. He was typical height for a fighter pilot, five feet seven tall, and sported a thick torso. Wherever he went, he was quite popular with his peers and superiors alike. Most importantly, it was his subordinates that truly liked him. Pepe's executive officer, Lieutenant Commander Jim Joyner, was one of those. Jim protected his boss from all the day-to-day pressures of such an important joint command position. Right now he was fidgeting in his seat as he listened to the questions.

His boss was doing fine. For the past forty-five minutes, he had answered every question correctly and completely. Never flustered, Pepe radiated the same quiet confidence all general officers in the nation's armed forces were famous for.

Congressman Smolen ended the session without giving the general any indication if he had succeeded or not. "Well, General Ramirez, thank you for your candid commentary. You will be hearing from us soon."

Twenty minutes later in his congressional office, the congressman called his military assistant Pedro Duque aside and said, "Pedro, I like this man. Make sure we put up the necessary public release critical of the Defense budget, but in the budget battle ahead, I want the Southern Command budget fully funded. After all, it is in our backyard."

Rafael "El Jefe" Terraza sat in his jungle hut in apparent comfort. A marked man, Rafael had been on the run for the past twenty years from Colombian government authorities. The army was looking for him, the police too; and now, various U.S. agencies were also on the hunt. He had seen and heard different types of U.S. aircraft, both manned and unmanned, quietly combing the countryside for his whereabouts. However, here in his jungle headquarters, he felt safe and secure.

He was in command of the Cucho Ramos Armed Front (CRAF), one of six independent groups that comprised the FARC forces. At his command were two thousand five hundred men and women that had committed their life to armed insurrection. His area of responsibility was southeastern Colombia—a terrain consisting of jungle habitat, navigable rivers, and borders with Ecuador, Peru, and Brazil.

Today was his monthly meeting with the CRAF leadership. This included his local commander Moncho Rivera, his second in command Manuel "León" Alonso, and his treasurer and life partner Mona Pedroso. Other section commanders would be informed of the decisions reached here. Distance and the poor condition of roads did not permit larger meetings of the CRAF leadership.

It was Moncho who arrived first for the meeting. He was a quiet but very effective leader; an observer, Moncho did not speak much normally, so it surprised Rafael when he seemed short of breath and excited. It was Moncho who spoke first, "I have terrible news, Jefe. It seems that there was a surprise attack on the river house early this morning, and we lost many men."

"Relax, Moncho, I have never seen you more excited. You know what the doctor said of your heart condition."

"Jefe, they got Mona. She is not dead, apparently they raided the house in order to capture her. It was an operation by the army's

Special Forces carried in and out by helicopters. They had direct knowledge of her exact location . . . I am sorry."

Rafael was speechless. *Mona, his lifetime love, captured?* For a moment, he did not think of her primary responsibility, the management of drug profits and arms purchases. He could only think of his partner and the thousands of little things they shared the past twenty years.

Still calm, Rafael asked, "How many men did we lose?"

"Fourteen killed, three of them women, and seven wounded. All of the wounded are doing fine. Only the cook was unharmed. He was found in the kitchen when my forces reached the house."

"I want the cook questioned, there must have been a mole," theorized Rafael out loud. He was slowly recovering from the initial shock from the news.

A voice from the door replied. "The cook is dead. I killed him myself, and my troops are tracking down his family to kill them also," said Manuel "León" Alonso the vice commandant of the CRAF.

"What? I wanted to question him. They took Mona!" Rafael said, almost shouting in desperation.

León answered quickly, "I did. He confessed that military officers had offered him money and resettlement for his entire family in the USA if he would turn in Mona. His family—wife, mother, and three children—are traveling to town to get resettled. Don't worry, they will not get far. Manolo is waiting for them at the first river transfer station, they will all soon be dead too."

"Still, León, the cook's life and that of his family were not for you to take. That is my decision and responsibility," countered Rafael.

León countered icily, "I thought you would be too emotionally involved with Mona's capture to react correctly on this, Jefe."

"Angry, yes," replied Rafael, now shouting. "Never underestimate me or my position as your commander, León. We will react to this, and it will not be an emotional effort. It will be cold and calculated, we most get Mona back. She is the key to our money, and that cannot fall on the government's hands."

Rafael thought, *No, it will not be emotional. We must do something fast to get her back.*

Rock, the agent's tactical name, had arrived at the U.S. embassy. As the field agent in charge for counterdrug operations, he kept quite busy. He worked for Warren Westback, a contemporary officer at the Central Intelligence Agency but now the embassy's Agency chief. He was now entering Warren's office. It was 7:00 PM.

"Success, Warren, we got her. Mona is now in custody at General Escobedo's headquarters."

Warren looked up and replied in his customary dry manner, "Hope these barbarians have not killed her yet. We need to get all the information we can out of her."

"Warren, how many times do I have to tell you that the Colombian Army is a very professional armed force? Sure, they have a checkered past and have been accused occasionally of brutality. But believe me, General Escobedo is a competent leader that abhors inhuman treatment. He will not tolerate it of his personnel."

"Rock, how many times do I have to tell you not to call me by my first name? I am your boss, am I not?"

"Whatever you say, Warren! Let me get back to my desk, the DDO will be happy to read my report of the abduction tomorrow morning."

"Our report, Rock," replied Warren.

"Of course, our report, Warren." Rock sighed as he walked back to his cubicle.

Rock had been quite busy the past three days with the planning and execution of Mona's capture. The messages had piled up in his in-box, and he had at least three weekly reports to send out to Langley. He took a look at his desk, disregarded all the work pending, and started to write his report.

It was a classic raid and abduction operation that the U.S. Delta Force was very capable of accomplishing. However, in this case, it was Colombian troops that performed the action. For the past three years, they had received training from the Delta Force and were now quite capable themselves.

The breakthrough in this case was provided by imagery from a Predator drone. Three days ago, a Predator had provided pictures of a group of twenty guerrillas disembarking at a known jungle stronghold of the FARC. What excited the CIA the most was the confirmation by CIA analysts that Mona, the financial officer of the southeastern terrorist cell, was positively identified as one of them.

Twelve hours later, General Escobedo had received confirmation from a mole that Mona was at a known safe house of the FARC. The only stipulation the general had was that the mole had requested movement and resettlement in the USA for him and his family. Although Warren at first balked at the idea, he reluctantly permitted Rock to request permission from Langley.

The permission was late coming, so was the response from the Colombian Air Force for the forces necessary to carry out the raid. In the end, however, all came about in three short but suspense-filled days. The operation was started by the infiltration of forty-four well-armed Special Forces ten kilometers upstream of the FARC safe house. They were dropped off UH-60 helicopters and carried their own assault rubber boats that they used to move downstream. The assault was done quietly and efficiently. Anybody asleep near the house was killed where they slept. The only reaction from FARC forces came after the abduction of Mona. The noise of the incoming helicopters and support aircraft woke other guerrillas in the area, and a firefight ensued. Colombian forces suffered two casualties, both minor wounds, and caused multiple casualties on the guerrillas when an AC-47 razed their lines with 20 mm and 7.62 mm Gatling gun support fire.

Rock finished his report about 10:00 PM. After Warren edited the report twice, he sent the message electronically to Langley and went home to his apartment for a well-earned rest. The messages and reports can wait until tomorrow, thought Rock.

Little did he know that the CIA report that would change his life forever was waiting to be read at the top of his in-box.

María Elena Borbón was at that moment waiting in the control room of the Spanish embassy in Honduras. She had ten of her agents deployed throughout the capital city, Tegucigalpa, in support of an operation to capture a well-known Honduran arms trafficker, Jose Manuel Padilla, "El Mocho." She had provided her agents in support of Honduran authorities. They feared that most of the local agents had been compromised with the traffickers and would be killed if they attempted to infiltrate the group.

María Elena had done this kind of operation many times before. Even though it was her first in Honduras, she was capable of completing special missions in almost any country that had diplomatic relations with Spain and, in one occasion, in one that was at odds with her country.

Watching a monitor, she whispered into her microphone a question to the lead agent forward, "Luis, are the exits covered?"

Luis Vigo, her partner for many years, took the question in stride for it was neither unexpected nor necessary. He replied, "Yes, when have I failed you? And you do not have to whisper, María, I can hardly hear you."

The trap was ready. The team of Spanish agents had lured the head of the largest Honduran arms for drugs trafficker to a Tegucigalpa hotel for a payoff after the transfer that afternoon of a truckload of AK-47s. He was invited to dine with the couple that represented ETA in Honduras and suspected nothing. In fact, he was very interested in dining with Johanna, one of the Spanish agents, since she would always tend to take his side and would make flattering glances at him whenever Luis, her husband, wasn't looking.

María Elena liked how Johanna handled men, and it reminded her of how she had done that early in her own career. For women like them, men were easy prey. Johanna was a striking beauty. Now twenty-eight, she was unmarried and enjoyed making men sweat when they approached her the first time. Most of the men in her team would gladly spend the night with her, but all of them were easily turned away. Johanna would not go out with married men. María Elena knew that when she selected her for the team.

In a way, María Elena and Johanna were the elite of Spanish secret operatives. Beautiful young women very devoted to the job. Most of them were unmarried, and most of them kept men at arm's length. In María Elena's case, love had only happened once, and she quickly put that instance away in her quest for service to her country. Her father had been the director of operations for the Center of Studies, Information, and Defense of the Spanish government; CEID was its Spanish acronym. In María Elena's case, the position of her father was in her sights, and she would give anything to rise to it as quickly as possible. She was not too far off; as the director of the arms trafficking office, she was only two promotions away from the job.

Luis interrupted her thoughts. "The party arrived. We are shutting down the hotel."

"Careful now," María Elena countered.

The operation was very efficient; the parties met in a conference room provided for business meetings. Johanna pulled the lead boss aside for a private conversation while his deputy counted the money. Once the signal was given, it did not take long for the agents to have everyone on the floor. Johanna took special delight in bringing her mark down. Imagine the surprise, one moment he was thinking of many romantic advances with Johanna; the next moment, he was laid spread-eagled on the floor by the very same woman he desired.

Once Johanna said, "All clear," Luis and his men went into the room and policed everyone quickly. The operation, two months in the making, lasted only ten minutes to unfold. Luis got on the radio and told his boss of the operation's success.

"Good, I can go home now to Charlie," said María Elena.

CHAPTER TWO

The next morning, Rock arrived at the embassy at 7:30 AM. In the early morning hours, Bogotá is just as peaceful a city as any in the world; it is a cosmopolitan city with many high-rises and several tourism-inspired areas where the night life is lively and the food is superb.

In 2004, the problem with Bogotá is the criminal element. It is the single most dangerous city in the hemisphere. Robberies, assaults, kidnappings, and terrorist events dominate the police blotter many times, transcending borders and making headline news throughout the world.

Rock felt very safe in his Toyota Land Cruiser. It was this year's model and was safeguarded with armored doors and bullet-resistant tinted glass. Of course, it could not survive a rocket-propelled grenade, but still it was the safest mode of transportation for a low-level embassy worker like him. He drove it daily from his apartment parking garage to the embassy lot in less than fifteen minutes and was never stopped by police due to the diplomatic plates his car sported.

When he got off his car, he was greeted by Pedro Muñiz, one of the local embassy drivers and a very friendly type. Pedro was recruited from the retired ranks of the Bogotá Police Department where he was a bodyguard for the police chief himself.

"Buenos días, Señor Cortes. Es un día muy bonito."

"Si lo es, Pedro," replied Rock as he quickly walked toward the marine checkpoint. As he processed his badge with the marines, he thought to himself that next time he should talk more to Pedro than he normally did. He knew of no one that liked being acknowledged with a short standard answer. Pedro was a very competent driver. He had once saved a previous ambassador from certain capture by everyday carjackers when he had expertly maneuvered the car out of a roadblock that was designed to stop the ambassador's motorcade.

Rock got to his desk and stared at the mountain of paperwork just waiting to be processed. Among his many duties, Rock was the security chief for the entire embassy staff and was responsible for the evacuation of the embassy personnel in the event a major disaster occurred or any other event that may put U.S. citizens in danger. That was enough work for ten people, but in most embassies, the job belonged to the CIA agent that was second in command. Rock would have loved for Warren to take up some of these responsibilities; but in Warren's case, it was a blessing he did not tackle these duties for it would be a disaster in the hands of such a mediocre agent.

His office was a spartan cubicle full of regional studies and historical books and an occasional picture. Of the three things that were immediately obvious when a stranger walked into his office, one was the ornate Mexican nameplate on his desk; it read,

Carlos Cortes
Agricultural Officer

The second was the diploma certifying that he had received a master's degree in agriculture from the University of California in Los Angeles. Lastly, it was the picture of a very happy couple in what seemed to be a European setting, and the girl in the picture was absolutely beautiful.

Before he made his first cup of coffee, he decided to read the message traffic that had accumulated the last three days. There were approximately ten reports in his In basket and thirty-five messages in his Outlook folder.

The top report on his desk, classified Top Secret/NF, was short, and it read,

FM CIA HQ/DDI

TO HQ PENTAGON JCS/J2/J3/J5

HQ USSOUTHCOM/J2/J3/J5

HQ EUCOM/J2/J3/J5

DOS/WHEM-AD/LATAM/NATO/EU

DEPSECDEF/SOLIC/INL

FIELD AGENTS/CENTAM/SOAM/CARIB/EU

Subj: Sting Operation-Arms Trafficking

Various methods used in obtaining following information. For details see URL: httpse://nisc.ref.gov/case_1256.9879/details.htm.

1. *Honduran police is setting up sting operation to capture arms merchant Jose Manuel Padilla, aka El Mocho. Operation is being run by Spanish CEID agents. Reportedly Honduran authorities requested the support of the CEID after other international police organizations refused cooperation.*

2. *Operation slated to conclude the week of 6-14-04. Operation being run by CEID field agent Rosario. NISC expects successful conclusion.*

End of Report

Rock closed the report and put it on his TS destroy box. As he was getting ready to read the second report, he stopped and, on impulse, turned to his computer and entered the URL address mentioned in the previous report. To his amazement, he found an update to the previous report that read,

TOP SECRET-NF

case_1256.9879

> *Reported by Spanish CEID agent Luis Vigo. Previous contact with excellent credentials and access.*

> *CEID team consists of agent in charge María Elena Borbón, Luis Vigo, and Johanna Valenz plus seven others.*

Note: Successful apprehension of El Mocho and three accomplices reported on 6-16-04, 1930 hours. Agent Rosario, tactical name, responsible for apprehension of Honduran arms trafficker.

There it was again, that name Rosario. *Could it be? No*, he said to himself, *coincidences like this only happen in the movies. Wasn't it Garth Brooks that sang "Unanswered Prayers" and the end result of that song was a very awkward meeting with a previous love interest?*

He attempted to return to the daily routine, but every time he dove into his work, his mind wandered; and after a few seconds, he went back thirteen years.

In the fall of 1991, the world was full of hope. The Iraqi Army was defeated, the international community had joined together in a common goal, and the world economy was busy in improving our lot. The only problem was the lack of confidence people in the United States felt toward their government's ability to bring about the needed changes to improve the economy.

If this was true of most U.S. citizens, it was not true of Carlos Cortes as he headed west again out of Southwest Asia and into the modern world. He was full of optimism and hope. His tour in Kuwait was very busy, sometimes predictable, and always boring. He had, in six very short months, come to admire the Kuwaiti spirit and despise the air of superiority that most Americans over there exuded. However, he was ready to change this. He knew that in the USA, the attitude was "If it is broke—fix it; if it isn't broke—leave it alone." All they needed was a dose of reality, one that surely would come with the communications revolution that was now evident.

However, his thought process had one detour; he was intent in visiting Rosario. For the last six months, he had not shaken her positive attitude or her beautiful body away from his conscious thoughts. So at the end of September, he had called her number in Madrid and left a note that he was coming back in November. The gentleman at the other end of the line seemed to know her very well, and he promised to pass on the message. He informed him that her full name was Rosario Marin. Three days later, he got a callback from Rosario herself, and she seemed truly excited that he had remembered her.

By early October, the date was set. Carlos would be in Madrid on Friday, November 1, 1991, All Saints' Day. Rosario had agreed to meet him at the airport and help him get settled at a nice bed-and-breakfast in the middle of town. She had promised to give him a tour of the city and was very open about her excitement about their upcoming meeting.

On that day, Rosario was waiting at the airport the moment he arrived. Their meeting was both cordial and sincere. Carlos saw her the moment he cleared the immigration booth at the airport. When they approached, Carlos, having learned the European-style greeting, kissed her on both cheeks. If only for a very short moment, he felt that the trip was worthwhile right then and there. To be close to her after six months, to be able to feel her presence, and to be able to peer into her eyes, life could not get better, thought the hardworking policeman.

Rosario said, "Carlos, are you all right? You are thinner now."

"I am fine, Rosario, what you see is the result of six months of hard exercise and no alcohol or fast food on my body."

"Mi vida. We will have to do something about that," said Rosario.

They did not skip a bit; the conversation while Rosario drove them to Madrid was as lively as he remembered. They talked about current events; about technology, a growing fad in the world; and about their own lives. Carlos was the most explicit; he mentioned his plans to complete his education and of a new opportunity he was made aware of in Kuwait. He was not specific on this but told Rosario that if he was successful in pursuing this job, he would have to move from Los Angeles.

Rosario did not say much. She let him speak at will and attest about his months of volunteer work. Approaching their destination, she said, "Carlos, get settled in your room, and I will come back to get you at two in the afternoon. Wear comfortable shoes, you will need them touring our museum of art, and later, I am going to take you to tapas bars in Plaza Mayor."

"I will be ready at two, can't wait," Carlos replied.

At exactly two o'clock, she drove up to the residence and found Carlos patiently waiting outside. "I can see you are very punctual, Rosario. A family trait?"

"Yes, something I picked up from my father, he was a military man."

"Oh, I am sorry, did he pass away?"

"No, thank God. He is retired and living in Palma de Mallorca. There, my mother takes very good care of him."

Carlos asked, "What was his line of work? I understand you must be well-off to retire in the islands."

To which she replied vaguely, "Oh, he was in my same line of work, he was very successful."

You can say that again, thought Carlos. They had been driving in a new BMW 525i, one that Rosario handled perfectly and a very expensive model. She even had one of those new cellular phones that were the rage. Very lucrative business indeed.

Twenty minutes later, they were in front of Spain's most famous art museum El Prado. They walked slowly the many halls and admired the work of masters in quiet admiration. Occasionally, Rosario would add historical information about the period of history the art came from. She new a lot about the art in exhibition there and also about the history of Spain. Carlos wished that Americans were as cultured and well-educated.

Eventually they stopped in front of a majestic nude. Carlos said that the painter was obviously in love with the model, to which Rosario replied, "Carlos, my dear, the painter was the master Goya. La maja desnuda is his most famous painting and is priceless. That alone shows how much he truly loved the model, who, by the way, was the wife of his benefactor. The Duke of Alba."

"You mean that?"

"Of course, the Duke of Alba was a very powerful man, but a poor lover."

"No, I mean . . . Did you just call me your dear?"

Rosario blushed. He remembered that reaction from months past, and he liked the color of her cheeks and the expression in her face. So he let the moment prolong a little longer and finally said, "Come on, I am hungry. Where are those tapas bars you talked so much about?"

Plaza Mayor is a large square in the center of Madrid frequented by Spaniards and tourists alike. Fridays, the square's restaurants and bars are teeming with people out to have a good time. Starting at around 7:00 PM, the meeting place for locals are the many bars in the area. Each individual bar has appetizers for sale, and as customary, each in one area has a different specialty snack (tapa). So most persons hop from one bar to another, ordering the house sangria or wine and trying out the different tapas in each.

Rosario chose her favorite bar and quickly ordered some sangria for both and an order of octopus and sausage tapas. When they arrived, the grease was oozing out of them.

Carlos did not care. It was late for him, and he was hungry. He told her, "I am so hungry I can eat a horse."

"You are eating horse," replied Rosario.

Carlos gasped, but quickly noticed Rosario smiling.

"There, I finally got you back. I owed you a couple if I remember right."

They hopped to two other bars, and Rosario ordered the specialty in each. By 9:00 PM, she decided that it was time for dinner and led him down some stairs at the far end of the plaza and onto Calle Cuchilleros where they stopped at 23. The name of the restaurant was Botin's.

Carlos stated, "Must be good, it looks old, stuffy, and small."

"Botin's was established in 1623. It is one of Madrid's most famous restaurants. By the way, the lore is that during the civil war, Hemingway ate here every night. Some say he got drunk here nightly."

"You had a devastating civil war in the thirties, didn't you?"

"Yes, and we are still recovering from it in 1991." They entered the restaurant, and Rosario was instantly greeted by the head waiter and led down the stairs to the basement. There Carlos noticed that all the couples were tourists. He also noticed that everyone had stopped doing what they were doing and were now intently looking at them. No, they were looking at her; Rosario was dressed in a tight-fitting evening pantsuit and had removed her sweater to reveal a cleavage most men dream of caressing. She must have been quite a sight, and for the moment, she was his. Carlos felt ten feet tall then.

He followed her cue and ordered the house specialty, roast suckling pig. After dinner, they were enjoying a couple of expresso coffees when Carlos said, "You were right, Rosario, the meal was delicious. From this point on, this is my favorite restaurant."

"I am glad you liked it."

Holding hands, they walked back to her car that was parked conveniently next to his residence. It was twelve, and Carlos was tired after having traveled all morning and losing a couple of hours on the clock.

Before he could say anything, she said, "Carlos, I know that you are tired and we will see each other tomorrow, so I will let you free now." Before he responded, she continued, *"How about a car ride? My uncle owns a cabin north of here, and we could go stay there until Sunday."*

"Free, Rosario? I don't want to be free, I will be your prisoner forever. Consider me captured."

"Caramba! I order you free. I will stop here tomorrow at nine in the morning since it is a long ride where we are going." She moved quickly, efficiently, and let go of his hand, grabbed his face with both palms, and planted a kiss that seemed to last forever.

Before he could react, she got on her car and said, "Now get some sleep, and that is an order."

To which he replied, "Your wish is my command, my dear."

Carlos was interrupted from his memories by Roger, the administrative clerk. "Mr. Cortes, I have your travel documents for Sunday. I hope you remember that you are representing Mr. Westback at the SOUTHCOM conference. It is a one-day conference, and I've attached the agenda."

"Roger, I had forgotten all about it. Why can't Warren go?"

"Well, sir, there is the ambassador's reception on Monday night, and I believe he wants to attend that."

"Ms. Universe, isn't it?"

"Yes, sir, she was crowned last week, and the ambassador wants to extend his congratulations."

"And Warren wants to get in her panties," added Carlos.

Roger left without comment. He could be trusted not to tell their boss about staff rumors. If anything was universal in that office, it was the total distrust all felt toward Warren Westback.

When he had left, Carlos reviewed the travel documents. Roger never missed giving him the preferred flights and hotel accommodations, so he focused on the conference agenda. It was a semiannual meeting of the different government agencies that worked with the U.S. Southern Command in Miami, Florida.

Southern Command, commonly referred as SOUTHCOM, is the combatant command arm of the Pentagon in the Western Hemisphere. Not counting Canada and Mexico, SOUTHCOM has military responsibilities in all other countries of the Caribbean Sea, Central and South America. Originally based in Panama City, Panama, SOUTHCOM had moved to Miami when the Panama Canal treaty negotiations mandated it in the 1990s.

The meeting was attended by several intelligence agencies from the U. S. government. In it, they shared current information that would help all agencies in their fight against criminal and terrorist elements in the hemisphere.

Carlos noted the agenda, the normal intelligence briefings and staff regional analysis of current events. One afternoon subject caught his eye and made him promise himself he would not miss.

— *1400 hours. Arms Trade in Central America. Presented by FBI agent Frank Records and CEID special agent Johanna Valenz*

Interesting, thought Carlos.

The meeting was called hastily; the entire CRAF leadership was recalled to discuss the next steps to take in response to Mona's kidnapping. The discussion was interrupted by Rafael to give his decision.

"Señores"—in deference to the three female commanders in the audience—"I have decided that we must kidnap a victim of our own in order to trade for Mona. The victim must be big, very high up, and hopefully an American."

León interrupted him, "I am ready to kidnap the ambassador himself, but I am afraid I would kill him immediately instead of trading him." Loud applause and catcalling ensued.

"No, León, we must kidnap a military man, as high ranking as we can, we must keep him alive and induce a trade for Mona. She is the key to the money and, regretfully, the only expert in moving it around that we can trust."

León sat down unhappy. The two men closest to him gave him some encouragement and commented quietly.

Rafael continued, "Juana and Jose, I want you to execute the U.S. embassy plan code-named Chofer. Take a select ten-man team to the capital, and let's get us a soldier quickly. At a minimum, I want the defense attaché Colonel James Platford in our hands by next week. And, Juana, I repeat, I want him alive."

Juana Montes, his First Group commander, immediately said, "Si, Jefe."

Lieutenant Commander Jim Joyner interrupted his boss during a regularly scheduled staff meeting. "Sir, the commander on the bat phone."

Pepe, ever trusting of his personnel, went directly to the black phone on the desk without dismissing them and picked it up. The phone screen showed the current status as secure. They could speak classified matters on it.

He said on the phone, "General Ramirez, sir."

"Pepe," the general answered. "Do you still have your bags packed? I need you to go to Colombia later this week and meet with General Escobedo. There is a nasty press report of atrocities in the area where our troops are giving training to the Colombian Army Special Forces. In particular, try to see if the reports of these atrocities are known by our men at the Meta brigade headquarters."

"Yes, sir. I will do that this weekend. I can travel and be back for the Component Commanders Conference on Tuesday."

"Okay, Pepe, I trust you to be thorough as always. Make sure that our on-site training team commander knows that this information is very important. We cannot permit or overlook inhumane treatment of their captives."

"Yes, sir, I will try to get access to their recent FARC captive. It is a woman code-named Mona. I understand that she is the lover of El Jefe, and she should give us clues about captive treatment at that headquarters."

"Very good, be careful." The commander of SOUTHCOM, General John Q. Goodman, United States Army, hung up his phone.

General Ramirez walked quietly to the front door of his office and hailed his XO. "Jim, please see me after this meeting. I have another no-notice trip to Colombia this weekend."

Lieutenant Commander Joyner nodded and thought to himself, *This poor man never gets a day off, I've got to force him to take leave soon. He and his family need one.*

Brigadier General Jose Luis Ramirez was a career airman. Now in his twenty-fourth year in the air force, he had an impressive resume. A fighter pilot and former wing commander, he had fought in three conflicts and was credited with the destruction of two enemy fighter jets, both during Desert Storm in Iraq. He was married with two children.

In 1993, he was promoted early to lieutenant colonel and received his first assignment to the Pentagon. What an assignment it was, he was fortunate to be selected as the executive officer to a hero of Desert Storm in Iraq. His boss had run the air war for General Charles Horner and was then the director of fighter operations within the operations directorate of the United States Air Force staff.

They made quite a pair and had taken over the air staff in the era where the marked improvement in space operations hardware and weapons technology was termed a new revolution in warfare. Now eleven years later, Pepe had risen to brigadier general and his ex-boss was the chief of staff of the air force.

In his current position as director of operations, he had made his mark and had been promoted to major general. Pepe was waiting for a reassignment that was due now any day. He was hoping to be assigned to the Air Combat Command staff in Langley AFB, Virginia.

Pepe was also the senior Hispanic officer in the air force. His career was flourishing, and better and greater assignments were expected. However, he would trade all of this for a chance to get back to the days where he led quiet family life and was joyfully flying the F-15 Eagle over the great expanse of the Gulf of Mexico.

CHAPTER THREE

The American Airlines aircraft had just parked at the arrival gate in Miami International Airport. Carlos stood up and glanced at his watch to see they had arrived on time at 6:00 PM. In his mind, he quickly went through his travel checklist to prevent any articles left behind.

He grabbed his garment bag and his travel suitcase, a Travelpro originally designed specifically for airline crews and now the preferred one of the business traveler. Hopefully today, the lines at immigration and customs are light, thought Rock.

He was wrong. Immigration alone was easily a ten-minute wait. The back and forth snake-type line was full for both U.S. citizens and foreign travelers alike. While he waited in line, his mind drifted off to review the events of the past month. It had been a very successful month for him and the Colombians. He made up his mind to talk up this success during his meeting with the other intelligence agencies tomorrow.

He had progressed halfway through, and his line had just snaked back to a view of the entire arrivals lounge when he saw in the distance a tall beautiful woman in the foreign traveler arrivals section. She was at the counter talking to the immigrations officer and was almost done with the process.

Could it be Rosario? thought Carlos. She looked eerily like the woman he had fallen in love with thirteen years ago. What could he do? He was trapped in the line, and any attempt to get off the line would cause too much trouble. He tried to rationalize that most probably he could catch up to her in the baggage pickup carousels prior to Customs.

This kind of thing had happened to him before. Even though he had great eyesight, he had been wrong before with women that looked like Rosario. Once recently in a soccer game in Bogotá, he had stopped a woman that looked just like her but was disappointed to find out her name was Clara and that she was married with children.

When he had cleared Immigration, he quickly checked out all the arrival carousels for the woman. He looked in vain for five minutes and came to realize that she was gone. She probably traveled like him with hand-carried luggage only.

Well, it was probably another Clara, thought Carlos.

María Elena Borbón got on the rear seat of the taxi taking her, Johanna, and Luis to their downtown hotel in Miami. Johanna had a meeting at SOUTHCOM headquarters in the morning, Luis had some business at the Spanish consulate, and she was bound for the beach in South Miami Beach. She told herself the one day off at the beach was reward enough for the past month of work in Honduras.

Miami was intriguing to her. They called it the capital of Latin America, and indeed, in the last ten years, she had noticed that the Spanish language had taken a hold of the city by storm. She frequented Miami a lot because most of the illegal arms exchanges in the hemisphere were either brokered, financed, or handled there.

Miami was as intriguing as beautiful, thought María Elena. They were going to her favorite hotel in Miami Beach. It was not much to look at, but it had her two prerequisites: a beach and fantastic restaurants and entertainment nearby.

As the taxi slowly progressed toward the beach, María Elena thought of her once lost American connection.

She was young then; what, thirteen years ago, she recalled. She had first met this stranger on a flight from the United States to Spain, and there was an instant bond formed between them then. Carlos, what a great-looking man; he was blessed with the charm of a politician and the honesty of a priest.

Maybe that was what he had become, a priest. She remembered her spontaneous invitation to Carlos for a guided tour of Madrid. How surprised and excited she had been when she heard from him four months later. Her fabulous weekend in November of that year followed by the remorse of having given herself to a man that she hardly new. Needing to see him again desperately, about three months later, to see if it had been truly love between them, and finally, the failure of her search for him.

Carlos Cortes had dropped off the face of the earth. Her search included calls to his bosses in Los Angeles. They claimed that in December of 1991, he had quit the job for a better offer elsewhere.

They also told her that they did not know who the new employer was or where he had moved to. Someone in his old office gave her the phone of a relative. When she called the number, she was treated with suspicion from the start from a lady that called herself his aunt. To María Elena, she was covering something up. She ended that conversation and came to the conclusion that Carlos had been married. That his family and fellow workers were covering for him and that further inquiries were going to be fruitless. In the middle of March 1992, she had given up the search for Carlos and committed herself fully to her career.

Johanna interrupted her thoughts and said, "Here we are, I am going to change to my swimsuit quickly and see you downstairs in ten, boss."

"*Si*, Johanna, I can't hardly wait too."

Carlos was dropped off at a five star hotel in an industrial area west of the airport in Miami. SOUTHCOM was reportedly no more than a few blocks away. It was the hotel where most of the out-of-town participants for the meeting were supposed to stay. As he entered the lobby, he saw a reception desk with a welcoming sign stating his conference name and a military officer taking down another guest's information in a separate conference table.

As he approached the desk, he was grabbed by the arm and turned around. He immediately recognized the friendly face that was about to greet him.

"Pepe, it has been a long time since we have seen each other, amigo. My, oh my, are those stars I see in your shoulders? Should I call you sir?"

"Nonsense, *hermano,* you keep calling me Pepe all day long. Do not make plans for dinner. I am taking you home tonight. You have never met my family, and my wife is dying to meet you."

"I never knew that you worked here. As a matter of fact, the last time I heard something about you was last year. If I am not mistaken, I believe you were the wing commander of one of our bases for the unpleasantness in Iraq."

"Yes, yes, but we can talk about that later with a cold beer in our hands. Go ahead and get settled first, I have some business to attend back at the office, but be ready at six sharp, and I will come get you in my car. Make room for a steak, Carlos. I am a good chef when it comes to the barbeque."

Juana and Luis Montes arrived in the capital at the main bus terminal. They were unarmed and looked like any other young couple. Bogotá was a very large city, and you could easily hide in it. However, it was now too dangerous to carry in any arms and explosives. This was the norm since the current political administration had taken over. Security was tight especially around all the high-value targets.

Her team was traveling individually to the capital. Only one man was the courier for the arms. That way, if his car was inspected and the arms were discovered, they would lose only one person of the team. By protocol, the courier would travel first and set up the safe house for the team. Once that was completed, the rest of the group could travel in relative safety.

The safe house was an apartment in an area of town where local government workers lived. It was a modest apartment complex with limited security and a high turnover ratio of renters. This was ideal to the FARC. Prior experience had corroborated that the apartment dwellers would not be curious of the new tenants for at least two weeks. This was sufficient time; they were planning to take no more than ten days for the entire operation. By this time in ten days, she would be either dead or have her captive in chains at the base camp for the CRAF.

Tonight, she was going to pay a visit to their dormant government servant. Of course, he new nothing of it and would be surprised to see her come calling. Hopefully, Pedro Muñiz had not gotten soft on them after ten years as the FARC's dormant plant at the U.S. embassy.

Pepe was on time. Not to his surprise, Carlos admired the baby blue Corvette convertible that he was driving. *These fighter pilots,* Carlos thought, *they get older and stop flying their fast jets, and they need to own something fast on earth. The Corvette is exactly what I expected he owned. Maybe one day I can own one also.*

"Hop in, Carlos. I live just a few minutes away in the Doral Country Club area."

Driving there, Pepe updated Carlos on what had happened to him since they last met in Kuwait in 1991. Of course, Carlos had not met Ana or the children; but after six months of living in the same apartment with someone, he felt like he knew them well. Plus Pepe was always talking about his family.

Things had definitely changed, both children were now young adults and away at college. The elder child, Jocelyn, was now twenty-one and a senior at the U.S. Air Force Academy. She wanted to be a fighter pilot just like her dad. The youngest, Junior, was a freshman at the College of William and Mary in Williamsburg, Virginia. He had the mother's genes and was on track to a political science degree and a career in the U.S. Foreign Service. Ana, of course, had her doctorate in political science and currently was a visiting professor at Florida International University.

"How about sports?" Carlos asked. "Your son was a great soccer player at six and your daughter an equally great tennis player at nine."

"Oh, Carlos, in those days, I was a was a hotshot fighter pilot that had just shot down two Iraqi MiGs, and my children were the proudest thing I had ever accomplished. I could have said they were the king and queen of Siam for all that matters."

"Seriously, Pepe."

"Okay, amigo. Jocelyn is the current singles champion of NCAA Division One tennis and Junior is on the JV soccer team at William and Mary."

"Now that's more like it, they are outstanding kids, just like mom and dad," said Carlos.

"And their parents could not be prouder," added Pepe.

Ana opened the door and was out to meet them at the porch to the house. There was no need for introduction as Pepe had always told his family about the cop from Los Angeles that had saved his life in Kuwait. Although they only heard from Carlos every four years or so, she felt like she knew him well. She received him with a warm embrace.

Carlos was impressed; she was very beautiful for a middle-aged woman. He spoke his mind. "Pepe if you ever divorce this woman, you are a fool." And he said directly to her, "You are as beautiful as Pepe told me and I understand a pretty good expert in your field also."

Ana was flattered. "I assure you, Carlos, your suave lines will not work with me. I am committed to this man we have in front of us."

Pepe added, "Hey, I am here! Will you quit romancing each other and let's get on with the cooking part of the show. I told you he was suave Ana, I don't know why a good woman does not have him in her grasp like you have me."

Later in the evening, while enjoying a fine Port wine, Carlos and Pepe talked about their time in Kuwait.

They met by coincidence; Carlos was working for the U.S. government helping the Kuwaitis reestablish the police force after the Iraqi occupation. Pepe was working for the Office of Defense Cooperation in support of the Kuwaiti Air Force. Due to a housing shortage, they shared an apartment in the city with two contractors of an American oil company.

It was three months into his tour in Kuwait when the accident happened. Pepe was riding in a government bus to the local air base when it rolled on its side due to high speed and a poor, combat-damaged road. Pepe was knocked unconscious in the accident and remained in the bus after the accident. When the local police responded to the accident, Carlos was in the group. Just as they arrived at the accident site, a careless smoker flipped his ashes in the vicinity of the bus, and it quickly caught on fire. Instantly everyone froze. Everyone, that is, except for Carlos. He went into action immediately, giving commands and asking the survivors if anybody was alive inside.

Getting no answer, Carlos dove into the burning bus. With some difficulty, he jumped over broken seats and twisted metal frames to find seconds later his friend and roommate lying unconscious. He pulled him out of the bus seconds before it was engulfed in flames. Unconscious but basically unhurt, Pepe recovered quickly.

To this day, Pepe swore to anyone he met that he owed his life to his newfound brother Carlos. If only he could pay him back some way one day.

Carlos started the conversation after dinner by stating how proud he was as a Hispanic that Pepe had reached the rank of general in the armed forces. "You have it good in the air force," Carlos said.

Pepe answered, "This is America, here, we all have it good, if we work hard."

"Yes, but we are not all rewarded in the same way, Pepe."

"What do you mean?" asked Pepe.

"I work hard too, *hermano,* but I am not rewarded the same way. I was not rewarded with a promotion at the Los Angeles Police Department. So I left them to hire on with the Agency for what I thought were exciting career opportunities. There too, when the time comes for a promotion, they look elsewhere. Let me tell you, I now work for the student that ended up in tenth place in my new hire class at the Agency."

"Tenth place, that is pretty good, isn't it? In the air force, you can still have your choice of assignments if you finish tenth in your pilot training class."

"What position did you attain, Pepe?"

"Carlos, you know I was number 1 in my class," answered Pepe humbly.

"You prove my point, Pepe. I was also number 1 in mine."

"So what is wrong, Carlos, let me help."

"Another time, another place, Pepe. The endemic problems of the Agency are ours to solve, not yours," said Carlos.

"Okay, we will change the subject then. Tell me, Carlos, any word on that hot flame of yours back in Spain? I know that you had given up hope of ever meeting her long time ago, but you are in the nation's intelligence service, you must have found out something about her since we last met?

"What was her name? Rosario, wasn't it?"

"No, Pepe, no change there. The woman has vanished from the collective mind, however, she is alive and well in my memories. I don't think that I will ever erase her memory until the day of my last breath."

Luis Montes knocked on the door of a simple apartment in Bogotá. After a short time, Pedro Muñiz opened the door.

"Cómo estas, Papá?"

Pedro's eyes suddenly swelled with tears. He had not seen his son for four years now. To most in his family, Luis was dead, the result of a clever way to disguise the fact he had joined the FARC. Luis used the last name of his lover Juana and was quickly rising in prestige with them.

"*Hijo!* What are you doing here, son? Come in quick, we must be careful. Evelyn, come here quick," he shouted.

"Papá, I cannot stay long, and what I came to do is not pleasant. Can I bring Juana Montes inside? I want you to meet her."

"Who is Juana, son, a new love interest?"

"Yes and no, Papá. She is my commander, and she is also my wife. She will tell you what we are going to ask you to do."

Juana came in and shook hands with Mr. Muñiz and his wife who had now joined him and was busy hugging her son. Mrs. Muñiz had not seen him in years and worried terribly for his safety daily. Pedro

45

approved quickly of his son's choice for life partner. He peered into Juana's eyes and saw a determined woman. She looked slightly older than his son.

"Mr. Muñiz, I come to you with orders from El Jefe. We are in urgent need of your services. He has ordered Plan Chofer into action"

"*Claro,* tell me what you need."

"Mona Pedroso was captured last Thursday, and you should know that she is the mastermind of finances for the Cucho Ramos Front, and her information on our funds is in jeopardy. We must get her back quickly."

"What do you have in mind, Juana?"

"Your son and I have a ten-man team in the capital, and our objective is to kidnap an American serviceman. El Jefe wants someone big like your boss Colonel Platford. After we capture him, we will trade him for Mona."

Pedro sat down. He invited the others to do the same and, after a moment, said, "That is going to be very difficult, he is a very careful man. He drives himself to work every day and selects daily a different route. His embassy driver is Ernesto, not me. I now work for Mr. Westback in the agriculture section. He pulled rank when he got to the embassy and got me because of my reputation as a good driver."

"Papá, you should be driving the ambassador. After all, you saved the previous ambassador's life," said Luis.

"Son, I know, but he has a marine drive him. One that got special training with the FBI, I believe. When do you want to do this kidnapping?"

Juana answered, "The sooner the better, we want to be done by the weekend at the latest."

"But that is not going to give you the necessary time to do surveillance. Without it, the operation might fail."

"I know," said Juana. "That is why we came here to you. El Jefe has ordered Plan Chofer. You may have to come out in order to assure the success of our mission."

"If we succeed, Juana, how do you know the Americans or the Colombians will agree to the trade? You know their stated policy on that."

"That is why it has to be Colonel Platford, sir. We need someone that knows as many secrets as Mona knows. And be positive, we will succeed!"

Pedro knew then that his son had picked the right woman. Little did he know or expect that it was Juana that had picked Luis.

CHAPTER FOUR

C arlos got up early the next morning and went out to the hotel lobby to ask about running tracks in the area. The very friendly concierge told him about a park only a few blocks away. What surprised Carlos was that the response had come in Spanish after he had asked in English. Boy oh boy, thought Carlos, *like they say in the news magazines, I am truly in the capital of Latin America.*

Even though it was six in the morning, the temperature was easily over 75°F, and it was muggy too. Carlos followed the instructions and was soon at the park and its running track. He started at an easy gait that would give him a three-mile run in less than twenty-one minutes.

The park had a mile-long track that wandered around in no specific shape. Halfway around the first mile, he noticed a large building just north of the park. The building was fenced and was guarded at the entrance to the parking lot. Carlos noticed three flags in the distance that he surmised were the USA and Florida flags and a third flag that looked like the one for Southern Command.

So that's where SOUTHCOM is? thought Carlos. *Funny, I expected a large campus with military establishments around a central compound.*

Carlos finished his three miles and was surprised to see that he had completed the easy run in 18:07. *Either the track is shorter than a mile circuit or the sea level altitude has me running faster than normal*, Carlos reasoned. *In Bogotá, I could not manage any better than seven-minute miles with the slow pace I had run.*

Across the city, María Elena and Johanna were finishing a punishing run on the beach that had lasted thirty minutes. Although they were very sweaty from the exertion of the run and the loss of traction caused by running on sand, they finished what was well over a four-mile run and did not even slow down after the run on their way to the hotel.

Johanna said to her boss, "Luis would not have finished this run today. We really pushed it hard."

"Yes, Johanna, he is slightly older than me plus he does not like to run like we do. I do not know how he finishes his training requirements year after year."

"Maybe he cheats, María Elena."

"No, I don't think so. He just strains himself hard once a year to pass his physical requirements and is happy with the mediocre results he gets."

"How come we are not that way, boss?"

"Oh, that is too easy, Johanna. We are women, are we not?"

"Have you always been this way? Have you excelled since day one, boss?"

"I have always tried hard, Johanna. The way to success in this man's world is to try harder than the best of them. But don't get me wrong, I have made mistakes in the past. Big ones, Johanna, however, I have managed to overcome those each time."

They arrived at the hotel lobby and made plans for dinner that night at a local restaurant recommended by the Spanish consulate. María Elena wished Johanna good luck in her briefing at SOUTHCOM and went to her room to prepare for a day of relaxation at the beach.

María Elena thought how fortunate was to have a day off in Miami after the month long duty in Honduras. She knew that the following days in Spain would be hectic since family duties and work issues would take up most of her time prior to the team's next assignment to South America. That assignment was very important, and it started in two short weeks.

I am glad that Johanna volunteered to give that presentation today. I owe her one. Little did she know that she was missing a chance encounter with the one man that had turned her world upside down just twelve short years ago.

Lieutenant Commander Joyner picked Carlos up at the hotel at 0800 hours sharp. Carlos was going thirty minutes before the other participants to receive a personal briefing on Colombia from the operations and intelligence staffers at the command.

"Hope the hotel was agreeable, sir," said Jim.

"More than agreeable, they gave me a free breakfast on the fifth floor, and everyone sports a wide grin in the morning. More than I can say of my work environment at the embassy."

They made a quick hop to the command and were greeted at the VIP entrance by Brigadier General Ramirez himself.

Pepe talked first. "Welcome, Carlos. I saw you approaching from my window and wanted to come greet you before this very fast-paced day starts."

"Something tells me that every day is fast-paced around here, Pepe."

"Well, weekends are off at least."

"All weekends?"

"No, I guess, sometimes we work those too."

"That's more like it, Pepe. I would like to know that my taxpayer's dollars are well-spent at SOUTHCOM."

"What? You don't work hard at the Agency also?"

"Touché!" *But here they are rewarded with promotion and increased responsibilities,* thought Carlos.

Pepe continued seriously, "Today you will get thirty-minute briefings from the operations and intelligence staffers about the situation in Colombia. I want you to give them instant feedback when you feel that what they brief you on is incorrect. You are the expert for Colombia, and I want my staff to know what you know."

"I am sure that I will learn something from your personnel also, Pepe."

"That is the beauty of this interagency cooperation. We both stand to benefit from mutual discussions in the subject area," Pepe added. "Sorry I cannot be with you the next hour, Carlos, I have to prepare for an impromptu visit to Colombia on Friday. Are you going to be there?"

"Of all the weekends you could have chosen to visit, this is not a good one, Pepe. I am taking the rest of the week off to visit my family in Los Angeles."

"We'll make it a point to meet in Colombia the next time I visit. Is that a promise?"

"That's a promise, Pepe."

"I know that you are in the Southeast a lot, Carlos. The first two times I visited Bogotá, I asked the military group commander about your whereabouts, and he never was able to tell me."

"Well, he is not the only one, sometimes not even I know where I am," added Carlos.

The situational briefings went very well. There was an outstanding exchange of information between the lieutenant colonels that briefed him and Carlos. After the briefings, Carlos commented on only one topic.

"Those were outstanding briefings, ladies and gentlemen. Let me comment on only one thing. In your presentations, you make mention of the FARC guerrilla in a masculine manner of speech. Do not underestimate the power of the female guerrilla in the FARC. Some statistics put their numbers in the 30 to 40 percent of all active combatants. In the last few years, we have noticed that several of their unit commanders are women also. In fact, that is the biggest difference between them and the Colombian armed forces. Their army needs to recognize that and act upon it. In the race to win the hearts and minds of the population, the FARC comes first and, I believe, the reason is their empowerment of the poor, disenfranchised Colombian woman."

They adjourned the meeting, and Carlos was led downstairs to the command main briefing room where the interagency crowd was meeting. They were about to start, and he was the last to arrive. He was led to the main briefing table to an assigned seat. The table was shaped like a horseshoe, and sitting across the room, Carlos noted Pepe looking at him. They smiled.

The morning meetings were all classified in a way that foreign visitors would not be able to participate. So Carlos noted that the audience was lacking the representation of the scheduled afternoon briefer from the CEID.

Sitting to Carlos's right was the FBI afternoon briefer Frank Records. During a break in the morning, Carlos asked him about the Spanish agent that would brief with him. "Frank, long time no see. Who is giving the afternoon briefing, you or the Spanish CEID agent?"

"Nice to see you too, Rock." Frank was aware of his nom de guerre and used it any time they met in a classified room setting. "When was the last time we met?"

"Wasn't it in Lebanon last year?"

"Yes, Rock, you were leading a Special Forces detachment into western Iraq, and I was providing a watch on terrorist activities inside Lebanon.

"That all went well, didn't it?"

"Yes, Frank, but you haven't answered my question about the briefing this afternoon."

"Oh, the briefing, I am not giving it. It is being presented by the undercover Spanish agent that actually arrested El Mocho. I've never met this Johanna Valenz, but I hear that she is a knockout."

"Is she code-named Rosario, Frank?" There, he had asked the question that had bothered him since the past week when he first became aware of the Honduran arrest.

"No, Rock, she is too young to be the famed Rosario. I hear Rosario is now retired and living in comfort back in Spain. She certainly amassed quite a reputation when assigned to the tri-border area between Brazil, Colombia, and Peru in the nineties. What was it, ten arms shipments interdicted and three top arms traffickers arrested all in a twelve-month period, a record that stands to this day."

"Well, we'll have to wait to the afternoon to see this CEID agent," added Carlos.

"Rock, I've never seen you so excited about a woman before."

"It's the Spanish women, Frank, only the Spanish."

Pepe took Carlos to lunch at a local restaurant famous for their ribs. They did not have much time for a large meal, so they both ordered the special that was advertised and guaranteed in five minutes or less.

Waiting for their meal, Pepe said, "Carlos, last night we heard a lot about my exploits the past ten years, but I have not heard much about yours. Did you not participate in the attack on Iraq last year?"

Carlos answered honestly, "Not much there, Pepe. I was given an area of responsibility in western Iraq and was in charge of the initial attack on H3, you know, the airfield."

"An outstanding success, if my sources were right," said Pepe. "So that means that you had been in country prior to the start, doesn't it?"

"A few times," answered Carlos modestly.

"I imagine too classified to talk about openly."

"Yes, Pepe, I imagine that our activities there will be classified for the next twenty years at least."

"Well, let me tell you, Carlos, that if I ever get in trouble again, I want you to be in charge of coming to the rescue. You are my guardian angel. Is that a promise?"

"Wait a minute, Pepe. You owe me, this is a two-way street, amigo. But if you want to hear it, of course I promise!"

"That's better."

María Elena turned around to face the midday sun at the hotel swimming pool area. She was wearing a conservative light blue bikini that accented her figure perfectly. She applied a bit of lotion to the exposed skin and resumed reading her book.

After a while, she grew tired of reading and began to appreciate better her human companions. There was an older couple that did everything together.

They must be married, thought María Elena. They were reading books, drinking mai tais, and seemed to be enjoying their time at the pool. There was a male couple that seemed to be enjoying each other as well. Then there was the gigolo. *Good looking,* thought María Elena, *but too plastic. Everything about him looks fake, certainly he is no Carlos.*

There he was again; every time that she looked at a good-looking stranger, she compared him to Carlos. Gladly, this did not happen often. But at thirty-seven, she still got mad that his memory was so enduring.

She remembered how committed she had been to a stranger only once in her life. Saturday, November 2, 1991. She was early to pick up Carlos at his hotel. They were headed to a house in the hills north of Madrid owned by her family. They had it to themselves, and that is just the way she wanted it. When she arrived, Carlos was waiting outside.

"Hola, Carlos, I am glad you brought a change with you since we may not be back until tomorrow." She noticed the instant grin come to his face.

The drive up to the cabin took two and a half hours. One stop to refuel and to purchase some provisions later, they arrived at a nicely designed but simple A-frame log cabin. The hill it was on reminded you of the hills north of Santa Fe, New Mexico. They were lush with vegetation but somewhat arid. The air was devoid of humidity, but with a temperature of 65° F, the atmosphere felt perfect for a weekend of quiet seclusion.

When they entered the cabin, María Elena remembered that they avoided the topic of sleeping arrangements for some time. Carlos had placed his carryall on a corner of the cabin entrance, and she had quietly gone to the single bedroom and placed her bag on the bed.

They finished unpacking the groceries they had purchased and decided to take a walk to the highest point of the hill they were on.

Although steep, the walk proved to be very easy for two young persons with finely tuned bodies. When they reached the zenith, neither had broken into a sweat even though they were wearing sweaters to ward off the chilly air.

María Elena recalled she was blunt when she spoke first that afternoon after settling down in a large rock that towered above the valley below. She posed for a couple of pictures, and when Carlos had put away the camera, she said, "Carlos, here we are. Two total strangers in the solitude of La Madre España. Tell me, what are you thinking?"

Carlos did not take long; he answered honestly and used what to María Elena sounded like romantic prose.

"María Elena, after six months of very hard work and intolerable heat, you descend in my life like an angel from heaven. You are mine to keep, which is my fervent wish."

All these years and she had not forgotten a single word of the reply. Immediately, she had kissed him. They kissed for a good while at the top of the hill. They slowly walked down to the cabin in quiet anticipation. Held hands, caressed, it was a magic moment.

Once at the cabin, there was no pretense. No questions to ask, they made love for three hours straight. María Elena now remembered fondly how he had carefully undressed her. How he had laid out her clothes before joining her in bed.

He had been prepared; they practiced safe sex that evening. The next morning, she awoke at nine in the morning to careful caresses on her back. Carlos had prepared breakfast and had already been out for a run. How can he do it? *thought María Elena.*

She ate ravenously while he took a shower and cleaned up. At around ten in the morning, they made love again.

María Elena caught herself smiling when she remembered the final funny happening of that wonderful weekend. The last time they made love, Carlos had told her, *"María Elena, I ran out of condoms, maybe we can just kiss and enjoy ourselves."*

Her reply still haunted her to this day. *"Go ahead, Carlos. Just be careful."* That was the last day she had seen Carlos Cortes.

The afternoon meeting at SOUTHCOM headquarters started promptly at 1330 hours. After a short introduction to the arms trafficking topic, the rest of the day's briefings were given by professionals from the U.S. Bureau of Alcohol, Tobacco, and Firearms and by Johanna Valenz, the guest presenter from the CEID of Spain.

When he saw her, Carlos had the same reaction as most men did upon laying their eyes on Johanna for the first time. Long black hair adorned her tall physique, and a model's cultured face was enhanced by a Mona Lisa smile that could topple several governments.

Wow! Are all Spanish women this beautiful? thought Carlos.

What followed was a very professional briefing about a carefully choreographed takedown in downtown Tegucigalpa, Honduras. During the briefing, Carlos noted that Johanna had twice stopped her scan of conferees and perceptively looked at him. He swore that the second time, she had smiled a little more as they traded glances.

After the briefing, the session took a fifteen-minute break, and Carlos quickly rose to meet the striking Spanish agent. He was not the only one, many conferees came to commend the success of the operation, and many others just wanted to be near her.

Carlos was surprised that it was Johanna that abruptly cut off another agent from the ATF and addressed him directly while laying her beautiful green eyes on him. "And you, sir, whom do you represent?"

A predator! And a beautiful one at that, thought Carlos.

"My name is Carlos Cortes, and I am very pleased to meet you, Ms. Valenz. I work for the 'Agency' in Colombia." There was no need to mention which agency. To intelligence operatives throughout the world, there was only one agency, the CIA.

"I may go to Colombia soon, maybe we can meet there and trade company information, Mr. Cortes?"

"Hopefully not too soon, Ms. Valenz, I have some vacation starting today and am on my way to Los Angeles to visit my family."

"Mrs. Cortes?" asked Johanna coyly.

"Yes, ma'am. My mother and father now are permanent U.S. residents and have moved to Brea, California."

"Brea?" asked Johanna. *So far so good,* thought Johanna. *No wedding ring and no obvious family ties. How could this man be single? I will look him up when we visit Bogotá in two weeks. That is if María Elena lets me.*

"A suburb of Los Angeles, the city is divided by many counties and towns. Brea is a town just southeast of the LA city center."

"I imagine that I can get a hold of you by calling the embassy operator, Mr. Cortes."

"Of course, any time of day, Ms. Valenz." *What am I doing? This woman is at least twelve years younger than me. I must be an easy mark to Spanish women,* thought Carlos.

Johanna excused herself as the meeting was about to start and she was scheduled to depart for Miami Beach. "I will see you soon," were her parting words. Carlos could not wait.

Juana came alone to meet with Pedro that evening. They met outside his local corner market.

"Buenas noches, Señor Muñiz."

"*Buenas noches, patriota.* Juana, I only have vague news. Today we got word of a visit to the Department of Meta on Friday or Saturday.

Of course, driving is only the backup means of transportation. Colonel Platford prefers to use a helicopter for such trips."

"So we will have to find a way to influence the colonel in taking a car this time, Pedro."

"Yes, and if we succeed, do not forget it will be Ernesto doing the driving, Juana."

"Just get me Ernesto's home address please. After that, all you worry about is getting us the agenda for the trip, let me worry about the car and Ernesto. That is my job, okay, Mr. Muñiz?"

"Si, Juana."

"Anything else?"

"Yes, there is one more thing. Traveling with Colonel Platford will be a high-ranking SOUTHCOM official from Miami. I still do not know his name."

"Find out, Pedro. We may get two targets instead of one. Let's meet at the same time but in front of the church tomorrow."

"*Si,* Juana, and please call me Pedro."

"No, Mr. Muñiz, you are the father of my lover and confidant. I will protect you and your family with my life. To me you are the father I never had." She kissed him in the cheek and, with nothing further to say, turned around and disappeared into the night.

Pedro's eyes filled with tears of joy.

That evening in Miami Beach, Johanna and María Elena excused themselves from their company at dinner and went to the ladies' room to refresh themselves.

That was something to emulate from the Americans, thought María Elena. *Here ladies' rooms also served as meeting places away from the male counterparts. Most of them were spacious and comfortable. If only the public places in Europe could copy this from them.*

When they met at the wash basins in the restroom, María Elena asked, "How was your day, Johanna?"

Johanna, young and impulsive, brushed aside the professional part of the question posed by her boss and said, "Fantastic, today I met a wonderful man, María Elena. He was tall and handsome and only a little older than me. I was most intrigued by his eyes, they never wavered when he looked at me. It's as if his entire soul was looking at me. In his presence, I felt naked, María Elena."

"What was the man's name, Johanna, and when will you meet him next?"

"If you permit it, I will try to meet him during our trip to Bogotá next month. He works for the Agency, María Elena, and his name is Carlos Cortes."

María Elena nearly fainted.

CHAPTER FIVE

The family is one of nature's masterpieces.
—George Santayana

F or Carlos Cortes, the trip back home was a long time coming. His mother was of ill health, and Carlos had not visited in six years. For his family's benefit, and company regulations as well; they did not know that Carlos was an agent for the most feared U.S. government agency in Latin America.

Carlos left Miami straight to Los Angeles in a nonstop United Airlines flight. The nearly six-hour flight was fraught with anticipation and dread. Carlos was happy that he was finally heading home but was not welcoming the many questions that his visit would ensue.

Let's see, since his last visit, Carlos had participated in three distinct wars, numerous other covert actions, and was now involved in the largest counter-guerrilla action in the hemisphere. None of which he could mention to his family.

He also took the risk of being labeled a failure by his immediate family. With his hard-earned master's degree, he should have accomplished something by now. Carlos dreaded the thought.

Let's even not think about family life, Carlos thought. *A distinguished Latino professional like me should be married by now?* He could sense the questions right there at thirty-nine thousand feet.

His thoughts were interrupted by an announcement by the chief purser that the in-flight movies were starting. He was looking forward to watching *Pirates of the Caribbean,* the monthly offering. *At least United showed free movies,* which pleased Carlos.

María Elena was by then over Bangor, Maine, on her trip back to Spain. She could not sleep; the nine-hour trip to Madrid was shaping up to be a nightmare.

She had heard right, "Carlos Cortes," a very tall and handsome man with great presence. *There could be only one like that,* she thought. *Oh, the irony of it. She should have gone to the SOUTHCOM meeting instead of Johanna.*

No amount of in-flight entertainment or good meals was going to get her mind away from her thoughts of Carlos. *Had she finally found him even though she was not looking?*

Pepe Ramirez arrived at his home late that evening. He was working three hard issues that had cropped up at work, all in the last week. First, he was wrapping up a very successful troop deployment to a Caribbean island. The operation had been fraught with peril and uncertainty, but in the end, the U.S. Marines that had deployed there had performed admirably.

The second issue was festering in Washington DC and with the world press. The situation in Guantanamo Bay, Cuba, was troublesome and getting worse daily. SOUTHCOM established a joint task force there, and problems with detention operations were tasking the command staff, and his operations directorate was not immune to the pressures.

Finally, the situation in Colombia once again merited his attention, and he was getting ready to visit there on Friday, the day after tomorrow.

Ana welcomed him with a kiss and tried to tell him a happening at the university that day. Although he looked at her and was apparently listening to her unhappy event, Ana knew that deep inside he was not listening. She stopped telling him about her and said, "Okay, Luis, what is bothering you?" She asked this question lovingly, disarming Pepe instantly.

"Nothing, honey, it is just that recently nothing is going well at the command, and I have what seems a large share of the burden."

"Then my problems can wait. Sit down in the family room, and I will get you a beer and listen to you instead."

"Where did I find you, Ana? You are too good to be true."

"You did not find me, I found you. Relax, one day when you retire, you will have time for my scholastic problems."

Carlos arrived at Los Angeles International Airport at eleven fifty in the morning Pacific time. He traveled by bus to the car rental office and rented a small convertible. *No other way to drive in Los Angeles,* thought Carlos. *At least here I did not have to take the life-saving precautions standard in Colombia.*

He took the Pacific Coast Highway followed by the 110 expressway to San Pedro. There were faster ways to get there, but he wanted to experience the stop-and-go traffic and sights of the Pacific Coast Highway, also known as the PCH. He grew up on the streets of San Pedro and, later, was a cop on the beat in Redondo Beach and Manhattan Beach. He could not believe it, but he found that he was homesick for the lifestyle of the area. *First you want to experience the world and get as far away from Los Angeles as possible, but after you have experienced other parts, you develop a slow yearning for your own backyard.*

These represented Carlos's present feelings, but he knew that it would not last. After a while, he knew that the life he had chosen was right for him. That was his justification anyway.

In Redondo Beach, Carlos visited with the police friends he had not seen in twelve years. They even convinced him to go to a late lunch at the Riviera Café right there on the PCH. He had a great time talking the cop talk he had not used in years. In particular, he was gratified to find out that his best friend back then, Wilfredo Colón, had been promoted to lieutenant in the highly regarded Detectives Division. He promised himself that he would try to get in touch with old Willy if he had time on this trip. About four in the afternoon, Carlos said his good-byes and headed for San Pedro, his boyhood town.

When he arrived in San Pedro, Carlos was dismayed to find out that his aunt's home was now a convenience store. A brand-new building stood where he grew up. This had happened recently as property values increased and the poor residents in town sold out and moved farther away from the city. His aunt, for example, now lived in Pomona over twenty miles away.

From San Pedro, Carlos got again on the 110 and, after one hour and forty-five minutes, was at his parents' new home in Brea. *The traffic was horrible at this time of the day,* he remembered. He arrived at seven thirty; it was a simple home, foreign to Carlos since he had not lived there. His mother kept a beautiful yard as always, and the porch was simple, but the necessary wood rocker was ever present for his father's use.

Not having told anyone of his visit plans, he started singing softly the same song his mother used to put him to sleep with a long time ago. Since he was right at the door, the sound of his deep voice traveled like lightning throughout the house. He next heard a loud scream and the sounds of breaking glass.

"Jesús, María y José!" he heard. "Dios mío, es nuestro hijo!" He was discovered.

His mother came rushing to the door, opened it, and gave him the biggest hug he had received in a long time. Carlos did not fight it; he needed it as much as she did.

She was joined a second later by his little sister. She hugged him too, grabbing on to a side since his mother had not released him yet. Then he noticed his younger brother and father slowly coming into the room with smiles on their faces.

"Mama, Sonia, let me go, I cannot breathe."

They reluctantly let him go, and for what seemed to be an eternity, everyone simply looked at one another. My, had things changed. Sonia was now twenty-two, and she was a gorgeous woman. His brother, Jose Manuel, was now twenty-eight and seemed delighted to see him. He was wearing his patrolman uniform of the Orange County Sheriff Department. His mother, Carlos noticed, was now crying uncontrollably tears of joy. Finally, his father was the most reserved, he looked well, now fifty-eight years old he had recently been promoted to foreman in his county transportation department job.

Carlos knew all this and more about his family's current accomplishments. Unknown to them, he exercised influence in their everyday life. For example, Jose Manuel's patrolman job was obtained after only two phone calls. After all, he was a capable and well-schooled young man. His sister was still in college at UCLA, and he had not influenced her life yet. His father, however, was an immigrant without citizenship. He had proven to be the most difficult. First, he had to get his parents a green card, and then he worked the phone lines extremely hard in order to get his father the county job he held. His promotion to foreman, however, was solely based on his father's own merits. Of this, Carlos was real proud.

Little did they know also that the loan his father had secured for the new home was in Carlos's name. After he found out that they were thinking of buying a new home, Carlos called his father's bank and had the loan guaranteed with his credit. His father was granted a loan that most immigrants would find inaccessible just for the mere fact of their status.

The first to speak was Sonia. Ever the self-assured lady of the twenty-first century, she put into words what the rest of the family was thinking.

"Carlos," she said, "you should be ashamed of yourself, the last time you were here was for my *quinceañero*, that was seven years ago!"

Then, like if a dam had burst, they all started talking at the same time. Carlos gave his apologies several times over. If he had not called home at every opportunity and sent his parents a monthly stipend these past few years, his family would be unforgiving. Anger gave way to joy, and the next few minutes were the sweetest Carlos had spent in a few years.

Late that night, Carlos and Jose Manuel were left alone by the rest of the family. Jose Manuel spoke first.

"Tell me, big brother, what do you do for the State Department?"

"I am the in the agriculture office at the embassy."

"Agriculture, if I am not mistaken, your education is in criminology to include your master's, *hermano*?"

"Yes, but—"

"Don't but me, Carlos. I am well aware of your phone calls that got me my job. Please don't misunderstand me, I am grateful, but you do not exert that kind of influence as a lowly paid government clerk."

"People talk too much," said Carlos.

"No, Carlos, people are very proud of your accomplishments. After all, I am a damn good policeman, and you well know that we can't be fooled, at least not all the time."

"Please, Jose Manuel, do not tell our family. It will be our secret."

"Our secret, I still do not know for which of the many secret U.S. government organizations you work for."

"Let's keep it that way. I am so proud of you, that patrolman uniform suits you just fine."

"Do not change the subject on me, *hermano*. One day I would like to work for your organization too."

"I am afraid about what it would do to our mother, Jose. Think of it, it could be disastrous in her present state of health."

"I can wait, Carlos, but do not forget me please."

"Of that you can be sure. I never forget."

Juana Montes was late for the Wednesday evening meeting. Procedures required for FARC members to wait at the predetermined place for no more than twenty minutes after the set time. It had been two hours, but Pedro was still there.

Pedro asked, "What happened, is everything okay?"

"Fine, sir, it's funny, I knew you would still be here. You are not worrying unnecessarily about your son, are you?"

"No, Juana, I am just curious," Pedro lied.

"Listen," Juana told him seriously. "I know you have never acted as a subversive in your life, if we are to succeed, I need you to worry only about your duties. Your son and I will be safe, yours is the dangerous part. Do we have that straight, Pedro?"

"Yes, Juana, and thank you. My son chose well in you."

Juana sighed and continued, "I have done the preliminary arrangements, and my plan is almost ready. I need three things from you. But first please tell me what you learned today."

"Sure, as I predicted, the visit to the Meta brigade headquarters is on Saturday morning, and they will depart by helicopter from the downtown police headquarters. The visitor is a big one, he is the director of operations for the command in Miami. Get this, he is a Latino too, his name is Jose Luis Ramirez."

"I don't care if he is the pope, he is our man, and we must get him, Pedro."

"What do you want me to do, Juana?"

"It's quite simple, please confirm a couple of things for me. If Ernesto cannot drive on Saturday, are you the official backup?"

"Yes, Juana."

"Also, if the police headquarters are unusable for any reason or if the weather is real bad, what is the backup plan for transport?"

"Short of going to Palanquero Air Base and getting on an air force plane, the most probable course of action is for them to travel by car. The road to Meta is considered real safe. Compared to Palanquero, it is the faster mode of travel also."

"So you are sure that they will travel by car?"

"They will, only if the helicopter or the police headquarters are out of the picture, Juana."

"Okay, tomorrow let's meet at the police courtyard at seven sharp. I will not be late, and we have a lot to cover. Please be there."

Friday, June 25, 2004; Madrid, Spain

At two thirty in the morning East Coast time and six thirty Madrid time, María Elena's aircraft touched down in Barrajas International Airport. She felt relief that time and distance had put her memories of the past on hold. It was a bright Thursday morning in Madrid, and her son was waiting for her. As always, he was under the good care of her aunt Clara and was probably up in anticipation of today's under-twelve match for the local youth soccer club.

I wish Charlie would be waiting eagerly for my return, thought María Elena. *I've been gone for three weeks and miss him terribly, but that cannot be said of him. He is busy growing up and having fun with his friends. Pretty soon, it will be girls and friends, and then I am afraid that I will lose him forever.*

After a usual quick pass through Customs and Immigration, she said her good-byes to Luis and Johanna and drove her car to her aunt's residence in the northern outskirts of Madrid. It was early summer, and Charlie's school had ended while she was overseas. This year, María Elena intended, would be different. She was planning to spend in August two weeks with Charlie at her parent's place in Mallorca. *The beach will be good for both of us, and we will have time all to ourselves.*

When she arrived at the residence, it was nearly eight in the morning, and she was glad to notice that she had been right. Charlie was waiting for her in the patio. Suited up for his soccer game in a brand-new uniform she had purchased, he came to her and could hardly wait for her to open the car door.

"Mamá, Mamá!" Charlie cried with joy.

Soon after, they were hugging and kissing earnestly, and it seemed that neither wanted to break loose. They stayed that way for an unusual amount of time. *Had something changed? Does Charlie notice something different in me?* María Elena was content in keeping this moment just like it was. A mother and son reunion, one that was very common given the nature of her work. *Maybe something has changed, but only the future will tell.*

CHAPTER SIX

Friday, June 25, 2004; Bogotá, Colombia

Juana and Luis were up early that Friday morning and parked in a side street of a quiet residential complex full of low-cost apartment buildings. The local residents were already exiting their buildings and walking on their way to work to the area bus stops. At the opposite street corner, about two hundred yards away, two additional members of Juana's team were waiting patiently in rented motorcycles.

Ernesto Davila, father of five young children and devoted husband, left every day for work at exactly seven in the morning. He usually wore the same light gray jacket that served as a wind breaker in the chilly morning air of Bogotá. Although it was late June, the high altitude of Colombia's capital kept the temperature most mornings in the range between 55° and 65°F.

Ernesto was a good provider. Thirty-seven years old and a previous serviceman, he had retired from his job in the Colombian Army to work for the U.S. embassy as driver and security officer. When he did that, his pay tripled.

Although now secure for life and with a salary that moved him into the middle class, Ernesto did not move his family out of their small apartment. Instead he saved 50 percent of his money for his children's education and what he expected to be a comfortable retirement.

He saved everything in dollars at the embassy bank. There the money was secure from the ups and downs of the Colombian economy. He also had many more ambitions that included sending his children to the United States to study. His job at the embassy would make it much easier for them to get student visas and attend stateside universities. Yes, indeed, Ernesto had great ambitions and an exciting future.

In a few seconds, Juana intended to change all that. Ernesto came out of his building at seven sharp. Holding his hand was a young child of about seven years of age.

"Damn!" Juana exclaimed to Luis; she did not foresee this eventuality. For some reason, he was taking a child to work with him today. *If only she had more time to study the mark!* This was not a typical operation, due to the crisis created by Mona's capture; the whole operation was compressed in time. *Hopefully, the next three days will go by with only this unexpected turn,* Juana wished.

Luis started their car and waited for her command. Juana did not hesitate; "Okay go!" she said and motioned forward with her left arm.

Luis started moving very slowly in the direction of Ernesto and his son and simultaneously blinked his headlights twice.

At the opposite end of the street, Pancho and Hugo started moving at twenty kilometers per hour in their direction. Pancho, the team's marksman, was first, and Hugo trailed three yards behind. They had practiced this method of approach several times yesterday afternoon until Juana was happy with the results.

Juana's last thought before the action was not typical: *Children, why they always have to get in the way?* she thought. *Have I become a cold killer and impart on the young the same cruelty that befell upon me?*

As Pancho approached the couple, he slowed down his motorcycle and pulled out his Smith and Wesson 9 mm automatic pistol. He slowly raised his arm and aimed.

The noisy street did not drown out all of the noise the approaching motorcycles made, and Ernesto started to turn his head toward them as they approached within ten feet. He clutched his son's hand tightly to prevent the child from darting toward the motorcycles as any good parent would. When he saw the gun, it was too late, and his next reaction sealed his fate. He turned his body to face the gun and protect his son from it.

Pancho had an even better target now. He fired twice in quick succession and hit Ernesto twice in his heart. One of the bullets went straight through his body and sprayed rearward Ernesto's blood on the wall behind and on his son's face.

Ernesto's body fell on the sidewalk as Hugo's motorcycle approached slowly. His son started crying and began to move to embrace his father, and he watched in awful horror as his father's face exploded when struck by Hugo's bullet and was disfigured forever.

Juana's job was to ensure that Ernesto was indeed dead before leaving the scene of the crime. After Pancho and Hugo had sped away, and before any other bystander had reached the body, Juana quickly got out of the car and went to Ernesto. The gruesome scene told all, and she was instantly convinced that Ernesto was dead. Instead of leaving, she instinctively grabbed Ernesto's son and clutched him in her arms. He was covered in blood and was quickly slipping into shock. She walked slowly with him in the direction of his apartment building. When she got there, she put him down slowly in the steps of the building and whispered, "Go to your mamá and tell her what has happened.

"You are a big boy now, hurry!"

Juana turned away and got in the car with Luis. As she closed the door, she only said one word, "Vamos." She looked outside as if to check for any approaching danger, but in reality, she was shielding her face away from Luis. Juana was crying.

Juana was born Juana Abel Martinez Matos. Her father was a good-for-nothing type that beat her mother and left the family when Juana turned seven. She was ten when her mother moved in with Manolo, a man that treated her mother with constant physical abuse and psychological disdain.

When Juana turned twelve, she started to develop into a beautiful young lady. The sexual abuse by her mother's common-law husband started one afternoon when he came in drunk from the corner bar and her mother was at work.

During the next year, the sexual abuse turned to rape, and through it all, Juana kept quiet. Manolo, the abuser, had threatened to harm her mother anytime that Juana refused sex or threatened to talk about it. In fact, the first time that Juana refused oral sex, he had forced all the children to watch as he lashed the back of their mother with his pet látigo. She was scarred for life.

When Juana turned fourteen, she made friends with a local boy that had joined the local guerrilla band. He was sixteen but was an amateur when it came to sex. She taught him everything she knew, and in return, he taught her how to shoot his gun.

A couple of weeks later on a Sunday evening, Manolo was returning late from the bar, and he took the usual shortcut through the local dump. That night, Juana was waiting for him. As he approached, he saw her and said, "Juana, I am a little too drunk for sex. So be a good sport and help me get home tonight, I can't see well."

Juana answered, "I want you to see well tonight of all nights you hijo de puta. *Tonight you meet the devil."*

Manolo tried to move the moment he saw the rifle, but Juana had practiced a lot, and she was now very good at firing it. The bullets cut through Manolo's body and rendered his body lifeless in seconds.

Juana approached him and said, "You are where you belong, Manolo, in the dump with the rest of the trash." She turned away and walked out of her current life and into the world of the guerrilla movement. She joined the Cucho Ramos Armed Front that same evening.

The embassy staff got word of Ernesto's killing at about ten thirty in the morning. The FBI and CIA chiefs got word to meet immediately with Paul White, the deputy chargé of mission, in his office. After the head of security briefed them all on the current events, Warren spoke first.

"Sir, I had my staff investigate Mr. Dávila, and we found an interesting fact that may shed some light on his murder."

"Go ahead, Mr. Westback."

"Sir, he has been employed by us for three years, and in that time, he has secured away $25,000 in his savings account at the embassy bank. He has used the post office privileges routinely. To me, he is a bit player in the drug business that got greedy and was gunned down by his own gang for some unexplained reason. This money implicates him, case closed."

"Wait, Warren, let's not rush to conclusions," Mike Malone, the FBI representative and embassy legal attaché, said in response.

"I am not rushing anything, how else can you explain that this yo-yo was able to save that much money in three short years. He only gets $19,550 paid a year, simply it's impossible, and may I add it is to be expected of these people. Aren't they the most corrupt country in the world?"

"Okay, gentlemen, why don't you go back and try to find out more about Ernesto's murder. We owe a rational explanation to the ambassador by this afternoon, and Warren, cut the yo-yo crap will you."

"Yes, sir."

It was mid-afternoon when word of the Bogotá killing of an embassy employee got to SOUTHCOM headquarters. The chief of staff called for an emergency meeting of the intelligence and operations directorates. They met at the chief's office.

Brigadier General Mike Huber, United States Marine Corps, was a decorated veteran and an astute administrator. He always had a keen awareness of when danger was brewing. He had in front of him two genuine American heroes: Brigadier General Omar Vazquez, U.S. Army, and Brigadier General Jose Luis Ramirez.

General Huber spoke first, "Omar, this situation in Colombia, did we see it coming?"

Omar Vazquez, native of Galveston, Texas, and the director of intelligence, replied, "No, Mike, the State Department has posted a standing caution to embassy employees that Americans are FARC or ELN targets, but at no time have we extended this caution to Colombian citizens working for us."

"And why is that?"

"The illegal armed groups and other underworld characters routinely kidnap Colombian citizens, but those are the politically connected or the rich and famous. The ordinary citizen is relatively safe unless he is caught in the wrong place at the wrong time. This is also true of assassinations. We have received very little information, but the preliminary report sure looks like a professional hit."

"Do you think this a new tactic to destabilize the support of the United States to the Colombian government?" Mike added.

"By all means, it could be the start of a new campaign of terror specifically directed at the U.S., but it also could be a specific act of violence. Bogotá is one of the most violent capital cities in the world."

"I agree with Omar. It is too early to tell what this incident was until we get further word from the embassy. We have our staffs trying to find out more. Believe me, Mike, if there is more to this, our staff will find out." Pepe Ramirez was very confident of his own people, and he had always got the best intelligence from Omar's directorate.

"Furthermore, I am going to Bogotá today and will find out personally why this happened."

"Yes, I remember. The human rights issue, isn't it?"

"Yes, Mike, and I know what you are thinking, you know I will be careful."

"Vaya con Dios," Mike said.
"I will be back by Monday, and thank you, amigo."

Carlos Manuel Cortes and son went to the evening game between the Los Angeles Dodgers and the Anaheim Angels. They found seats in aisle 19 just between home plate and the Dodger dugout. The Dodgers had a forgettable team, even though they were in first place in late June; instead, every one came to see the Angels. They were the new kids on the block even though the franchise was years old by now.

Who cared about Gagne, Lo Duca and Nomo. The Dodgers had no truly recognizable player and were starting to show the lack of appeal true of a second-rate team. This year, even the Chicago Cubs had it right. They had surrounded their marquee player, Sosa, with a host of major-league stars. They and the crop of impressive young pitchers were the future of baseball.

It had been quite some time since his last visit to Dodger Stadium. He was here last during the 1988 World Series when, as a young rookie cop, he was assigned to crowd-control duties. Assigned to the Dodger dugout area, he had finished his duty after the miracle ending of the second game in the series when Manager Tommy Lasorda came to him and presented a baseball signed by Orel Hershiser and himself. Carlos later felt some disappointment when the Dodgers won the series in Oakland and did not return to Dodger Stadium for more games that year.

However, Carlos was happy to be here with his father. They had a good seat right behind first base and were settling down to watch the game when Carlos's cell phone vibrated. It was Roger, his administrative clerk. *Funny, he normally does not call me while on leave.*

"Yes, Roger," Carlos answered, slightly surprising his father. "How is everything at work? You are working late."

"Sorry to bother you, Mr. Cortes, but we have a situation at work, and the boss would like you to call him tomorrow at noon."

"Okay, Roger, anything else?"

"Call him at home, and, boss, hope you are having a great time with your family."

"As a matter of fact, I am. The Giants are visiting us, and we are hoping to see Barry Bonds hit a long one tonight and the Dodgers to emerge victorious regardless."

"Enjoy the game."

"Thank you, Roger. I will call tomorrow."

Carlos hit the End Call button and thought to himself, *Now what. 'Tomorrow at noon' was the code to call ASAP and secure. Only Warren Westback would think this up late on a Friday night.* Carlos knew one thing; Warren normally overreacted like this only when pressured by above. That meant the embassy or headquarters. He decided to call the latter.

Carlos pulled out a headset cord and connected it to the cell phone. He hit and held the number 8 button to connect to the twenty-four-hour Operations Control Center in Langley, Virginia. When the phone was answered by Langley, Carlos hit the code for his controller and waited to establish communications. A small red light lit up on the screen to confirm he was connected securely.

"Hola, Rock."

Carlos recognized the sweet voice of Shirley Miller and wanted to say something nice in return but was forced by protocol to speak in code first. "What's up?" This was the code to tell her he was not secure on the other side and could not speak about classified topics. However, she was not so restricted due to the technology that allowed her to speak openly and automatically have her words scrambled on her end, transmitted, and quickly unscrambled by Carlos's cell phone on the other end.

"I don't know, Rock. We are waiting from word from your office about an embassy worker that was murdered early today," she continued knowing that Carlos was restricted by SOP. "His name was Ernesto Dávila, and he was the military group driver. Preliminary report from your office calls it a drug gang hit. They suspect Mr. Dávila was mailing drugs for them through the embassy post office. I'm sorry, but there is nothing else."

Carlos absorbed the news and swallowed hard. Ernesto was a very good worker and was very proud of his family. One thing his instinct told him instantly was that Ernesto was not a drug mule. He spoke next, "Thank you, Shirley, I guess I have to call the office. I hope you are well."

"John and I are well, and thanks for asking." Like many other CIA female employees, Shirley once had a crush with Carlos Cortes. They had gone through training together and were very close; but time and distance were great hurdles, and eventually, Shirley fell in love and married a fellow worker. "Rock, do me a favor, will you?"

"Yes, Shirley."

"Get done with that assignment in Colombia soon. We need you at headquarters. You are one of the most experienced and decorated agents we have. Your skills are being wasted on the field."

"Like always, Shirley, you are most kind. Get me a promotion, and I will consider it. I hope to see you soon. Good-bye."

"Good-bye, Rock."

Carlos put his phone away and decided to wait a while to call Warren. *I am going to enjoy the game first and will wake him up later,* he thought.

"Work issues, son?" asked his father.

"Yes, Dad."

"I was not aware that agriculture issues were that important, son. Is the coffee crop going bad?"

"No, Dad, just issues at the embassy. I will call my boss later."

"You must find a job that uses your education in criminology. What a waste, after you dedicated so much time and effort to get an education, you should put it to work for you. Why don't you come back to LA, son? Your brother should be able to get your job back."

If he only knew the truth, thought Carlos. "*Cálmate,* Papá, I know what I am doing. I have a good career and should get a promotion soon, maybe even move to Washington DC."

"You are no longer a young ranchero, son. I hope this promotion happens soon. How about this Shirley, is she a sweetheart?"

"No, Papá, just a work acquaintance. She is happily married. Don't start—please—on my personal life now, let's enjoy the game."

"Okay, son, let's enjoy the game. I still have that ball you got me during the '88 Series. It is one of my proudest possessions."

The team of five patriots was meeting near Pedro's house in front of the courtyard of the local police headquarters. "Safest place I could find," Luis had said. Indeed, the location was the safest in the neighborhood to meet and plan the events of Saturday.

Juana asked the first question. "Are you set to drive for Ernesto tomorrow?"

"Yes, I volunteered to cover for Ernesto today and was asked by Colonel Platford to work overtime tomorrow. Today we picked up General Ramirez at the airport, and he is staying in his hotel tonight. Tomorrow at eight in the morning, I am taking them to the police heliport for their trip to Meta."

"Good," said Juana. "That will never happen. We have plans for the police station tonight."

"Is your backup plan to drive to Meta?"

"Yes, there is no other way to get there expeditiously."

"Okay, Pedro." Juana was talking in an operational tone, so determined to succeed that she forgot her loved ones were involved. "I have decided that we must kill Colonel Platford. There simply is no room for him in the truck we have secured for the getaway."

Pedro looked down after receiving the news. *What a change to my livelihood,* he thought. *Colonel Platford is such a good man with a beautiful family.* One last brief thought passed through his mind before he gave his answer. *Can you do this, Mr. Muñiz?*

Slowly, Pedro raised his head and assented. He said quietly, "You can count on me, Jefa."

Juana and Luis spent the next fifteen minutes describing to Pedro how the plan would develop. Nothing would happen until the car was south of Villavicencio. Exactly twelve kilometers after passing the village of Acacias, there was a bridge over the Cabuyaro River. If all was normal, Juana herself would be at the side of the road just two kilometers short of the bridge to give the all clear signal. Once Pedro received the signal, all he had to do was stop at the side of the road immediately passing the bridge and stop just short of a car driven by Pancho. He would use his pistol to restrain the car occupants until Pancho could finish the abduction. Juana, Luis, and Hugo would pull up to the embassy car with the produce truck and transfer General Ramirez. Once that was completed, Pedro and Pancho would get rid of the embassy car at the next large turn of the road. There was a three-hundred-meter drop at that location and would make the abduction actually look like an accident.

After the plan was covered three times, Pedro asked the last question, "Juana, are you sure we will succeed?" Pedro let a little of his insecurity show.

Juana reassured him going back to her usual deferential tone. "Mr. Muñiz, get used to it, *patriota*. Our business is a dangerous one, but one that when taken seriously can be very rewarding. Rest assured tonight, tomorrow we will succeed."

It was ten thirty at night when Carlos finally called Warren Westback. At the other end of the line, a very irritated chief of station answered in an angry tone, "Rock, do you know what time it is? I needed to talk to you hours ago."

"Why, Warren, I could not find a secure room until now. We are going to talk classified, aren't we?" Carlos was speaking from the parking lot of Dodger Stadium. "Anyway, what happened back home that you need me for?"

"Ernesto Dávila, the military group driver, was shot dead this morning, and the ambassador is throwing a fit. I think it was a drug gang-related hit and need to convince him not to raise the alert level at the mission and make such a fuss over it."

"Ernesto was a good man, Warren. I doubt that this was gang related."

"Hogwash! The man had a large sum of money saved in the local bank. He was obviously crooked, Rock, these people are all crooks. The bottom line is I need you here on Monday to track down the police investigation into the killing."

"Warren, have you forgotten about my training at the Agency next week?"

"I have asked Roger to excuse you from that training. Get back here ASAP!"

Carlos ignored him and continued, "Malone, what does he think Warren?"

"You know him, he is noncommittal and wants more time to form an opinion."

"Wise man, I think. Maybe you should agree with the ambassador and, as a precaution, add a layer of security to any activities we have planned for the weekend, Warren."

"I am certainly not going to overreact, just get here by Monday, Rock. It's an order."

"I am just being cautious, Warren. I will be there on Monday." Carlos did not wait for the reply and cancelled his connection from his end. At the headquarters in Langley, Virginia, Shirley Miller tagged the recording as "Conversation regarding Ernesto Dávila's murder—24 June 2004" and went back to her work.

Carlos slowly returned to his seat to break the disappointing news to his dad. The Dodgers were down 12-0 in the bottom of the seventh inning, and Carlos suspicions about the team were further reinforced. "Papá, I have bad news. I will not be able to see you in two weeks during the League of United Latin American Citizens convention in San Antonio. I have been recalled to work and may not be able to come back."

His father understood; he was used to his son being gone by now. All he said was "Still very unusual, son. You are being called back to work on agricultural problems late on a Friday evening. It must be one big insect infestation all right."

To that, all Carlos could say was "I love you, Papá."

CHAPTER SEVEN

"Que viva la revolución!"

Saturday, 26 June 2004; Bogotá, Colombia

For security forces of the Colombian police, the day started early. At 12:15 AM, the evening calm was ruptured by an angry blast of exploding surface-to-surface rockets aimed at the main heliport and headquarters of the city police department in what seemed a scene stolen from recent similar attacks in Iraq.

Three members of Juana's team had just released twenty-three rockets from the back of a pickup truck at the police headquarters. The rockets were unguided, but the experience of Juana's main explosives expert Roberto Suros ensured that the main target was hit.

In a second, two of the four helicopters resting in the yard were in flames. Seconds later, the main fuel tank of one exploded, ensuring that the simple attack was immediately successful. Due to the lateness of the attack, there were no immediate casualties. The fire was put out in two hours, the yard cleared by five in the morning, and the two remaining helicopters were readied for flight; then, the second rocket attack happened.

This time the attack came from a different angle, and neither of the remaining helicopters was hit directly. What the attack caused was instant confusion and numerous casualties. The Colombian police immediately went into lockdown of the entire zone surrounding the headquarters and other possible targets of interest to the guerrillas.

By six in the morning, the decision to cancel any helicopter operations that did not directly support the search for the guerrillas were cancelled for the day. Juana's plan was working.

Luis Montes woke up Juana at six. Juana could feel his erection but felt very uneasy about a romantic moment with her lover today. She was feeling faint and felt as if a bug in her food had unsettled her stomach. She used the excuse of the pending kidnapping to brush off the advances and rose slowly to prepare for the day's events.

When she rose, it took her at least three minutes to feel better again. However, she decided that the kidnapping was more important than her health and quickly forced herself into the cadence of operations that she was famous for among her FARC comrades.

By then, Roberto and Papo Suros had ditched the rocket launcher from the back of their pickup and were heading south of the city with a load of plantains in the bed of the truck. A quick phone call revealed that her first two team members were safe and were returning to base.

Pepe Ramirez rose early also and went down at seven in the morning to the hotel lobby for breakfast. There were very few patrons in the restaurant, but one caught his eye immediately.

Pedro Duque, military liaison assistant for Congressman Dan Smolen, was a friendly face in the room and was rising slowly to greet him. "Pedro, how wonderful to meet you here today," said Pepe. "Why are you in Bogotá?"

"Same reason that you are here for, I would imagine, sir. General Goodman probably wants to ensure that the accusations on human rights abuses are false, doesn't he?"

Pedro Duque was a very smart man; he held a doctorate in foreign affairs from the University of Notre Dame, came from a very wealthy Cuban family in Miami, and was an aggressive young member of his party—a rising star.

"I am meeting today with General Torres and with two different human rights NGOs. I will nip this problem at the bud, sir. I know that the Colombians have come a long way in their fight to ensure that both their police and military forces respect the rights of all Colombians. What we need is a plan to ensure both sides are happy with the state of affairs and, in particular, with the status of Mona Pedroso. I understand that she was high up in the organization of the FARC."

"That is very kind of you to clue me in, Pedro. You guess correctly, and I will work the issue directly with Generals Torres and Escobedo this weekend. Maybe we can meet here tonight and compare notes?"

"It's a date, sir. By the way, did you hear the large explosions last night?"

"Yes, I tell you what, the worst part of this job is that I cannot control what is going on around me. During my last assignment in Iraq, I knew everything that was going on around my air base. I am most proud that all of my troops came back safely to the U.S. after the year was up. I should get an update from my military group commander this morning, and by tonight, I will let you know what happened from the U.S. point of view."

"And I will ask General Torres for the Colombian angle. After all, he is the deputy minister of defense."

"Okay," added Pepe. "I will see you at seven sharp."

"I will be here."

While Pepe was having his breakfast, Colonel Platford walked in to the restaurant and sat down with him. After normal pleasantries, he said, "Sir, we are driving to General Escobedo's headquarters today. There were several guerrilla attacks in and around the city yesterday and last night, and the police are using all of their available resources to track them down."

"Of course, Colonel Platford. How will this affect our schedule today?"

"I had to move our meeting with General Escobedo to 11:00 AM and cancelled the meeting with General Torres that was scheduled for 2:00 PM. He has graciously agreed to meet with you tomorrow morning before your trip back to Miami. I don't think he is the kind of man that spends Sunday mornings in church."

"Well, believe me, the Lord will definitely treat him kindly when it's time for his final judgment. He has done great things for his country trying to solve the problems that plague his society. I have never met a more resourceful and original military planner in my life. So when do we leave?"

"As soon as possible, sir, I have a car waiting."

"Okay, let me pay my bill, and I will be ready in five minutes."

It was five forty-five in the morning California time when Carlos rose, unable to sleep anymore. He put on his jogging clothes and went outside for an early morning jog. Carlos took his secure phone with him.

The call to Mike Malone took seconds to connect. In the four short months since he had met Mike, Carlos knew that he had found a true partner in the common fight to stop the illegally armed groups in Colombia and their link to the drug trade.

"Mike?" Carlos asked.

"Yes, Rock, isn't it early in Los Angeles for you to be calling me? Plus aren't you on vacation?"

"My vacation ended yesterday, Mike. Warren recalled me, and I am flying there later today."

"What for?" asked Mike. "Warren thinks he solved the problem already. In fact, he is trying to convince the ambassador of his theory this morning."

"He is full of it, Mike. Ernesto Dávila was a good man and definitely not a drug trafficker. I can put my reputation on the line on that one. He was the most trustworthy Colombians working in the embassy. In fact, I am happy that Warren recalled me because I am going to track down his killers and get them to justice."

"I agree with you on Ernesto, Rock. So what can I do for you? Things are hectic here, there were two rocket attacks on the police headquarters last night. Two helicopters were hit and destroyed. The whole city is in lockdown looking for the perpetrators."

"I am calling you because I think the ambassador should raise the alert level at the embassy. What you just told me about the rocket attack further reinforces my feelings. Last night, Warren shrugged off my concerns, and I think that kind of attitude is incorrect. We are all in danger, Mike, I think the attacks were caused by Mona's abduction."

"I see. And you don't want to go over your bosses' heads. That's probably a pretty smart move calling me, Rock. I agree with you that the situation calls for caution. We do not know their next move, and if I am the only one that believes you, that's enough. I will go with your instincts and recommend the raise of the alert level this morning. The ambassador has to follow my counsel. After all, I am partly responsible for the security of embassy personnel."

"Mike, one more thing, is there any distinguished visitors in town this weekend?"

"Yes, Rock. It is a normal weekend. There is a congressional group in town inquiring on the latest human rights abuse allegations, the Department of State Special Ambassador to Latin America, and, of course, your friend General Ramirez."

"My god, I forgot about Pepe. Do me a great favor, Mike, babysit these visits this weekend, and I will help you tomorrow morning after I arrive."

"Trust me, Rock, I will. The only one that is out of my control is General Ramirez, they are soon on their way to General Escobedo's headquarters in Meta and will be back this afternoon."

"How are they traveling, Mike?"

"By car, I believe, Colonel Platford and his driver are taking the general to his meeting."

"Mike . . . the Milgroup's driver was Ernesto."

"No kidding, Rock. I did not think of that, and I have to admit, I do not know who is driving them. I will find out however, trust me."

"I trust you, Mike, get busy on the other two visits, and I will call Colonel Platford directly at his cell phone. That is all I can do this far away to help, Mike."

"Okay, Rock. See you tomorrow." Mike Malone hung up the phone and diverted his attention to the country's visitors. *Another Saturday gone!*

Carlos dialed the number for the Milgroup's commander Colonel Platford. On the other end, Pedro Muñiz answered, "Hello, this is Mr. Muñiz, can I help you?"

Carlos instantly knew who was driving Pepe today, and he felt relaxed for the first moment since yesterday evening. *You could trust Mr. Muñiz, accomplished driver and hero, nobody better to replace Ernesto,* thought Carlos.

"Hello, Mr. Muñiz, is Colonel Platford there? This is Mr. Cortes of the agriculture section."

"No, sir, he is inside with a visitor. I am driving them today on official business."

"Well, Mr. Muñiz, I am calling on behalf of the director of security. We are worried with security due to recent events in the capital. Can you tell him to give me a call at this cell phone number when he gets back to your location please?"

"Yes, sir, I will."

"Pedro, drive safely please. See you on Monday."

"Pedro out, adios."

Pedro Muñiz carefully removed the battery from the rear of the cell phone and destroyed the terminal connectors. He replaced the battery and took pleasure in noting that the phone's screen was now blank.

Carlos thought how odd the last words of Pedro Muñiz sounded. *It seems like he was on a military mission and was signing off an HF radio transmission.*

He did not know that his perception was absolutely correct. Pedro Muñiz was playing his role; from this day on, he was a guerrilla.

Thousands of miles away, María Elena Borbón was watching as her son ran with the ball down the left side of the *fútbol* field. He was quite adept at handling a soccer ball, and most kids his age could not keep up with him.

What drove him apart from most fast players was the devastating left foot he possessed. Charlie was the top scorer on his team. He had a decent shot with his right foot; after all, he was right-handed. But in the field, his coach quickly noticed his left foot, and a lifetime dedication to the left-wing position was slowly developing.

In Spain, if you were this good, a professional team would recruit children as young as fourteen to sign contracts with their youth development teams. Charlie was twelve, and the best team in the land, Real Madrid, was already coveting purchasing his services for their development.

At that moment, eighteen yards away from the goal and on an extreme angle, Charlie let loose with a shot on goal that was simply amazing. The two teams just stopped and admired as the ball gathered speed and began a sharp left arc to the goal. The opposing goalie lounged at the ball but was not quick enough. The ball crossed the goal line no more than one yard from the ground still arcing and deposited itself in the net behind the goalie. It was Charlie's twentieth goal of the season, a team record.

María Elena rejoiced at experiencing only the fourth goal of the season of Charlie's twenty. She resolved right then and there that she would devote more time to her son. *After we come back from Palma, I will tell my boss to transfer me to a job at the headquarters. I must spend more time with my son. Only trip left is the Colombia operation, that's it!*

For some reason, Juana Montes had lost her focus once again this morning. In her late twenties and in the middle of an operation, she again permitted her mind to wander what the future held in store for her and Luis. Her thoughts betrayed her concentration. What had happened? She could not understand it; one thing for sure, she had not lost her devotion and determination or her will to fight. What was different she could not understand. Was it meeting Mr. Muñiz and acquiring a new family?

What Juana did not understand was buried deep inside of her; her body was changing. With these changes came a transition, a whole different attitude about the survival of the species. Juana would have to battle these urges in the coming months. For now, it would be days, maybe weeks, before she found out the truth. She was going to be a mother.

Luis woke her from her thoughts, almost startled her. "There they are. The embassy car is approaching, I will follow it carefully."

"Don't be too obvious even if it is your father driving," cautioned Juana.

In the car, Pepe Ramirez noticed the little green car as they passed it. *The young couple in it seemed innocent enough with a beautiful girl in the right seat,* thought Pepe, *yet you can never be too careful.* It was the fighter pilot sense that was engrained in him since pilot training, or maybe even from before, long before in the streets of Rio Piedras, Puerto Rico.

Pepe lived in an exclusive neighborhood of San Juan. From there, he took a daily public bus to his private school in Rio Piedras. Colegio San Jose was a Catholic high school run by the Marianist Brothers of Dayton, Ohio. It was a college preparatory school, and the entire school body consisted of sons of the elite families in San Juan. There were one or two underprivileged children attending classes with them. These kids also merited being there; they were smart.

One such student was Lino. He was not only intelligent; Lino was also street-smart. During the four years of high school, Pepe formed a lasting friendship with Lino. From him, Pepe learned the value of checking your back, of developing a sixth sense for survival. This training had saved him from dangerous situations in later years. It also was applicable to the training given a fighter pilot in the military. Pepe was always ready for the unexpected. He was constantly, as they say in fighter pilot talk, checking his six o'clock.

Pepe remembered how this sixth sense helped him destroy his second MiG during Desert Storm. It was a daylight encounter between Iraqi fighters and a four ship of American F-15s on the second day of the war. He was the lead pilot for the second echelon and was following his leader's maneuvers when he noticed a single MiG-27 approach the flight from slightly behind and below the four-ship formation.

Calling out the intruder and keeping him in view, he waited for his leader to make a determination on how to counter this lone fighter. Flying flight lead that day was Ed "Too Tall" Huber; like his name implied, Ed was tall in stature but not in ego. Recognizing that Pepe's formation was in a better position, Ed said, "Pepe, you take him, I'll cover."

Pepe acknowledged the order and did a high yo-yo to fall in position directly behind the MiG. However, the Iraqi pilot was good. Acting alone, he decided to take on Pepe's two-ship and countered by pulling his aircraft straight into Pepe to attempt a high-altitude reversal on him. Pepe's senses tingled as he watched the experienced pilot attempt this new maneuver. He coolly went to zero gravity while turning the formation on his own reversal to the right and fall directly behind the MiG at almost zero airspeed.

The F-15 has powerful engines; for the MiG to out accelerate the American fighter, he must be heading down in full power to get an edge. So the MiG pilot swept his wings back while turning upside down and beginning a maneuver known as a split-S.

Pepe immediately recognized this last ditch attempt to lose him and calmly permitted his aircraft to mimic the MiG and follow behind. Next to him, he quickly noticed his wingman Lieutenant Roger "Rocket" Mann follow the events from slightly behind the pair of aircraft standing in reserve if needed. "This kid is good." Pepe made a mental observation so that he would debrief his wingman later at the base.

The aircraft were all screaming at the ground; now heading straight down and passing five hundred knots indicated airspeed, Pepe's senses warned him about three things in quick succession. First, the MiG was in fact outracing his aircraft. Something that the missile Pepe was locking on to the aircraft would hardly notice. It had plenty of catching up ability in its arsenal. Second, the MiG pilot was pulling 6 Gs in the split-S recovery, apparently the maximum that he could tolerate with his training. Since all F-15 pilots were trained to tolerate 9 Gs, or nine times the pull of gravity on their bodies, Pepe knew that they had a tactical advantage there. Third and most alarming was the rate at which they were closing in on the ground. They were at six thousand feet in their altimeter and still at sixty degrees nose-low attitude.

If his formation continued to follow the MiG, they would hit the ground! "Pull out! Pull out!" Pepe's command was followed by Rocket immediately, and both aircraft instantly went to a 9 G recovery, momentarily forgetting about their quarry. Once they leveled off at one thousand feet above the ground, Pepe looked low and to the left to see a smoking hole in the ground where the Iraqi pilot had impacted. That was Pepe's second confirmed kill of the war, and he had not even fired a shot.

"Señor," Pepe said to Pedro, "please watch that car that pulled out behind us. They seemed like if they were waiting for us to pass to fall in behind."

92

"I will, General Ramirez," Pedro answered.

Colonel Platford added, "Pedro is one of our most accomplished drivers, sir. He once saved the ambassador from a certain kidnapping by maneuvering his car around a trap. He is the hero of our little embassy."

Twenty-five minutes later, Pedro told Colonel Platford that he felt a problem with the steering mechanism of the vehicle and was going to stop at the next opportunity. Having lost the green car in the distance and sensing no danger, the colonel assented, and Pedro began looking for a good spot. Straight ahead and exactly twelve kilometers after the town of Acacias, there was a truck stop on the side of the road where a white cargo truck was parked on the far end of the clearing.

Pedro's training included instructions to park away from any structures and vehicles when stopping short of the destination like this. So he stopped the car just after passing a small bridge and as far away from the truck as he could.

After stopping, Pedro started to move across the front seat in an attempt to exit the vehicle on the passenger side away from oncoming traffic. At the same moment, two men left the vicinity of the truck and started moving toward them. One of them was carrying a blue pail.

Pepe's senses started tingling about possible danger. Immediately his mind raced through a survival checklist that seemed engrained to his brain. *Gun? In the briefcase on the front seat. Safety? Bulletproof body armor and car. Escape route? The river below and behind.*

But before he could act on any of his suspicions, the only person that could betray them inside the bulletproof car did.

Pedro stopped his motion to exit the car and instead turned toward Colonel Platford from the passenger side and fired twice into his face. Pedro did not miss; he was once a champion marksman and bodyguard to the president of Colombia.

Colonel Platford's expression of shock and incredulity did not change in death. His lifeless body slumped in his seat.

"No, no, General Ramirez. I am not here to harm you unless you try something funny. Please stand still."

For once in his life, Pepe Ramirez—brigadier general, war hero, leader, and devoted father and husband—was trapped. He did not resist capture for now. He noticed how the little green car stopped next to his vehicle and out of the front seat came out a very beautiful young woman and a nice-looking young man that resembled a much younger face of his driver Pedro Muñiz. His senses had not failed; only the cruel treachery of an embassy employee caused his colonel's death and his capture.

His side door was opened by one of the men from the truck, and immediately, a rag he was carrying was thrust to his face. After a slight struggle, Pepe felt his senses failing, and unconsciousness take hold of his body.

Juana stood over his slumped body and said, "General Ramirez, you can now consider yourself a prisoner of war."

CHAPTER EIGHT

The best flight Carlos was able to get on was one that left Los Angeles International Airport at 12:55 AM. He was flying Mexicana Airlines followed by a change of aircraft in Mexico City to an Avianca flight direct to Bogotá. He would arrive there at one ten in the afternoon the next day. This was the fastest and most direct way to travel between the two cities.

To Angelinos, it was very difficult to understand why the world's airlines refused to fly direct into LAX. Only a handful did to a city that was the capital of entertainment and the hub of air and maritime commerce for the region.

Carlos was lucky; his total travel time was ten hours and fifteen minutes. Most other connections would take him over fifteen hours to complete.

Since his early morning run, Saturday had been a blur of activity for Carlos. He took an afternoon nap in preparation for a family dinner his mother had planned for Saturday night.

The dinner was delicious, and meeting all his relatives living in the Los Angeles area was very gratifying for him. In the end, he had very little time to say his good-byes, pack, and once again hug his mother for an inordinate amount of time. Carlos wished she would last him a few more years, but the cancer she had was resisting treatment.

Luckily the drive to the airport only took forty minutes since traffic was light that evening. At the airport, Carlos had time enough for a quick beer. The bar in this location had microbrew selections that were difficult to find in Latin America.

Carlos settled into a barstool and permitted his attention to focus on *CNN Headline News* now starting the 11:30 PM segment. The news was predictable; the beginning segment mentioned the top news of the day including coverage of the turnover of government in Iraq. Other headlines were less interesting, and Carlos let his mind wander back fifteen months when he was a team leader of CIA and Special Forces operatives the opening night of Operation Iraqi Freedom.

It was the last headline that refocused his attention back to the newscast. The announcer said, "Two U.S. servicemen and a Colombian U.S. employee missing in Colombia. Late this evening, the Pentagon has confirmed that two high-ranking members of the U.S. Southern Command are missing from a day trip in the vicinity of the capital of Colombia. CNN has just confirmed that the embassy car they were driving was spotted down a deep embankment as sundown cancelled rescue efforts for the evening."

"Damn." Carlos's remark made other patrons look up and wonder what had caused his reaction. Most were not interested in the news and were caught up talking to others or simply, desperately staring at their beers.

Carlos dropped some money on the counter and quickly exited the premises while pulling out his secure phone. Moments later in a quiet part of the airport, his secure connection to Shirley Miller was completed.

"Hello, Rock, you call so soon, miss me?"

"No, Shirley, I just heard a headline on CNN that scared me. What happened in Colombia today?"

"Are you referring to the rocket attack on the police headquarters, the shoot down of a spray helicopter over the coca fields, or the car accident? Today was a busy day down there."

"The car accident, Shirley, give me the details please."

"We don't have much, Rock. The accident happened in the morning hours south of Villavicencio, Colombia. It took all day to find the vehicle after it was reported missing by the Colombian Army. It seems the Milgroup commander had an appointment with Major General Escobedo and failed to show up. The car is in a deep crevice, and this is odd, it was found on a side road and not the one used to travel between the capital and the military base they were visiting. The personnel missing are Mr. Muñiz, an embassy employee; Colonel Platford, the Milgroup commander; and Brigadier General Ramirez, the J-3 at Southern Command. The embassy fears the worst."

Carlos cringed when Shirley confirmed what he feared most, his friend was missing and was presumed dead! He reacted and quickly transitioned to an operational tone with her. He told her, "Shirley, I need your help tonight. I am about to get on an all-night flight back to Colombia and will be out of touch for ten hours.

"Yes, Rock, of course."

"Call Mike Malone at the embassy, you know, he is the legal attaché there. Talk to him and tell him this exactly, ready to copy?"

"Why, you know we record these conversations, go ahead."

"Suspect accident staged, in reality, kidnapping attempt. Car would not be off course on a side road, this does not follow SOP. Ask embassy security coordinator to request that Colombian armed forces shut down the surrounding area and search all vehicles for the three missing personnel. Rock sends."

"Got it, Rock, you can count on me."

"Thanks, Shirley, gotta go!"

"Ciao, querido," and the conversation was ended.

Manuel Alonso walked in to El Jefe's jungle home in an ebullient mood. He walked into the room that served as conference center, living room, and courtroom, depending on the need. Rafael Terraza was sitting in his normal rocking chair quietly smoking a pipe.

Manuel nodded to his boss and said, "The operation was a success. Our radio operator just confirmed that Juana's team was victorious and is safely on its way home. 'Team plus two and victory,' was the message passed."

"*Caramba*, that is certainly great news. She did all I asked in the time allotted and is bringing us truly a wonderful gift, an American!"

"That makes four we hold, Jefe."

"No, the others are being held by someone else's group. This American is mine, and he is high-ranking to boot. Let's celebrate tonight."

"Sorry, Jefe, I will help you draft the message that will carry the ransom demands for the American. A colonel for Mona, that should be our only demand to the *cabrones*."

"I like it! You will go far, Manuel, you even have a catchy phrase. What is your best guess of Juana's arrival?"

"Ten days at the most, she should be here next Monday at the latest."

That very moment, Juana and her team were settling down for the night in the small town of Malabrigo. It had been a smooth ride so far; after the abduction of General Ramirez, the team had split in two. Pedro and Luis had driven the small car and the embassy car to a side road for disposal. They had no problem finding a deep canyon and had pushed the embassy car with Colonel Platford's body off the side down a six-hundred-meter steep grade. Then they had returned to Villavicencio to pick up Pedro's wife. She too was now embroiled in the fight toward a better life for all Colombians, not only for the rich and powerful Criollos.

Juana, Hugo, and Pancho had continued in the delivery truck with precious cargo. The general was sedated and sleeping on a space between the truck cab and the cargo area. Today's load was rice; Pancho was a known food distributor, and they carried what appeared to be a full load of rice in the truck.

When stopped by the police, which happened frequently, Pancho would bribe his way out of trouble by giving some of his cargo away. Today they had presented two large sacks of rice so far. Never was there any hint of trouble in either police checkpoint. *Good,* Juana had thought. *So far the plan is working.*

On one occasion, they were surprised by a new checkpoint close to their destination. Since Pancho did not recognize the military personnel involved, he asked Juana to share the hideout between the driver's cab and the load of rice with General Ramirez. They did not want to risk Juana being noticed by strange soldiers and risk the entire operation on the sexual appetites of young men with guns.

To clear this new checkpoint, Pancho had to bribe them with two sacks of rice. This was small change for Pancho who made most of his profit by being the conduit of small quantities of drugs to the capital, where rich Colombians would buy an ever-increasing quantity of drugs to satisfy their addictions. He carried his load in the same cavity where his most precious cargo was sedated for most of the day.

The house they were in was a FARC home. It was safe for the captors to permit their captive to awake from his slumber, but as a precaution, they covered his mouth to prevent the shouting fits that most captives demonstrated.

Juana noticed how this captive was somewhat different. He had risen from his sleep in a most alert manner. His eyes were not confused or misguided. Juana noticed how the general had slowly studied everyone in the group and was now studying her specifically. He had found the leader.

It would be days before they could remove his gag and permit him to speak. Juana wondered what kind of man he was. She surmised that he had to be a great leader to become a general for the gringos.

For his part, Pepe had wakened suddenly and alertly. From his bindings and his memory, he quickly determined that he was a kidnap victim. *Who are these people, FARC, ELN, or AUC? What do they want? The driver! The reason they succeeded was that the driver turned. I must escape!*

Although his thoughts were somewhat ragged, jumping from one thought to the other, he was quick to study his environments and the people surrounding him. He was in a small home. He was sitting on the floor, and his hands were tied to a structural post between the kitchen and the room that served as entry and living area. As far as he could tell, his bindings were strong, and no movement he could muster would break them in a sudden move.

The people surrounding him were a mixed bag. Some, like the man who walked toward them at the kidnap site, were of the type that he called Jíbaros back in his island of Puerto Rico. Darker in complexion than most and with rugged features, he was not pleasant to look at. His eyes too told the rest of the story; he had the eyes of a killer. He had seen those eyes many times over in his career.

The embassy driver was there too. He and a woman his age were sleeping on a couch next to the entry door. He was light-skinned; obviously, his family had less contact with the Indian and African influence that colored the Jíbaro.

Most worthy of his attention was the young woman of the group. She was a dark beauty. Small and thin, he had seen her face before in a somewhat fleeting moment when they passed on the road from Bogotá. She was very controlled in her actions and words. Spoke softly to the members of the group that were awake and exhibited all the traits of a leader. Pepe's thoughts drove him to one conclusion: *I am the captive of the FARC. She is the reason the FARC has been so successful, they give women leadership roles!* Pepe knew this fact before, but somehow his present situation made this fact take added significance. *It will be difficult to escape from the claws of this seductress, but I will try!* Soon enough, the stress of the day caught up with Pepe, and he fell asleep.

Sunday, 27 June 2004; Bogotá, Colombia

The flight from Los Angeles via Mexico City was early by twenty minutes. Carlos got up from his seat and was out in the immigration area quickly. As usual, he was spirited through the process by eager clerks that recognized him instantly. Carlos was respected and admired by all of the Colombian government personnel he met and dealt with regularly. *If only U.S. personnel were this courteous, we would have a better reputation throughout the world,* thought Carlos.

His ride was waiting outside. He recognized an air force airman dressed in civilian clothes and driving one of the embassy cars, a sure sign that things had changed since his departure. He knew better than to ask for a crash update from the airman, so the ride to the embassy was filled with idle chitchat.

They were at the embassy in twelve minutes a lot less than it would take on a workday. Carlos thanked the airman and quickly went to his office to drop his carry-on luggage. There, his section appeared deserted. None of his counterparts were at work. It was at the embassy's command center that he found both Mike Malone and Jack Smith, the security officer.

"Mike, Jack, what's new?"

Jack answered, "The personnel of General Escobedo were able to reach the crash site about an hour ago. They were assisted by two U.S. Army Special Forces NCOs assigned to Escobedo's brigade."

Carlos feared the worst. They were about to tell him that his friend was found lifeless in the car, and he dreaded that fact. *Was he wrong, did he lose his buddy?*

Jack continued, "The body of Colonel James Platford was recovered, and they are combing the crash site for the missing passenger and the driver of the car. It appears that all three were thrown from the vehicle. We fear the worst."

Carlos interrupted him abruptly, "Jack, hold it. Mike, did you get my message last night that I believed this was a kidnapping attempt?"

"No I did not receive it. Yesterday afternoon, once we secured all other distinguished visitors, Jack and I traveled to the crash site to assist in the recovery. I'm afraid my phone was out of range most of the evening. We came back once the army sergeants were on station and were better suited for the recovery than us, Carlos."

Jack in turn interrupted Mike, "Carlos, what do you mean kidnapping?"

Carlos calmed down a bit and told them, "When I got on the airplane yesterday, I left word with my control center in Langley to pass word to you that I believed the accident was staged. Why on the world would they crash on a road other than the direct route from the capital to General Escobedo's brigade headquarters?"

"It does not follow SOP," added Jack. "My god, why didn't we think of that? We were so worried to recover anyone injured that we skipped over the obvious!"

"What was Colonel Platford's cause of death?" asked Carlos.

"We have not asked, unfortunately, we assumed it was the crash," now Mike chimed in. "Sorry, Carlos, I know how much you like General Ramirez."

"Jack, find out the cause of death ASAP please. Also, can you coordinate with General Escobedo on my theory of a kidnapping attempt? Maybe he can ask his patrols downrange to look for the general and his driver?"

"I will, Carlos."

Carlos turned to the CIA desk in the command center and dialed directly his controller in Langley. On the other end, the day-shift agent answered, "Jim here—"

"Jim, this is Rock, how are you?"

"Fine, Rock, busy days in Colombia lately, I imagine."

"I don't have much time, Jim, can you check in the log and find out who got my message here that I left with Shirley last night about midnight California time?"

"Sure, Rock, Shirley debriefed me on it. The message was passed to Astronaut at 0830 GMT. She tried the other personnel you named but could not contact them. They were out of area, Rock. And Rock, Astronaut was not happy to get this message at 0230 local time."

"Life's a bitch, Jim. Thank you, now I know what happened." Astronaut was Warren Westback's tactical name.

The door to the command center opened, and the ambassador walked in followed by his deputy and a man that Carlos did not recognize. They went straight to Jack Smith and asked about the search for survivors. Carlos approached the group.

Ambassador Peter T. Nimitz was a tall Texan with an instantly recognizable name. He made his money selling furniture and was now comfortably retired from the business. The current administration had hired him onto this very difficult ambassadorial spot due to his party affiliation and his close working relationship with the current secretary of state.

As Carlos approached, he could hear Jack Smith telling the gathering of their new suspicion about a kidnapping attempt. He then heard the man he did not recognize speak.

Pedro Duque asked, "Mr. Smith, are you sure of a kidnapping? What kind of operation are you running here that a United States general officer gets kidnapped in broad daylight?"

Jack answered quietly, "Sir, let me confirm first the kidnapping angle. For now, I am insisting that the Colombian personnel at the accident site continue looking for survivors. Carlos, can you explain to Mr. Duque your theory please."

"Absolutely," Carlos answered.

The ambassador spoke next, "Mr. Duque, Carlos Cortes works directly with the Colombians in support of the counter narco-guerrilla effort. Carlos, Mr. Duque is the military assistant for Congressman Dan Smolen of Florida." There was no need to include Carlos's affiliation with the CIA.

"Sir, two days ago, an embassy driver was murdered on his way to work in front of his child. He was the driver of the military group assigned to this embassy. Although murder is common in this city, this particular one had the attributes of an assassination instead. Two days later, the military group car, now with a new driver, is discovered down a one-thousand-meter embankment. The driver, a longtime employee and one of the safest drivers of the embassy, is not found. Likewise, the distinguished visitor in the car is missing. And finally, the car is found on a road not normally traveled by our personnel and not even on a route that would take them to their destination. Sir, the only conclusion that I can come up with is a kidnap."

Jack Smith interrupted the group with a report from the field. "Gentlemen, the military personnel responded to our query on Colonel Platford. It is obvious to them that the colonel suffered a bullet wound to the face also. The kidnapping theory is becoming stronger every minute."

At that moment, General Goodman had assembled his staff and had ordered to commence twenty-four-hour operations at U.S. Southern Command with the sole objective of recovering his director of operations who was now feared dead. He would have to appoint a general officer to investigate the accident and another to accompany the body home. The same protocol would be followed for Colonel Platford with the exception that a colonel would be appointed to be the escort officer for the body all the way back to his home and burial.

The general started his comments with a poem he had written years before when he was a cadet at West Point.

Who are we to fear death,
Who are we to test the Lord,
Just soldiers obeying orders,
Runners crossing the final ford,
Heroes preventing darkness,
For you, me, and all.

"I know that all of you are saddened by the news that we have lost two of our own. General Ramirez and Colonel Platford were two of our best. I want no stone left unturned for the preparations and final arrangements in support of their families. We must remember these gentlemen quietly and continue our work so that Mrs. Ramirez and Mrs. Platford sense our determination and are comforted by the fact that they are part of this SOUTHCOM family and that we, not them, will work tirelessly to effect the funeral preparations."

The general's words were interrupted by Lieutenant Commander Joyner who entered the room abruptly. He approached the head of the table and spoke quietly to General Goodman. "Sir, the embassy just called the JOIC and confirmed that they had recovered the body of Colonel Platford. The embassy report continued with the startling fact that the colonel was murdered and that they now fear General Ramirez was kidnapped. We are waiting for further clarification, sir."

The commanding general said quietly, "Thank you, Jim." He turned to the table and told the director of intelligence, "Omar, assemble the crisis action planning staff immediately. I want an update of the situation in Colombia by 2000 hours tonight. It appears that our General Ramirez is alive." To the chief of staff, he said, "Mike, please ensure that preparations for the recovery of Colonel Platford continue unabated. Ladies and gentlemen, we have a job to do, let's get to it!"

The ride in the truck had been both short and rough. Pepe Ramirez was again in the small room behind the truck cab, but this time he was awake. Still muffled, he was very uncomfortable due to the high humidity and the rising temperature. When the truck came to rest and was shut down, someone opened a panel that permitted the warm air to at least keep a breeze flowing through his cramped quarters.

Father Frank was a known Catholic priest and a bush pilot. He flew to bring the church to the people and weekly made the rounds to airports throughout Eastern Colombia. When Father Frank arrived in your town, there was mass celebrated whether it was Sunday or not. Father Frank, locally known as Padre Chico, was also an FARC sympathizer.

Today he was landing in Veracruz Airport for only one purpose, to assist Juana's operation and transport a high-value prisoner. He would be flying them south to Calamar, a town approximately forty-five miles away. Father Frank showed no remorse in doing this. All he asked from the FARC was for them to show some restraint in their treatment of the people throughout his area. The FARC leadership obliged.

To Juana, the priest was a problem solver. The most perilous part of her journey was ahead, and the airplane gave her the tool to bypass it completely. The Colombian Army had started a new operation in the area, and the road to Calamar was teeming with troops and checkpoints. Once in Calamar, Juana had a vehicle waiting to take them away from the troops and into friendly territory. Only she, Luis, and Hugo would accompany the priest since the aircraft could handle only five passengers. Pancho would stay with his vehicle and continue his delivery truck business. The others would travel by road to Calamar.

To transfer the general to the plane, Juana had to untie him and remove the gag. So she headed to the truck to talk to her captive for the first time. She found him awash in sweat. "*Buenas tardes, mi general,* I hope that you are comfortable and ready to take a short airplane ride. Now we are going to remove your bindings and gag, but I need you to promise me something. I need you to stay quiet and make no attempt to escape. Hugo here will have a gun to your back, and any false move will be your last. We even have a priest to give you your last rites if you fail me."

Pepe saw the determination in her face and assented with a short nod. He noticed how Hugo tied a rope around his waist, one that later would be tied to Hugo's left arm. *These people take no chances. They have done this before to perfection many, many times,* thought Pepe.

When his gag was removed, he spoke immediately to Juana; he did not raise his voice or show alarm. "Señorita, I recommend that you release me immediately. You have no idea the international problem you have caused and the serious consequences that it will have."

Juana answered, "It's señora, and I am under orders to bring you to my commander. Now you are a military man and understand following orders. So I want you to walk near me to the airplane that waits for us and do so without raising any suspicion. *Comprende?*"

Once outside the truck, Hugo released the arm restraints and pressed his gun deep into the ribs of the general. For good measure, Luis also showed his gun to the general and walked by his side the thirty feet to the plane.

Pepe saw the airplane and instantly recognized it; he had learned how to fly in one of them. It was a Piper Cherokee built around 1970 and was capable of sitting six passengers. When they got to the airplane, the pilot was not there, and the hatch was open. In order to hide their captive, Juana ordered the group to get in the plane and secure the general again. "Tie him up real good, we don't need him to try anything foolish while we are airborne. I am going to find Padre Chico."

Pepe went in first, and the plan in his mind was cemented when he saw the cockpit layout and recognized it. He appeared to stumble while slightly pulling Hugo with him into the plane and stopping his fall with his hands. Then as quickly as he could, he changed a panel on the center console where the owner had added on a system called the Identification, Friend or Foe Transmitter, better known among pilots as the IFF. He noticed the panel was set to 1200 and was set to run anytime the airplane power was on. This was the code normally set for visual flight rules, and he quickly figured that the pilot would ignore the panel prior to their departure, assuming that it was on and set right. He changed the panel to read the international code of distress and prayed that Hugo had not seen him.

"Levantate y sientate hijo de puta."

Pepe answered in a calming tone, "Lo siento."

The stumble made his captors more determined than ever to secure their man. Hugo tied him up in the rear seat, ensuring that he could not make any foolish moves, and later sat next to him. Throughout the process, Luis kept a 9 mm automatic pistol aimed right to his face.

While being tied, his captors did not notice the look of satisfaction that Pepe had; nobody had noticed him changing the code.

Juana and the pilot returned after a few short minutes. She spoke first, "General Ramirez, I hope you are comfortable back there and that you are not afraid of flying."

So they could not recognize his uniform or his wings! *This is good,* thought Pepe.

His hopes were dashed immediately when the pilot spoke next. "Juana, *mi hija,* don't you recognize the uniform? This man is an air force officer and a command pilot. Undoubtedly a fighter pilot, most generals are. Tell me, son, am I wrong?"

Pepe fired back, "You are American, your accent betrays you. What are you doing helping these people?"

"I help because they need love and compassion, not guns and bullets. In time, my son, you will learn that not everything is resolved by conflict. As to being an American, I gave that up long time ago, I belong to the world and to God."

Juana interrupted the conversation, "We have to go, Padre."

"All at the right time, dear. Is everyone buckled up?"

Father Frank turned on the battery and cranked the engine. It started with no problem, and Pepe noticed that it ran very smoothly. *So this man is a priest and a bush pilot and most probably an able mechanic too*, thought Pepe.

They were soon airborne and flying at 145 knots indicated airspeed in a southerly direction. The moment the aircraft lifted off, the IFF transponder started reporting the distress code that Pepe had set. Pepe hoped that the system was working properly. As he had figured, Padre Chico had not looked in the direction of the panel the entire flight. He was unaware of the distress squawk.

Since they did not cover his eyes, Pepe looked outside to orient himself but found that the jungle below appeared similar in every direction. *He must be following the road below to the next airport*, thought Pepe. To him, it was impossible to figure out where he was or where they were taking him. All he knew was that they were heading south, deeper and deeper into the Colombian jungle.

There is an IFF receiver and display console at every Federal Aviation Administration Control Center and at most air traffic control towers in the United States. In Eastern Colombia, there are none. Most air traffic flies visual flight rules, and there are no air traffic radars east of the Andes. Flying at five hundred feet above the jungle, there was no chance for a receiver in the populated portions of Colombia to get the signal that Father Frank's aircraft was transmitting.

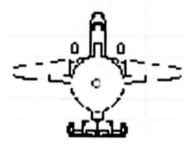

E-2C Hawkeye

High above the Andes, however, an E-2C naval patrol airplane was slowly advancing to a scheduled stop in Bogotá. They had taken off from Ecuador and were transporting the commander of the USS *Ronald Reagan* for a coordination meeting with Colombian Air Force personnel. The *Reagan* was the newest commissioned aircraft carrier in the U.S. inventory and was under way on a cruise throughout South America to introduce its capabilities to partner nations and to exercise its forces with friendly counterparts.

The E-2C Hawkeye is the U.S. Navy's carrier-based early warning and control patrol aircraft. This same type aircraft would occasionally provide support to U.S. drug interdiction efforts in the region, and Colombia benefited directly from the information provided by its air traffic control radar.

Lieutenant Ramón Cintrón was the only person in his console at the rear of the aircraft. He had just finished his training as an aircraft control officer and was practicing with the radar that afternoon. In front of him was a circular screen that he controlled from a console; a mouse assisted his movement on the presentation, and the screen gave him a clear picture of other aircraft flying in the area.

He was interested in a flight of slow movers that were low and very distant from their own position. These aircraft were not squawking with their IFF panels. *Pretty sure that is a combat patrol of helicopters by the Colombians,* Ramón thought. The moving target identification had them pegged traveling at 140 KIAS. *Blackhawks, no doubt!*

At that moment, a blinking light in his panel drew his attention. Ramón efficiently pressed its button to display the information in his screen. He now noticed how an aircraft emergency return was being displayed about thirty miles south of the helicopter operations he had just monitored. *This one is squawking emergency and probably has no Mode C since he is not reporting altitude.* Traveling at 144 KIAS, this return was on a southerly heading.

"Captain Honeycutt, this is Lieutenant Cintrón, sir. I have an unidentified bogey squawking emergency. He is approximately 145 nautical miles east of our position heading south."

The ship commander, Captain Honeycutt, always flew his airplane any chance he could. Certainly the command pressures did not give him many opportunities. Today he was enjoying one of those rare opportunities, and the clear skies and tall mountains of the Andes certainly were beautiful to watch. They had forty minutes to destination to a strange field that was covered with tall mountains. He took the information from the lieutenant and made the only decision he could make; his years of experience told him it was the right one.

"Thank you, Lieutenant, pass the information with coordinates if possible to Commander Lewis. He will call Colombian authorities and warn them of the in-flight emergency. Sorry, crew, but the fuel situation and the unfamiliarity with our destination prevent us from going to the rescue today."

CHAPTER NINE

The report by Mayo 11, the E-2C Hawkeye, was received at the traffic control center run by the Colombian government and by a military control center run by the Colombian Air Force. The Colombians had no resources in the area except for combat helicopters now involved in operations south of San José del Guaviare.

The Colombians made note of the report and did nothing. They would wait for reports of missing aircraft and people before taking further action on the matter.

Training the Colombian Air Force controllers were a couple of U.S. Air Force air traffic control technicians. Although it was a Sunday, they were at work due to a training schedule that was complicated by the inexperience of the recruits being trained. They took notice of the events and agreed with their hosts that there was no platform available to assist the stricken aircraft. However, they were required to relay the information to the control center at the U.S. embassy.

The information was received by another air force controller at the embassy and logged into a list of significant events for the day that the watch officer kept.

Carlos Cortes had done everything he could. He had talked personally with General Escobedo and succeeded in getting him to accept the possibility of a kidnapping. The general had warned his road patrols to be in the lookout for suspicious groups of men. Carlos had also warned the police commander. To do so was almost futile since Carlos was convinced that the abductors were heading to the jungle where there was no police presence.

He had also put in a request for IMINT. This was the acronym that the U.S. intelligence community had for image intelligence. The pictures were taken mostly from above; in Colombia, the pictures could be taken by airplanes and spacecraft. To the requester, the type of craft was of no consequence; it was the results that mattered.

Carlos had requested the entire zone south and east of the town of Acacias. In Colombia, particularly in the eastern zone, there were few roads. So the request included only three major roads. Carlos gave the highest priority to the road heading south to the major town of Guaviare.

The area in question was vast, about the size of the entire country of Iraq. In order to narrow the search, he placed a restriction of three hundred kilometers from Acacias. *No car or truck could travel much farther in the unimproved roads of the area,* he deduced correctly.

That was all he could do for now for his friend. Jack Smith was in charge of the investigation and would handle the sudden lack of security for employees and visitors to the embassy.

He next picked up the phone and dialed directly to the residence of Pepe Ramirez. This was a task that he had avoided all afternoon. At the other end, a voice identifying herself as Carolyn Huber answered.

"Hello," Carlos said. "Could I please talk to Ana Ramirez? This is Carlos Cortes, a personal friend of her husband. She knows me." Carlos did not identify himself further.

Mrs. Carolyn Huber, the chief of staff's wife, tried for the next several seconds to prevent him from speaking to Ana. Carlos assured her that he knew the events of the past two days and had some words of comfort for her. "Just wait a moment and let me see if she wants to speak to you." She laid the phone down.

A few seconds later, a soft voice on the phone said, "Carlos Cortes, is that you?"

Carlos could sense the state of mind Ana had with just that one sentence. He spoke softly back to her, "Ana, you only met me recently, but I hope that the friendship between your husband and I are enough to convince you of one thing. I believe that Pepe is alive. Although you do not know the nature of my job, I can assure you that I and the organization I represent will not rest until he is back in your arms. Ana . . . *esto es una promesa de todo mi corazón.*"

"Are you sure, Carlos . . . are you sure he is alive?" Her soft style betrayed the self-doubt and uncertainty she was feeling right now.

"No doubt here, Ana, although he is in danger, he knows that the might of the U.S. is behind him, that and his training will keep his spirits up. Most important right now is that you and your children are well. Please promise me that you will take care, and I promise that I will bring him back to you safe and sound."

His words seemed to perk her up some. She spoke back a little clearer now, "I promise, Carlos."

"Then it is a deal, Ana, I will call you soon."

"Good-bye, Carlos."

Carlos placed the phone in its receiver and felt better. *That's done, now I hope that my word was not in vain.*

Monday, 28 June 2004; Madrid, Spain

At 0800 hours, María Elena Borbón assembled her staff for a briefing detailing their next operation. The topic of discussion was

Anatoly Kuprikin, the kingpin of arms traffickers in the Ukraine, a former state of the old Soviet Republic. Anatoly was a supplier; he bought arms from willing distributors and supplied them throughout the world. There were never any questions asked, just cold hard cash passed hands; U.S. dollars were used, the currency of choice for most of the smugglers in the world.

He was wanted by the Interpol, the FBI, and several countries to include Spain. María Elena was herself committed to bring him in. This man would pay for the pain and suffering his arms and explosives had caused. He was the prime suspect for having supplied the explosives used for the horrific train bombings that rocked her country in March.

Anatoly was very wealthy, and he only had one weakness, his fondness for beautiful women. This fact was the key ingredient in the Spanish plan to rein him in. The morning briefing was being given by Johanna Valenz after having worked all weekend to present a comprehensive plan on the capture.

Reaching one key point in the brief, María Elena interrupted her, "Johanna, why do you think that Anatoly will travel to Aruba with such certainty?"

"Our researcher discovered why," pointing at a young man that did analyst work for the team. He had an obvious infatuation toward Johanna and would have done anything for her.

"José, tell me about your discovery," María Elena asked.

José Arias, of medium build and slightly overweight, answered her, "I was reading transcripts of Interpol cell phone taps related to Mr. Kuprikin and found out that he has a deep desire to make love to a particular Venezuelan beauty. It seems that he saw her last year in the Ms. Universe pageant and told his men to move mountains in order for the two to meet. I call that an exploitable weakness in the man."

Johanna added excitedly, "And I went a step further and called this woman in Caracas. She is a medical student at the university there. After a pleasant conversation about her reign as Ms. Venezuela, she faxed me some publicity photos taken of her. Here she is."

A series of publicity photos of the Venezuelan beauty showed in the screen in front of María Elena, and all could admire the beauty of the woman in question. When the photos were finished, Johanna left the last one up and continued, "Although this lady is deep in studies at the present time, I found a way to use her to lure Anatoly." Johanna paused.

"What is it?" asked Luis Vigo impatiently.

"Look at the screen, Luis. This last picture is of me in a blonde wig and made up like Ms. Venezuela."

There was loud laughter in the room as all realized they were looking at a picture of Johanna in a formal dress and a fancy hairdo. They were all duped; Johanna was herself a striking beauty.

"No room for mistake here, Johanna, are you both of the same height and weight?" asked María Elena.

"Perfectly, we could be twins."

"Okay, we have found the weakness. What is your plan, Johanna?"

Johanna went on to outline a beautifully crafted plan that got the immediate approval of the team.

María Elena thanked her team and promised to have it approved by the end of the week. She gave tacit approval for Johanna to start laying the foundation for the plan. She figured correctly that the capture of Anatoly was so important that even mediocre plans would be approved by her superiors. In her estimation, this plan was brilliant. She figured that the chance for success was 95 percent.

It was early on Monday when Carlos reached his office cubicle after spending only four hours resting in an embassy lounge they

116

kept for such occasions. He turned on his light and noticed that he was the only one in his section. He turned on his computer and went about cleaning up his e-mail in-box. This was a simple process since very few messages were addressed to him directly.

Ten minutes later, he was cleaning up the printed message traffic that Roger had accumulated for him the last two workdays. This was also a simple process; Carlos simply put them all in the burn basket. *He figured that he had more important things to do.*

Next, he cleared his phone messages. Having only three, it did not take long. He replayed the last one three times to ensure that he had heard it right.

"Carlos, this is Johanna Valenz. We met last week in Miami, and I told you a trip to Colombia was in the future. Well, the future is now, and I will be arriving on Wednesday at 11:30 AM your time. I hope this is not too forward of me, but can we meet for dinner on Thursday? I am afraid that I must depart Friday morning on another leg of my trip. I'll let you choose the restaurant. Be a good boy, and don't say no. Call you then."

Mi madre, *this woman is really aggressive. How can I say no to this fortune cookie that you dropped from heaven, Papá Dios.*

Carlos got up from his chair and started to depart the office to visit the control center and get an update of the events that had transpired since 1:00 AM. When he turned out of his cubicle to the front door, it was opened by Warren Westback; he was alert and refreshed.

"Carlos, welcome back."

What a hypocrite, Carlos immediately thought.

"Warren, it's been a tough two nights for me, but when I come back from the control center, will you explain to me why you did not act on the message that Shirley passed you on Saturday night?" He did not wait for the reply and continued by his boss and out of the room. *Won't even defend yourself when you know you are wrong. What an ass.* A faint smile could be seen form in his face as he walked away.

Forty minutes later, Carlos returned to the office and found Roger at his desk. Carlos blurted, "Good morning, Roger, let me know when Warren gets back from the ambassador's staff meeting, will you."

"My, are we direct this morning. I'm sorry, but Warren has left for the day. Personal business, he said, and good morning to you too."

"So John went to the staff meeting?"

"Yes, Carlos."

"Let's meet at the conference room once he gets back." Carlos turned into his cubicle, leaving Roger with an answer in his mind, an obscene one.

On his desk, Roger had placed two folders clearly marked with the following words:

Coded Message—Barnstormer
Personal for—Case Officer

He had forgotten all about Juan Miranda, his personal infiltrator to the FARC leadership. The time was right; this young man was a paid informant and plant of the CIA. His predecessor had recruited him two years ago at the Catholic University of Quito, Ecuador. After a fast six-month training period in the United States, Juan had been returned to Ecuador where it was easy for him to become a recruit for the FARC.

His cover was easy to figure. Juan was of Inca blood, and his face matched the features of most Ecuadorian recruits to the Colombian guerrillas. He had Israeli training in weapons to include air-to-air weapons. He used the cover of a dissatisfied Ecuadorian Army recruit at the air defense unit defending a fighter base near Guayaquil, Ecuador.

His reports were infrequent; Juan only got time off from his unit about twice a year. Receiving two reports from him was then highly fortunate. Carlos, however, had no way of communicating with him.

The first report was a month-by-month account of the FARC activities Juan had participated in. It was filed in a border town between the Ecuador and Colombia borders. Filed on Friday, it contained no information on the kidnapping of Pepe.

The second report was the jackpot, the reason why Juan had been inserted in 2003. The report, first in Spanish and later translated by an analyst into English, read,

> *Major purchase of air-to-air weapons expected soon. I have been told to expect fourteen Russian Strela missiles and to train in their use approximately fifty members of two different armed fronts (CRAF and FMAF). Training is to commence in early August if missiles are received soon.*
>
> *Missiles expected to be used in the defeat of Colombian Air Force airplanes and helicopters. Also intended for high-value reconnaissance aircraft belonging to the U.S. and used to support operations in the theater.*
>
> *May put into service "Orion" if the situation warrants. Next report in December, will be given time off in Ecuador due to my outstanding service to the cause.*
>
> *Current location: N01° 36.22' W071° 41.10'*

This was indeed good news; Carlos half-expected this project to fail and was really surprised when he read the reports. Orion was the code word for the only piece of technology that the CIA had given

Agent Miranda. It was a beacon with enough power to continuously transmit its position to CIA headquarters in Langley, Virginia. To conserve the small battery and to ease communications, Juan was to use the beacon only if air-to-air missiles were received at his location, or if by chance, he found the three American hostages being held by the FARC. Thus the use of the beacon invited an armed attack to its location.

Can't forget Pepe, but this is important too. I am certainly going to be busy in the near future, Carlos thought. He let his eyes wander in the direction of the picture of Rosario Marin; she was ever-present in his thoughts in times of trouble. *Sorry, Rosario, but you are also out of the picture for now!*

Manuel Alonso and Moncho Rivera were meeting with El Jefe to discuss battle plans and future operations. Today, they were discussing two major events, and the meeting was specifically intended to discuss them.

"First, let's start with the purchase of the missiles. Manuel, give us an update please."

"*Sí,* Jefe. I was able to recover the papers where Mona had recorded the details for the purchase. We are dealing with a dependable dealer with whom we have dealt before. His name is Abdul Al Kassar, and he is based out of Suriname. He delivers his weapons on time, and we have never been shortchanged by him, not even one bullet."

"What is his motivation, Manuel?"

"I don't know, boss, he is affiliated with other dependable dealers of the area. Of course, Mona could tell us more about him, but I simply can only retell what Mona had on the books, sir."

"When is the delivery and how much, Manuel?" Moncho Rivera asked impatiently.

Rafael Terraza looked at Moncho unapprovingly but added, "Yes, Manuel, how much?"

"Too much, boss, a Russian Strela-2 missile can be bought for approximately $15,000 U.S. in the open market. Our forces have owned a few of them through the years but have had no success in shooting down an airplane with them."

"So why are we spending money on these?" Moncho blurted out.

"These are Strela-3s," Manuel said excitedly. "They are much better and, may I add, much more expensive. The total price for fourteen missiles and the training to complement the purchase is a cool one million dollars."

"Are they that good, Manuel?" Rafael asked.

"Better! Guaranteed to shoot down a fighter plane at four thousand meters, and that means we will be able to destroy those enemy helicopters easily, Jefe."

"If we shoot down at least six helicopters with these missiles, they will be worth the money we paid, Manuel. The enemy does not have that many helicopters, and the more we shoot down, the better the possibility for them to cancel their current operations against us."

"And may I add, we still have money to spare, sir. I have found three accounts in your name with at least twenty-one million in them. Mona was a great money manager. She moved money around like candy and has protected our resources quite well."

"Is, Manuel."

"Excuse me?"

"Mona 'is' a great money manager. We are getting her back," El Jefe added with conviction. "Manuel, I want you to go get these missiles personally, and once you get them, please don't let them out of sight. Now let us discuss the ransom demands for our captive. I want those out before Juana even gets here."

That statement perked up his deputy; he was obviously left out of the previous conversation, and that slight was always perceived negatively by Moncho. "I am ready to transmit a message to the government telling them of our captive and instructing them of our terms. The colonel for Mona."

Manuel contradicted him immediately, "The general for Mona and two other FARC leaders!"

"What?" both Rafael and Moncho asked loudly and incredulously.

"Just as you heard me, boss, we have received reports from Calamar that the person missing is a general from the Southern Command in Miami. The colonel in question was found murdered in the embassy car. It looks like Juana was successful beyond our dreams," Manuel stated confidently.

"What makes you think that we can get even one prisoner released for that gringo, Manuel?" asked Moncho softly and menacingly.

"A general of the United States of America, why, they will move mountains to get him back," added Manuel.

"Which is exactly why this is a very dangerous situation. It could be a catastrophe." Now Moncho's tone was angry. He had been outmaneuvered by a subordinate twice in the last few minutes, and he did not like it.

"Calm down, Moncho. Manuel will be leaving soon to get these missiles, and I want you to handle the negotiations to get Mona back. That should appease you. I also agree with you that the Americans will not let a stone unturned in order to get their man back, so be extremely careful. The bottom line is, get Mona back at all costs."

On hearing these words, Moncho stormed out of the room and said in passing as he closed the door, "I will get your querida back, now get us those damned missiles, we are losing the war, and we need to turn the tide."

Rafael Terraza—guerrilla commander, patriarch and hero of the revolution—looked down in disgust and said softly, "We were such good friends once."

It was late afternoon in Madrid, Spain, when María Elena met Johanna for an update. She spoke first. "Johanna, as we expected, the approval came quickly. The March bombings, as unfortunate as they were, are a catalyst for action. All our bosses want is to get our man, yet do it safely."

"Good, I will confirm my plans for travel. I intend to go to Colombia first to inform our embassy of the missile purchase plan. Then I travel to Suriname and to Aruba where I plan to meet with you in three week's time. The plan hinges on my ability to convince Al Kassar that our men are the best Strela instructors in the world," Johanna said.

"That is the only part of your excellent plan that I am uneasy with. I agree the ETA cover story is good, but you know my style by now, I like to bait them enough that they are absolutely convinced these are the right personnel. I am at the point of resurrecting Rosario Marín for this caper."

"Boss, you are too well-known in that part of the world, somebody may recognize you."

"The world is full of danger, Johanna, and I am not going to skirt it if the actions I undertake are necessary." María Elena then changed her topic of conversation to a different topic. "Tell me, Johanna, are you going to call on this Carlos Cortes when in Bogotá?"

"Of course, I told you that man is too good to pass up. And don't worry, I will not compromise the plan."

"No, Johanna, I am confident of that, if you meet him, ask him if he knows a Rosario from Madrid. Will you do that for me please?"

"María Elena!" Johanna said softly with a devilish grin on her gorgeous face. "Of course I can. I will tell you what I find out."

The early afternoon staff meeting started without Warren Westback's participation. In attendance were the other three CIA personnel of the Bogotá office with Mike Malone and Jack Smith. John Minor, field agent in charge of reconnaissance and surveillance, spoke first.

"I have ordered the target you gave me as the first priority, Rock. We have tasked National Reconnaissance Office to supply both infrared and foliage penetration radar images for the coordinates in question. By the way, I found another interesting fact while researching the activities of the weekend. On Sunday, we had a report from a navy E-2C that an airplane had squawked an emergency signal in that same area. They tracked the signal for fifteen minutes and then lost it as they began their approach into Bogotá."

"How close to the area in question?" asked Jack Smith.

"About forty-five miles, but what is unusual is that there was no crash reported in the area. The Colombian authorities passed the information to their air force and police forces, and they had no mishaps that day."

"No airplanes missing?" asked Mike Malone.

"None, nada," added Minor.

"What if . . . what if a passenger on that plane, one with intimate knowledge of procedures was responsible for the emergency squawk and the aircraft did not crash at all?" Carlos seemed excited as he asked his question, one that he did not expect an answer to.

"Interesting, Rock, I will ask SOUTHCOM's public affairs personnel to track where that airplane was headed and possible landing sites. Do you think we should narrow our search to that area?" asked Jack.

"We have nothing else but hunches and suspicions, Jack." Addressing now his fellow field agent, he added, "Nice work,

John, I need you to keep looking at this angle while I visit with the Colombians and try to energize the hunt for Pepe."

They had been on the move since early Sunday with only minor rest periods. The travel was acerbated by the difficulty in walking with your hands tied to your back on the deep jungle paths they had taken. Pepe was exhausted; he had fallen several times, and his face and arms were cut in several places. In addition to his arms, Pepe was tied to a tether that tied him to Hugo behind him.

Pepe also knew he was in danger. Not as worried about his captors, who evidently were kidnapping him for ransom. He was worried with the many and different dangers that he faced in this jungle. For example, he had recently heard how some very small mites were carriers of a disease called leishmaniasis. This particular disease would attack his exposed skin and create horrid-looking sores that if left untreated would scar him for life and could even cause death.

He knew because he had ordered mosquito netting for the U.S. troops now working with the Colombians in the vicinity of this same jungle. The netting was of a special type, one with a tight weave that would prevent the mites, smaller than a mosquito, from passing through.

His situation was hampered by the fact that he had lost all sense of direction. *Nothing worse for a pilot and military man to lose than that,* he thought. The double-canopy jungle in this area was at least 150 feet high, and Pepe could not see the normal clues that would tell him what direction and whether they were going in circles or not.

They finally came up to a river and met with two other guerrillas that were camped out there, apparently waiting for them. There were greetings and salutations, and Pepe noticed that the two men were respectful of their leader.

They all sat down where they could, and Pepe noticed Juana walking toward him, carrying a sack that was passed by one of the men they had just met.

"Dear General," Juana said, "let me treat those cuts you have on your body. I would not want anything to happen to you now that I have you. You are my very special cargo."

Pepe was not as pleasant. "Young lady, I could care less what you think I am. I am telling you now, if you do not want to bring death and destruction to your people, turn back now and release me at the first opportunity you have near any town of your choosing. To do less will only bring you misery and the demise of persons you love."

"My, aren't we feeling important today! Relax, General, now lay back and let me clean your wounds. You do not want to see them infected. Not a pretty face like yours."

While she was cleaning his wounds, Pepe noticed how careful she was. The woman had a soft touch and a sense of motherhood in her own way. When she was finished, Pepe said, "Tell me, ma'am, what drives you to live like this? You are obviously a mother and a caring wife. I would think you should leave this life and concentrate in your family."

"No, General, I am not a mother. What I am is the face of dissent of our nation, a nation that gives to the rich and lives off the poor. No, sir, I will not rest until we get equality for the poor, the Indian and the Colombian woman most of all."

With that she rose and strode off. *Wow, what conviction she possesses. Give me ten like her, and I could straighten up the Colombian military high command.*

It was late in the afternoon when John Minor walked into Rock's office. He was carrying a piece of paper and seemed excited.

"Rock, I am glad you are still here. Look what just arrived from our signal intelligence site." With that said, he handed the piece of paper to Carlos who read,

This is Commander Terraza. Please pass the following message to the American embassy. "In custody of a military general that belongs to you. He is deemed an enemy of the Colombian people and will be executed in the next week if Mona Pedroso and ten other FARC captives are not freed immediately. Signed, Rafael Terraza, Cucho Ramos Armed Front."

"Holy shit," Carlos looked up and stared at John who remained standing quietly. It was six o'clock on June 28.

At the U.S. Southern Command in Miami, Florida, General Goodman received the message and ordered immediately a state of alert for his staff. At the present time, he was finishing a telephone conversation with Ana Ramirez. "Ana, I assure you that we will do all that is in our power to recover Pepe safe and sound. You are a strong woman, I will call you soon with updates on the situation, and trust me, we will not rest until we capture his kidnappers."

When he finished the conversation, he looked up to see a crisis action room full of personnel and preparations for his "stand-up" meeting proceeding at a frantic pace. He called one of his general officers aside.

"Omar, can you give me a quick update of the situation before we start our meeting?"

General Omar Vazquez responded to the query immediately, "Sir, we really don't have much. Comandante Terraza is one of the wiliest commanders the FARC possesses. His personnel are well-trained and rarely commit mistakes. We have confirmation from our intelligence sites that he was responsible for the weekend attacks in Bogotá. To me, they were all preplanned to coincide with the kidnap attempt, sir."

"That is certainly obvious, Omar. Wily and smart, we must watch this man carefully and prevent at all costs that he does something rash with Pepe."

"Sir, your entire command is primed to find Pepe fast. We will get him back pronto. And, sir, Comandante Terraza is a dead man, you have my word."

CHAPTER TEN

Wednesday, 30 June 2004; Bogotá, Colombia

S he arrived in Bogotá at 11:30 AM on an Air France direct flight
from Paris. Johanna was resplendent even after the long flight.
Having traveled in business class, she was one of the first passengers
to reach the immigration counters. As if on cue, every man stopped
what they were doing and looked her way.

Johanna noticed the attention. *How satisfying it is to be ogled at even
in a country known for their beautiful women.* She then breezed through
the immigration and customs process and took a cab outside to the
Spanish embassy.

Arriving thirty minutes later at the embassy, she was rushed to a
meeting with the ambassador and what seemed to her every other
male employee in the embassy. It seemed to her that they all wanted to
get a glimpse of her. After all, this was her first visit to South America,
and her reputation preceded her.

Johanna was very proper when she met the ambassador, but she
quickly reminded him that her briefing was classified at the highest
levels of government, and she could only brief the ambassador, his

deputy, and the embassy chief of security. Everyone else was dismissed by them, and a very disappointed crowd left the room noisily.

Once they left, Johanna gave the three gentlemen the details of the plan. They were surprised by the insightful and careful professionalism with which Johanna approached the issues. To their amazement, they were all convinced that the plan stood every chance of success once she had finished presenting it. *No wonder she was the future of Spanish operatives,* thought the ambassador.

He spoke first, "Tell me, Señora Valenz, if I got all the details right, you are the only operative that is in real danger throughout the operation. If the Strela missiles make it to this hemisphere, they will only get as far as Aruba, and the end result is for Spain to capture and return to justice their number 1 fugitive?"

Johanna answered quickly and with a sense of triumph, "Yes, Señor Embajador, my goal is to have him in Madrid in the next two weeks."

At exactly the same time, Carlos and Warren Westback were meeting for the first time since Carlos returned from the United States. The location was Warren's office.

"Welcome back, Warren, where did you go the last two days?"

Westback's reply was short and rude. "I am having you replaced, Carlos, the events of this weekend are indicative of your lack of professionalism and poor organizational qualities. The paperwork left this morning, I expect you out of the country on the last plane tonight."

Carlos froze where he was, considered jumping this excuse for a man and beating him senseless; but in the end, he simply turned around and walked off without saying a thing. It took guts to do that.

From his desk, Carlos placed a call to his mentor at the Agency. The deputy director of operations for counterdrug ops was Mike Dunn. Almost a father figure for Carlos, he was not a powerful Washington insider, but he was a good friend and counselor.

Carlos explained the situation to Mike and discussed how he viewed the relationship between him and his supervisor. He went into greater detail on the situation as it unfolded the past weekend and the events of the last three days.

Mike was a good listener. He took in all the details and let Carlos vent his anger before he spoke. At the end, his answer and counsel was equally considerate and reflected the years of experience of a true Agency veteran.

"Carlos, what you described to me I have seen countless times before. It is the normal course of events when the Agency places a bureaucrat and an operator in a boss-subordinate relationship. Either way you match those two, the end result is the same, and that is failure. I see and understand your side, but the DDO is going to side with his protégé, and you know that."

"I know, Mike, but I cannot leave this place now. Not with the kidnapping of General Ramirez, why, I am the only embassy officer with the connections to work with the Colombian military now that Colonel Platford is dead."

"Who said you have to leave? I can detail you to the Colombia mission even if Westback does not want you there. If the decision is made today, I will detail you as a personal representative to the Colombian government immediately. Keep working, Carlos, I know you are busy and good luck."

"Thank you, Mike, how can I ever repay you?"

"Oh, don't be so humble, Carlos. Your successes are legendary to this section, and even when I detail you to play GI Joe every once in a while, you are a true champion. Don't worry, and find your friend Pepe."

"You knew about our friendship, Mike?"

"I know everything, Carlos, I am even aware of the telephone conversations on Friday and Saturday nights where you tried to warn all concerned about the danger represented by the simple murder of an embassy employee. If everyone had your vision, Carlos, we would be much better off."

"Thanks, sir, you are too kind."

"My pleasure, Carlos, now get back to work."

Carlos hung up the phone and decided to stay right where he was for now. Even if he had to move, he was not going to be in a hurry or rush off like a scared chicken. As he figured, Warren was not enough of a man to challenge him while he was present. He always did his dirty deeds alone and in close coordination with his mentor at Langley.

After a few minutes clearing up his things and taking care of some due paperwork, he started reading the message traffic. Here he found another interesting report from the Spanish agent of the CEID. The message read,

FM CIA HQ/DDI
TO HQ PENTAGON JCS/J2/J3/J5
HQ USSOUTHCOM/J2/J3/J5
HQ USEUCOM/J2/J3/J5
DOS/WHEM-AD/LATAM/NATO/EU
DEPSECDEF/SOLIC/INL
FIELD AGENTS/CENTAM/SOAM/CARIB/EU/
MOSCOW/KIEV

Subj: Sting Operation—Arms Trafficking

Various methods used in obtaining following information. For details see URL: httpse://nisc.ref.gov/case_1270.1356/details.htm

Reported by Spanish CEID agent Juan Vigo. Previous contact with excellent credentials and access.

1. *CEID headquarters has approved plan to lure and capture arms merchant Anatoly Kuprikin. Ukraine native is number 1 suspect in the provisioning of high explosives used in the Madrid train bombings in March. Reclusive and highly protected, the subject has plans to visit the island of Aruba under false papers.*

2. *Operation is scheduled to commence in three days and come to a successful conclusion in two weeks. Suspect is tentatively visiting Aruba the weekend of July 10. He will be traveling by private charter and is coordinating sale of fourteen Russian-made Strela missiles to arms smuggler Abdul Al Kassar based in Suriname. The missiles are being purchased by a Colombian IAG.*

3. *CEID operation is being led by Director María Elena Borbón. Spanish agents are briefing the government of Colombia, Suriname, and Aruba. Objectives include the capture and extradition of Kuprikin to Spain, Al Kassar to Colombia, and the intercept of Strela missiles in Aruba.*

End of Report

So this must be the reason for Johanna's visit to Bogotá. She must be here by now, thought Carlos.

It was three thirty in the afternoon when Johanna called the embassy and asked to be connected to Carlos Cortes. He answered the phone and was immediately elated to hear her soft voice. *This day is not all bad after all,* thought Carlos.

"Hi, Carlos, it is Johanna Valenz, and as promised, I am in your city with plenty of time to get to know you. Can you show me around tonight?"

She had not lost her direct approach, what a woman! "Johanna, how pleasant to hear your melodious voice again. I am truly honored that you have not forgotten me, and I must admit, neither have I forgotten your beautiful face."

Johanna felt herself blush even though she was talking to a phone. "Why, Carlos, you are so kind."

"Listen, Ms. Valenz, things are very hectic here, and I am very busy, but I can come to pick you up around 9:00 PM and take you out to a wonderful restaurant that is my favorite."

His sudden change in tone and formality was disconcerting to her; however, it made her more determined to get inside this man's thoughts and maybe share something more intimate if things went right. "Mr. Cortes, make that the last time you are formal with me. Call me Johanna or the deal is off, please."

"I'm sorry, Johanna, things are not going smoothly today. I promise to be familiar tonight and leave all my worries behind."

"Okay, I am staying at the La Fontana Hotel. Nine o'clock it is. See you then."

At U.S. Southern Command, General John Goodman was on the phone with his boss, the secretary of defense. The secretary was speaking with an authoritative voice.

"Now listen, John, we have to tread carefully on this. I know that General Ramirez is a national hero especially for the Hispanic community, but that does not give you permission to put troops in harm's way in Colombia. Furthermore, the NCA has not given us the go-ahead on any rescue attempt."

"But, sir, we know that they have taken the general to an area close to the Macarena Mountains, and we can narrow down the search area to approximately one hundred square miles or less. If we wait any longer, they can move Pepe, and you know well the southeastern part of Colombia is the size of Iraq."

"Calm down, John, I ordered the entire intelligence community on this mission. Finding Pepe Ramirez is the department's number 1 priority."

"Sir, forgive my frustration. I promise not to leave a stone unturned and narrow down Pepe's location. Then you will forgive me for calling you again and asking permission to go hunting."

"If, and only if, the president agrees with us, John."

"Yes, sir."

Carlos was on time for his date with Johanna. As he expected, she was waiting inside the lobby of the hotel dressed in resplendent clothes and looking as delicious as always. *My, this woman knows how to dress, how can anyone resist her?*

Carlos kissed her on both cheeks and said, "My, Johanna, you look beautiful tonight. It is indeed a pleasure meeting you and sharing this wonderful evening."

Johanna replied coyly, "Now this tone of voice is much better, Carlos."

"I have chosen my favorite restaurant known for its great meat and seafood platters. Shall we eat?"

"Why not," said Johanna and extended her left arm cocked for being led out of the hotel.

"The night is young, let's enjoy it," said Carlos.

At the restaurant, everything went beautifully through the first three courses. Carlos did not want to ruin the evening to talk about business, but deep inside of him, the trouble Pepe was in, the Spanish Strela operation, and the ever-present reminder that one of the operatives was named Rosario kept him wondering if he should broach these subjects.

To his surprise, it was Johanna that broke the trend of the evening and spoke of business first. *Had she noticed that I was preoccupied and detached?* He never expected what she asked next.

"Carlos, did you ever know a Rosario Marín?"

Carlos's face betrayed him immediately. The unexpected question was received, and in an instant, his attention span was focused in what Johanna had said. He looked submissive; Johanna understood she had information that was both desired and valuable. *I wonder what happened between them. Guess I should find out.* She also understood that any chance for romance tonight went out with the question.

"Rosario Marín, yes, I knew someone with that name back in the nineties. Do you know her?"

"Not only know her, Carlos, I work with her. Tell me about you two."

So her real name is María Elena, and she is Johanna's boss. Even though Johanna did not say that, Carlos quickly deduced the truth.

"I don't have much. We met back in 1991 and dated once, but, Johanna, I have never forgotten that weekend." Carlos continued with an edited version of the passionate weekend, never betraying the romantic passions unleashed by them.

When he finished, Johanna knew that this man truly cared for her boss. All the years did not dim his enthusiasm for an old romance. And yes, there had been romance; the way he told the story betrayed the level to which this couple once cared for each other. María Elena's curiosity also confirmed that she had not forgotten this man. *Why did I ask the question? The night is over, and I am not going to bed this man. What a pity.*

After they finished dessert, even Carlos knew that the evening was coming to a close, and he decided to broach the other subjects that worried him tonight. Driving back to the hotel, Carlos used the excuse of giving Johanna a windshield tour of the capital to discuss more business.

He explained Pepe's kidnapping and the inability to get a good fix on his location. He also confided a bit of the possible locations and the FARC front he suspected of having carried the kidnap.

It was Johanna that supplied the next bit of information. "Well, Carlos, let me tell you in confidence about an operation we are conducting soon in the area. I think it will interest you."

"Go ahead, Johanna."

Johanna went through a quick review of the arms trade deal and that the intended target of the sting was the arms trader himself. She did mention in passing that the middle man in the operation would also be captured and that the arms in question would not make it to the FARC. She failed to inform Carlos of the highly classified portions of the plan.

Carlos, not satisfied with all that he heard from her, decided to reveal a bit of his ongoing investigation. "Thank you for confiding with me. Let me tell you a bit of my investigation that is related to your operation. So far we know that the same group that kidnapped General Ramirez is the one intending to purchase your Strelas. Can you confirm to me that the purchaser is the Cucho Ramos Front, Johanna?"

"You mean that the Agency knows about the arms deal?" Johanna's question was blurted out as if surprised he knew about it.

Carlos waited a bit to answer. He pretended to concentrate in his driving while he composed his reply carefully. After a few seconds, he reassuringly put his right hand on Johanna's left arm and said, "We know that someone is providing Russian missiles to the FARC and that fifty guerrillas are going to be trained in their use. This is not acceptable to the U.S. government, it must be stopped. You can count on our full cooperation to ensure that does not happen. Please tell María Elena that that is a promise."

He had revealed a lot with those few words. Johanna quickly figured that Carlos was an astute analyst. Although she had been vague in her story and had never revealed María Elena's real name, Carlos had put two and two together quickly, and he even knew about a highly classified portion of the Spanish plan. She decided to end the evening and not reveal any more of their plan. "Carlos, be a gentleman and take me back to the hotel please. It is getting late, and I must travel tomorrow."

"I will, Johanna, but promise me something first. Please take our offer of full cooperation to your boss. At the Agency, we have complete trust in your organization, however, if we work in partnership, we can be even more successful. Do you promise?"

"First thing in the morning, Carlos, now promise me something in return. Please do not name me in your report to headquarters in the morning. You never heard anything out of my lips."

"I promise, not even when I call them as soon as I drop you off."

"My, you Americans, does anyone at the Agency ever take a night off?" she said this with a tone that reflected the lost passions that could have been unleashed that evening.

"Not when their dearest friend is kidnapped, Johanna," giving a personal answer to a general question.

Carlos called Mike Dunn while driving back to his apartment. Mike answered, and it was evident he was trying to get some sleep when the phone rang.

"Yes, Carlos, do you believe in rest hours or is your first name Count?"

"Sorry, Mike, but this is important." Carlos told him about every detail of the investigation. He wound together the kidnapping clues with the report from his informant. He then proceeded to reveal all he knew about the Spanish operation without revealing Johanna as his contact. At the end, Carlos said, "Mike, we could convince the

Spanish to permit the sale of the Strelas and their transfer to the FARC. However, we would substitute the missiles with some we have and jimmy the guidance mechanism so that they fire but fail to guide on aircraft. In addition, we can put a transmitter on the missiles so that we can fix the front's position exactly. With luck, Mike, the missiles may end up where they are holding Pepe."

"The radio gadgets, Carlos, they may be found."

"Not the current technology, Mike. I have seen them. They are the size of an insect and include a GPS transceiver."

"How long does the battery last?"

"That's the trick, Mike. They use the missile battery, so when they turn on the missile, they transmit."

"Okay, Carlos, you convinced me. Now let me shake the bushes tomorrow, and let's see what we can do."

"Thank you, Mike, sorry to wake you up."

"This is important, Carlos, you will have an answer by noon. Good night."

Oh god, I hope that what I told Mike about the radio technology is right, thought Carlos.

CHAPTER ELEVEN

Thursday, 1 July 2004; Eastern Colombia

Pepe woke up in a ten-by-five-foot cell in a strangely good mood. He was the sort, no matter how dire the circumstance; Pepe was always cheerful, never gloomy.

In part, that was the reason for his successful career. Life had thrown a few obstacles Pepe's way; nevertheless, he usually found a way to clear these with minimum damage to his reputation or self-respect. Certainly his current situation was dire, but how can you compare this to matching your aircraft against a determined enemy at supersonic speeds? To Pepe, the current situation was manageable, and now he was at least safe from the dangers of the Colombian jungle, not the worst for wear.

He was still a little groggy, and his mind drifted far away to his native land, Puerto Rico, the "Land of Enchantment" and also the birthplace of Ana, his wife for twenty-three years.

The normal color of the sky in the island is grayish blue, the result of too much humidity in the atmosphere. It was such a day, very few clouds in the sky, and Pepe was rushing from one class to another at the Rio Piedras campus of the University of Puerto Rico.

His next class was in the architecture building that was near the entrance to the university and that made it the farthest walk he had for classes. He was nearing his building when he looked right to the entrance of the library and noticed a female student with a very nice figure. She was talking to another student and had her face turned away from Pepe.

I guess it was the hunter in him for he slowed down his pace and looked her way as he approached the pair. At that moment, she laughed and turned his way. Suddenly, the day became brighter; his pupils dilated automatically as he focused on the most beautiful woman he had ever seen.

Ana Luisa Mendoza was a drop-dead gorgeous first-year student. About five feet seven inches high and sporting long black hair, she was a typical Spanish beauty with a faint streak of native Indian blood and the light bronze color of skin that makes you look permanently sunburned. She looked directly at him and smiled.

The courtship lasted four years. What was love at first sight consummated itself in vows of love, respect, and dedication; it was January 20, 1980. What a wonderful day!

Pepe came back to reality when he heard the door to his cell opening. *It was a double door, so no chance of making a sudden attempt to escape here.*

He instantly recognized Juana Montes and noticed that with her was a much older man. Juana told him to stand at the far end of the cell with his hands up. She was sporting a 9 mm automatic that Pepe saw no sense in challenging. He obeyed.

"Siéntese, General."

Pepe sat down and studied the stranger. *This must be the boss, I wonder what he wants.*

"Buenos días, mi general, es un placer conocerlo," the man said.

"Buenos días," Pepe responded alertly.

Juana came in first and quickly went to the left side of the room. Pepe made a mental note of this.

Comandante Rafael Terraza came in next; he spoke first in an accented but perfectly spoken English. "General Ramirez, it is my pleasure to meet you. I am—"

"El Jefe Terraza," Pepe interrupted him. "Commander of the Cucho Ramos Armed Front and a feared man."

"You are very impressive, General," Rafael laughed to mask his surprise. "I welcome you to my camp and home and wish that I could make your stay more comfortable. However, the circumstances that brought you here make you my prisoner, and I need you badly to recover Lieutenant Mona Pedroso."

Your lover, you mean. Pepe kept his thought to himself and instead said, "I regret to inform you that my country has a policy of non-negotiation with kidnappers and criminals, I hope you know that."

"Let's, for your sake, hope that the policy is not followed in this case. I would regret to try you for crimes against the revolution. A charge that carries the death penalty I am afraid."

"We are soldiers, Comandante, if you do not follow the Geneva Convention, that makes you a criminal. But," Pepe said sarcastically, "I called you that already."

"General, I treated you so far with respect. I hope that in the future you return the favor in kind." That said, El Jefe turned and left the cell. On his way out, he said out loud to a guard outside, "Hoy no le den de comer, ni tomar."

Juana followed out the door, keeping Pepe in sight and never pointing the gun anywhere but at him. She said, "Please keep your sharp tongue in check when you talk to the comandante. He is an *unprediáctionable* man."

"Unpredictable, Juana," Pepe said correcting her English. "I wanted to see how far I could ride him."

"He is not a woman, General, be careful." Juana smiled and closed the door.

Johanna finished her run, showered, and was ready for the morning meeting at the Spanish embassy at 9:00 AM. After the meeting, she called her home office and asked to speak with her boss.

"Haló," María Elena answered her phone with a slightly higher tone of voice than normal. Johanna had noticed that of her when the conversation was through a secure telephone connection. *Normal for someone that did not mature during the last ten years,* she thought.

Johanna went ahead with her report on the two meetings she had with the country team in Colombia and the statements of support by the ambassador. She reminded María Elena of the plan to shield the second half of the operation from the country team. It was meant to prevent any leak that endangered the team that would infiltrate the FARC under the pretext of training guerrillas in the correct tactical operation of the Strelas.

"Johanna, I know you too well. What else is in your mind that you are dancing around with?"

"Oh, you noticed, I also went out last night with Carlos Cortes."

More than five thousand miles away, María Elena's heart seemed to skip a bit, her brow moistened, and she started to slightly hyperventilate.

"I made a mistake by asking him out, boss. At the end of dinner, he gave me a tour of the city and surprised me with questions of our pending operation. He knew the type and quantity of missiles, and somehow he found out about the training promise made to the FARC. I have to admit that he caught me by surprise, and my gestures and tone of voice may have confirmed his suspicions that it was the CEID that was conducting the operation." Johanna decided to not tell María Elena that it was her that had started the conversation in order to salvage the evening.

"He must have found out about the operation through one of his moles in-country, Johanna. What else did it lead to?"

"He promised the full cooperation of the Agency if we let them in the operation. I guess the threat posed by the Strelas is too big for them to ignore. Plus it looks like the general that was kidnapped last Saturday in Colombia was a personal friend of Carlos. He called him Pepe."

María Elena instantly made the connection. The General Ramirez that CNN was talking so much about was none other than Major Pepe Ramirez from Carlos Cortes's days in Kuwait back in 1991. The same one that Carlos so proudly boasted he had saved from a certain death after a horrific car accident. *So this Carlos Cortes and hers were one and the same after all.*

"When will we know, Johanna?"

"He promised to get back to me by noon today. That is half an hour from now. One more thing, María Elena, the man still cares for you. Take this from a woman that once considered him a catch. All I can say is that a woman named Rosario Marín stole his heart in Madrid many years ago and that heart still belongs to her."

"So you asked, Johanna?"

"First thing, boss, what do you think started me on the wrong line of conversation at the end of the evening? My night was shot, and now I have put the whole operation in jeopardy."

"Nonsense, Johanna, we have worked with the Agency before, and we can do that again. However, we cannot put in jeopardy the capture of Anatoly, because if we lose him, our heads will roll."

"I promise to call you back the moment he calls. Thank you for your vote of confidence. Adios."

"Adios, Johanna." María Elena put down the receiver and smiled. *Carlos Cortes cares for Rosario Marín; after all these years, I judged him right from the very first day!*

When Carlos showed up to work that morning, Roger met him by the entrance to the embassy and told him that his belongings were moved to the defense attaché office. He told him that when Warren Westback had found out Carlos was still in country and that it was with the full consent of the deputy director for operations (counterdrug), he had gone into a wild tantrum.

Roger had saved his belongings and moved his personal effects before Warren had them burned.

Carlos thanked Roger and went to his new office space in the second floor. He wondered how this would work since his embassy cover story was in the agriculture office, and now he would sit with the office personnel least concerned about the plight of agriculture in Colombia. He decided to create a cover story that temporarily assigned to him to the DATT concerning the coca leaf eradication program of Plan Colombia.

He spent all morning in overseas teleconferences with his mentor and other key personnel in the Agency with which he had strong personal and professional ties. In the middle of the morning, Warren had made an attempt to railroad his plans by requesting that the plan be dropped. Not having proposed a counterplan himself and the Agency seeing the threat posed by fifty air-to-air missiles in the wrong hands, Warren's effort failed even with the support of his boss Marc Higgins.

At twelve noon, Carlos visited the Spanish embassy. After a few minutes, Johanna met him and took him to the office she was using in a safe room.

"Johanna, I am so pleased that you waited for our response before you continued on your trip."

"For you, anything, Carlos."

"I know that I caught you by surprise last night. But let me confirm that the Agency will support your operation fully with all of our resources and with minimum meddling. I know you worry a lot that we could overpower your operation and cause it to fail, but let me assure that this will not happen. In fact, tomorrow morning, the director of intelligence will call your director personally to state just that."

"No meddling, Carlos?"

"None until you capture and secure Anatoly Kuprikin. Once that is done, the director will ask for CEID's consent for two things. First, that our technicians make some changes to the guidance mechanism on the Strelas, and second, that it be me who accompanies the missiles into the Colombian jungle for the training branch of the plan. I am trained in their use and will ensure for my bosses that the missiles are not used for nefarious intent."

"Do we have a choice, Carlos?"

"Don't ask like that, we do not like to impose our will on you, and there are a thousand details to cover before you can say that we are imposing on you."

"But the plan is ours, Carlos. You are meddling."

"Johanna, your country does not have over one thousand military and civilian citizens supporting Colombia's effort on the road to peace. We have the right to ensure their safety and hope that your director sees it the same way we do. I hope that you can recall that since 2003, the FARC has in their possession three U.S. civilian contractors and, since Saturday, a general. We do not want that number to grow."

"You realize, Carlos, that as a consequence of this operation, we may find your hostages."

"The thought had crossed my mind."

When he returned to the embassy, Carlos called General John Goodman on the secure phone. His call was answered at thirty-nine thouisand feet; the general was headed to Washington DC to discuss the situation in Colombia directly with the Joint Chiefs of Staff.

"Goodman here," the general's voice was soft and warm. It did not betray the stress the general must be under, and it characterized the reason why the general had been so successful in his career.

"Sir, Carlos Cortes, special agent in charge of counterdrug operations in Colombia, if you don't mind, I would like to discuss the rescue of General Ramirez with you, sir."

"Carlos, anything we can do to conduct a safe and expedited rescue of the general does interest me, go ahead."

Carlos described the situation as he saw it presently, covered the information on the surface-to-air missiles and the upcoming sting operation in Aruba to great detail, and told the general about the link between the arms sale and the Cucho Ramos Front. He did not cover information on his mole at the front since he considered that privileged information that he would reveal only with the permission of his superiors.

When he finished, the general asked, "Carlos, do I understand your proposal correctly, if we do this right, we catch an international arms dealer, an FARC arms supplier, and the possibility of fixing the position of General Ramirez?"

"Well, technically, sir, the Spaniards are doing most of it. I hope that as an endgame, we fix the location of Pepe and conduct a rescue. If we are lucky, we could recover other hostages being held presently by the FARC."

"And that poses a problem to us, Carlos, will our president permit us to mount the rescue attempt, and will the Colombians permit us into their country?"

"Sir, I understand the difficulties. The director asked me to contact you and proposes a joint effort to get this approved by the White House and the Hill."

"Does the State Department also approve?"

"We have not approached them yet, and that includes the ambassador, sir."

"I think I can help with that." General Goodman was a good friend and former assistant to the secretary of state, so he was confident of providing support on that end. He then asked a final question. "Carlos, how will we be sure that we fix the position of the hostages correctly, and will we trust the Spanish agent that does it?"

"That, I can assure you, is no problem, General, for the agent taking care of that is yours truly. That is, if the Spaniards let me."

"Very well, Rock, I know that the Secret Angel of the Western Iraqi desert is a man to be trusted," betraying the fact that the general knew who he was talking to all the time.

"Sir, your staff is good. How did they find out?"

"Not my staff, Rock, it was Pepe who boasted of your exploits in the desert during Operation Iraqi Freedom. He always reminded us about his friend in the Agency when we covered your drug reports at the command."

CHAPTER TWELVE

Friday, 2 July 2004; Madrid, Spain

"Charlie, muy pronto cumples trece años, vas a ser un jovencito." María Elena Borbón was telling her child nuggets of motherly caution as she prepared him for his visit with the *abuelos* for the summer vacation. "Promise you will be safe at all times and no visits to the rocks by the point without my papá, do you understand?"

"Sí, Mámi."

"I will come to visit you in four week's time. I promise that we will spend the best two weeks of summer together, no work, just fun."

"This time, Mámi, don't cancel like you did last year."

"No, *hijo*, I promise. We need to sit down and talk seriously when we see each other next, now that you will be a young man, I have a story to tell you."

"A good story, Mámi."

"I hope so, *hijo*, I hope so." Her voice trailed a bit as she let her mind wander some. "Now, let me finish packing, I also have a long trip this evening."

Warren Westback reached his boss at the Agency using the secure phone of his residence. "Marc, I am really mad that this asshole Carlos got away with staying in Colombia. I don't know what else to do to get his pompous ass from fucking up the works here. I tell you, he is bad news."

"We have to proceed carefully, Warren, Carlos has a few friends in the headquarters. That, by the way, was obvious yesterday when they countered your wishes and kept him in place in Bogotá."

"What about this operation he is working on, boss, anything you can tell me about it?"

"Not over this phone connection, Warren, you should know better. Plus it is classified at a higher level than even the phone is cleared to. Tell you what, I will send you a personal message detailing the plan and suggesting how you and I can profit from the operation. I would like to take credit for its success."

"How can it succeed, boss, this guy is a fuckup."

"He certainly has not exhibited those traits in the past. In other words, everything he has touched has turned to gold, if you know what I mean."

"Lucky, Marc."

"No, luck has nothing to do with it. Preparation, he is always better prepared than most. We just got to be better than him this time. And, Warren—"

"Yes, Marc."

"You can be familiar with me since I am your father-in-law, but do you have to use profanities all the time?"

"Sorry, sir, I talk this way when I am mad as hell."

"You don't talk to Ophelia like that, do you?"

"No, sir, never."

Juana stirred in her bed next to her husband. She was again not feeling good to her stomach, but this time she knew why. *Preñada?* She had been incredulous at first, but the camp's midwife had convinced her that she was at least three months pregnant. *How am I going to do this? If it happened to one of my female warriors, an abortion would be required. I better talk to El Jefe.*

Juana got up without waking her husband and suited quickly in her trademark combination of black jumpsuit and green camouflage hat. The jumpsuit tightly silhouetted her beautiful figure, the object of desire of many men since the age of sixteen. She grabbed her weapon, one that was never far from her since she shot her first man, and headed for the tent of her commander.

When she got there, El Jefe Terraza was up drinking coffee. He was a father figure to Juana, and the affection was clearly two-sided. He motioned for her to sit next to him and greeted her. "Juana, mi hija, siéntate."

"Jefe, I have something to tell you. It is both great news and sad ones for me," she paused.

"Go on, *mija.*"

"You know the love and affection I have for Luis, well that love has rewarded us with a child. I am pregnant and will give birth in six months. That is, unless you order something else, Jefe."

El Jefe was taken aback; this was one of his best commanders in the field. He did consider the mandatory abortion but only for a split second. Instead, he quickly hatched a plan. "Juana, General Ramirez is a big prize, knowing the Americans will take their time with negotiations, I need someone really capable leading the forces guarding him. If you like, I will put you in charge of his continued incarceration. You go on and have a beautiful child, one that can grow up to be a *patriota* like us."

"Ay, Jefe, how can I repay you?"

"You already have, Juana, the operation in Bogotá was a masterpiece. Only you could have done that. Hurry up and have a child. I need you back in action after that."

"Gracias, Jefe."

Johanna Valenz arrived in Suriname aboard an Avianca flight. She would check in at a local hotel and call her mark from there. There was no hurry; in two day's time, they would head to Aruba and put her plan into action. She felt excited about the opportunity this plan presented. The Russian, Anatoly, was public enemy number 1 back in Spain.

No need to spend any time with the arms merchant, she said to herself. The man is probably despicable, an excuse for a bullet if ever she had the chance. At least she had received the go-ahead to permit Carlos Cortes in the operation. She was looking forward to witness as Carlos met María Elena again.

It was late that evening when Warren Westback read his classified e-mail detailing the plan crafted by Johanna Valenz. *How did we know so many details? The Spaniards must have a mole that reports directly to us.* He was bothered by one detail and the overall perfect scheme the plan represented. First, the plan was going to succeed in apprehending Anatoly. Carlos would probably screw up the Colombia piece, but at least the missiles would be rendered useless. The detail that bothered him was that he was going to lose the one arms merchant that Warren considered his personal go-to guy for arms transfers. He had used Abdul several times to deliver untraceable weapons in Eastern Europe and South America. To lose him and to lose him due to Carlos was unacceptable.

Impetuously, Warren got up from his desk; he had an idea and was going to put it into action. He walked out to the embassy courtyard by the cafeteria, took out his untraceable cell phone, and placed a call to Suriname!

Saturday, 3 July 2004; Bogotá, Colombia

Carlos called headquarters and was patched to the home of Mike Dunn. "Boss, the Spaniards just called and confirmed my participation. I am packing and should be on the next flight out to Aruba."

"That's good, I will have John Miller meet you at the Miami airport. He will be carrying the equipment to modify the Strelas and some other equipment for your personal use. I am impressed with the beacon our technicians have come up with. They guarantee reception at this headquarters even if you are underneath three hundred feet of foliage in the Colombian jungle."

"I hope all of that comes with a user's handbook."

"No, not really, it is intuitive. Plus John is checked out on all the new gadgets. He will be your guide."

"Well, Mike, I will be able to report daily until we take the flight into Colombia. After that, I trust the Spaniards have all the angles covered."

"This woman Rosario, her reputation precedes her, I don't think it can go wrong. I am happy if you return safely and will be overjoyed if you return with General Ramirez."

"So long, Mike, I'll keep in touch."

It was 5:35 PM when Carlos finally walked out of his flight at the Miami airport. There was no other way to get to Aruba; as a government servant, he had to travel in American carriers. As they say in the Americas, for them, all roads lead to Miami.

Waiting patiently at the gate was John Miller. Carlos had not seen the agent for a few years, and to him, John looked a little heavier. *Well, the good life in Georgetown no doubt!* Carlos thought. John had a somber look, and that was not typical of him.

"Hello, John, what's happening?"

John did not speak. Instead he handed out an envelope he was carrying. It was a personal, eyes only note from Mike Dunn.

Carlos opened the note and read,

> *Personal for Carlos Cortes. Suspend all operations and head back to Washington DC ASAP. Spanish agent Johanna Valenz was found brutally murdered in her Paramaribo hotel room by an employee this* AM. *Spanish embassy has sent a demarche to the State Department officially questioning the actions of the CIA and, in particular, of special agent Carlos Cortes. Report to the deputy director's office this evening.*
>
> *Mike Dunn*

A written note was attached to this typewritten faxed message; it read, "Carlos, sorry, the Spaniards have called the entire operation off. See you at the agency. Mike."

CHAPTER THIRTEEN

Three years later, August 22, 2007

It was getting late. Carlos sat in his usual bar seat at an Applebee's restaurant in the city of Fountain Valley, California, just off the 405. His two close friends having left, Carlos was left with Jamie the bartender and his thoughts. *No use going home,* he said to himself, *my mind would wander off ESPN to my memories there too!* So he ordered another drink without specifying the type. No need, Jamie knew him well.

He also noticed a man sitting alone at the end of the bar. He occasionally would look up in Carlos's direction. *Odd,* Carlos thought.

Jamie brought his drink, Dewar's and water, and left with no comment. *I know your body language, dear Jamie, you think it's time I leave. But go where?*

ESPN took his mind away from memories for a minute. It was a big day in baseball. True, the Dodgers were fighting for a chance at the wild card entry for the World Series, and they had beaten the Phillies 15-3 tonight. But the news was even more sensational out of Baltimore. There the Texas Rangers had routed the Orioles by the score of 30-3. "First time since 1897 that a major league team scores thirty or more," said the ESPN announcer.

The television shifted to commercials, and Carlos's mind again wandered off.

The sequence of events that followed his return to Washington DC back in the summer of 2004 was blurry in his mind even now. First, he had undergone the shock of the loss of a beautiful woman, one he had some affection for and was looking forward to working in partnership with her. Second, he was fingered and presumed the guilty party in the fiasco that preceded the outing of Johanna to the enemy.

That his record was excellent and his many friends in the Agency vouched for him was inconsequential to the internal affairs investigation that followed. At the Agency, he was presumed guilty from the start. The director of operations Marc Higgins had led the efforts to remove Carlos from the CIA.

The final blow came two months later when his long-term ally Mike Dunn was caught in the web of firings that the administration had instigated in response to the intelligence failures of the Iraq War. Just one month later, Carlos was on the street, another casualty in the fight against terrorism.

However, what mattered most to him was the loss of contact with Rosario. He had been so close! He was sure they were going to meet in Aruba, and that opportunity was gone in a flash. Even worse, what did Rosario think of him after this? Was she the accuser? Did she believe the charges?

Dios mío! *Why do I keep thinking of the past?* Carlos was looking at his glass as he slowly extricated his mind from the daydreaming. He looked up and noticed the stranger looking intently at him. When their eyes met, the stranger quickly looked away, but the many years of covert work gave Carlos a sixth sense when it came to coincidences like this. Even more, the guy was probably armed. If not, why was he wearing an oversized coat on a summer night like today? After all, it was eighty-five degrees outside.

Carlos got up from his stool and asked Jamie for the bill. After he paid, he went outside and started a slow walk to his apartment. He lived right across the street from the restaurant. His apartment was fourteen miles south of the California State University campus of Long Beach where Carlos was a professor at the Department of Criminal Justice.

Carlos walked slowly at first; there was a crosswalk fifty meters from the Applebee's, and Carlos waited for the light to change even though there was no traffic on the street. As he started to cross the street, his peripheral vision noticed someone else leaving the restaurant and walking his way.

His apartment complex was modern, and there were very few places where one might spring a trap from. The only one was provided by the first building on the left and a very large bush. Carlos decided there was where he needed to wait for his uninvited guest.

Am I crazy? Is this guy really following me? Carlos was overcome with self-doubt, but his training as an operative took over, and he waited patiently.

It did not take long; the man with the large overcoat walked slowly in the direction of Carlos's apartment as he passed that first building. For Carlos, taking the man down, disarming him, and pointing the gun directly at his prey took less than five seconds.

"Okay, *hermano,* why are you following me?"

Luis Vigo, now looking at the other end of his own gun, did not speak; instead, a disarming voice was heard loud and clear.

"*Basta,* Carlos, the man has done nothing to you."

Startled, Carlos lowered his guard immediately. He had not heard that voice, that melodic voice, for sixteen years. He did not have to look her way; it was Rosario, at last!

Carlos stood up still holding the gun and turned her way. Standing just ten feet behind him were Rosario and another man. He was holding a gun pointing in his direction. But Carlos did not care; that was Rosario standing in front of him. He was safe.

Juana Montes came into her prize captive's hut in the Colombian jungle. She was carrying a couple of newspapers, a glass of juice, and no gun.

Pepe Ramirez was doing push-ups when she opened the door. He said, "*Hola,* Juana, what do we have here?"

"Just a couple of newspapers, one of them includes an interesting article where they mention you, sir. And yes, there is a direct quote from your wife in it."

Pepe stopped his exercises when he heard this and stood up. "Let me see them, Juana."

"Your wife is not like the other ones, while others shun from a military rescue attempt since we are under orders to kill our captives if that happens, your wife seems to encourage it. Here, see for yourself."

Pepe grabbed the newspapers and commented, "That's my wife, Ana, a true military wife. Although she's a civilian, she lives by the motto of never surrender and never quit."

"How about you, Pepe?"

"You know my motto, 'Never say impossible.' It has been with me since my college days in Puerto Rico."

"That's what you kept repeating after your escape attempt last year, wasn't it?"

"After ten days in solitary confinement, I cannot remember what I said. That was the low point of our relationship, Juana."

"Pepe, I kept you alive. After the military attacked and killed fifteen of our troops including El Jefe, León wanted you dead in revenge against the death of our leader. I think it was his way to assume command with little difficulty. It took all my powers of persuasion to convince the leadership you were more valuable alive than dead."

"And the ten days in the can, what was that?"

"I had to demonstrate some leadership myself. A renegade captive is treated with a cruel punishment so that they don't forget."

"And kept locked up at night, right, Juana."

"Yes, and guarded at night by one of my best troops in case you get ideas again.

"Here is your juice, I have to run and put Pepe Luis to sleep. He is growing like a weed. My husband should be coming back this week, and he is bringing joy to our front, new arms that will make the Cucho Ramos Front even more powerful."

"*Gracias,* Juana, but remember what I said. You fight a lost cause. The Uribe government is going to succeed, and your best bet is to give up your arms and join the political process."

"We'll see. I like you, General, after El Jefe died, you have become like a father to me. We just do not agree, we don't see what you call eye to eye."

Carlos closed the door to his apartment after letting in the three CEID agents. They had not said much after the encounter in the parking lot. Just pleasantries after Carlos returned the gun to Luis and they had shaken hands.

"Make yourselves at home, can I get you anything to drink?"

María Elena answered for the group, "No, Carlos, we are here on business, we need to talk."

"Rosario, of course we can talk."

"And please don't call me Rosario, the name is María Elena. Let me start by telling you that the Spanish government has just completed an extensive review of the brutal murder of Johanna Valenz and the investigation into the leak that caused it. We are prepared to exonerate you of any complicity in this tragic chain of events. I am sorry."

She is reserved and serious, maybe it is because we are in the company of her men, at least I hope so.

Carlos would soon find out that was not the case.

Friday, August 24, 2007

At SOUTHCOM, Marine General John Strange sat down to review the situation surrounding General Ramirez's captivity. He was the newly appointed commander and had changed the frequency of updates from weekly to every two days. He had also changed the organization favored by General Goodman to one where a general officer was directly responsible for Pepe's rescue and could effect changes in all of the command's subordinate organizations.

This move had been blessed by the new secretary of defense and was highly criticized by the military services who felt the new boss was treading heavily on their turf.

Major General Mike Huber, the old chief of staff and recently returned from the Afghanistan theater where he earned his second star, spoke first, "Sir, it is a pleasure to brief you directly on Operation First Strike. I have spent a month in Bogotá and can honestly say that everything we can do is being done to effect the recovery of General Ramirez."

"I have to be honest, Mike, since I arrived here in April, I have not felt comfortable with the overall effort to rescue the general. The reason I have transferred you to Colombia and put you in charge of all operations is that I feel your leadership is the necessary ingredient to make it happen."

"Yes, sir, I also understand that you want me to integrate the effort going forward. Even though everyone is trying their hardest, it is exactly that factor that is missing from the equation. Everyone is operating on their own agenda, and they are not coordinating with each other. I ask for your patience since I am dealing with foreign forces, other intelligence agencies, and the State Department."

"No easy task, Mike, I understand what you are telling me, but my patience has its limits. In short, I want results."

"Yes, sir." Major General Huber continued his briefing. "Today I will give you a glimpse of where I believe we can get the most for our time and effort."

This officer is the right man for the job. A decorated marine and war hero, I can trust him to complete this very difficult task. I just hope he catches a lucky break, I think we'll need one this time, General Strange said to himself with concern for his protégé Mike Huber.

The next day—Saturday

María Elena Borbón arrived at the appointed hour. At precisely 1:00 PM, she rang the doorbell of Carlos's apartment.

He opened the door and was surprised to see she was alone. "Good afternoon, María Elena, please come in."

As they walked to the sitting room, María Elena said, "We have no time to spare, I hope you have made up your mind."

"You almost sound like an American, where's the civility? Can I offer you something to drink?"

"No, Carlos, I really must go." María Elena sat down in the only straight-back chair in the room, leaving the entire couch for Carlos to use.

"I'm here as an official representative of the Spanish government. Yesterday we offered our apologies, something even your own government has not done, and offered you an opportunity to get even with those that treacherously backstabbed you three years ago. This time we have a plan that is not compromised and that I will personally see through to a successful conclusion."

"I believe you, in fact I trust you completely. I have two reasons why I asked you back today before I agreed to do this. First, I need a job after this and had to request an emergency leave of absence from the university. To my delight, they extended me one although I am not tenured on the job."

"They must like you, Carlos."

"Most importantly, the students like me, I am very popular during registration week. However, I have a very capable assistant that will take over for me while I am gone."

"The second reason, Carlos?"

"Oh, you had to ask."

"Well, you brought it up, *caramba!*"

"It is personal, María Elena, I want you to give me your word that you trust me and that you are comfortable working with me. I will not do this unless you say you do."

"I trust you, Carlos," María Elena countered. *If you only knew how much I have throughout my life,* she thought.

"Then I'm in. When do we leave?"

CHAPTER FOURTEEN

They did not meet again that day; María Elena left behind tickets for American Airlines to San Juan, Puerto Rico. He was to sign in as Jose Hernandez at the Caribe Hilton Hotel. Also included in the package were an American Express card, a U.S. passport with the same fictitious name, and $1,000 in cash. *How did they get my picture?* Carlos thought, *Their skills are similar to ours.*

When he finished packing, Carlos drove north to Brea to visit his family. It was 5:00 PM, and the traffic was heavy.

I am happy that Sonia and Jose Manuel will be able to make it. Carlos was mostly thinking of his family as he drove the Los Angeles freeways. *We have not seen each other much since Mother's funeral. Mama, if only I had been here more when you got sick. Maybe I could have done something to cure you, make you go to the doctor, help pay for treatment,* Dios mío, *so much I could have done!*

Someone cut in front of him without warning on the freeway. That snapped Carlos out of his tormenting daydreaming, and he corrected his curse quickly to prevent an accident. *Wow, that was close, better pay attention to what I'm doing.*

When he arrived at the house, he noticed his two siblings had not arrived yet and his father waiting for them patiently on the porch. "*Hola*, Papá, como estas?"

"Cada día deseando tenerlos a todos en casa," his father said, and he meant everyone including his lovely Eugenia.

"*Si*, Papá, Mother is always with us no matter where we are in the world." Carlos tried to change the conversation. "Papá, that is why I am here today, I know I have not traveled in a long time, but tomorrow I start a very long trip."

His father was not listening. Instead he turned Carlos around and said, "Here comes Sonia and Jose."

Carlos waited till much later to tell all the truth about his upcoming trip. When all were seated at the dinner table and it was time to say grace, Carlos knew they would all be paying attention to what he said.

Pepe heard the helicopters early. He never slept deeply, and any such noise would wake him readily. He knew that any day, someday, the forces of either Colombia or his own would knock on the door of this guerrilla army and rescue him. But it had been three years and still no rescue, and this always demoralized Pepe for a few weeks.

Maybe tonight's the night, Pepe was thinking as he got ready for the inevitable. He knew that at any moment Juana and a group of guerrillas would take him away from the camp and to a safe zone where he could be guarded better.

Like clockwork, Juana arrived with two other men and took a handcuffed Pepe away from his hut. They immediately started down a known path that led to a freshwater stream. In the distance, Pepe could hear the faint sounds of a firefight. *Maybe three to four miles away,* thought Pepe. *If we had daylight, maybe I would know from which direction the bomb blasts were coming. East/west, who knows in this jungle?*

When they arrived at the stream, there was urgency to cross it for the other side was considered safer. The stream was five to six feet deep in places, and Pepe knew the area well. Juana was about to start crossing when Pepe said, "Juana, take my handcuffs off, or I may drown if I slip."

Juana thought about it for a second and started taking the handcuffs off. "Don't get any ideas, General."

"Where could I go?" Pepe said as he began crossing the stream.

Just at that moment, fortune smiled Pepe's way. First, a large explosion was heard in the distance followed by another just seconds later. All in the group except for Pepe were startled by them. Then, a few seconds later, very loud aircraft noises were heard approaching the group.

Jets on their escape maneuver! Maybe KFIRs, thought Pepe. As he considered that silently, Pepe noticed the other members of the group looking away from him and in the direction of the incoming jets.

Not a moment to lose! It was a dark night, but Pepe knew exactly where he was. He used to swim in this area during the rare times he was allowed to bathe. So he slipped into the water and began swimming below the water downstream and away from the group. Even though he was underwater, he heard the jets charge overhead just seconds later. *The sound of freedom! Boy, do I love the roar of afterburners.*

Just at that moment, Juana realized her prize captive was gone. She turned around after looking directly at the jets' bright red exhaust, momentarily losing her night vision.

"General, where are you?" Juana shouted. She turned to her men immediately and gave orders to split and find their man. Her orders were clear but met an unsuccessful end. Pepe had slipped away!

Carlos sat down with the family at the dinner table. They were all at their appointed seats. Carlos and Jose Manuel sat next to their father who was at one end of the table, and Sonia sat next to Jose. The place setting at the other end of the table was prepared but would not be used; it was reserved for Mamá.

They finished their meal, and as Sonia was serving dessert, Carlos said, "Papá, I have not told you the truth about my work for the U.S. government that ended three years ago. This was because I was restricted from doing so even after I was fired."

All three of his family members reacted with surprise when he said "fired."

"Yes, I was fired from the primary intelligence agency of this nation due to a misunderstanding, Papá. I did not quit and move home like I told you."

"I knew it, the CIA!" Jose said out loud from the other end of the table.

Carlos continued, "For a time, I was a decorated agent for this agency, and everything I touched turned to gold. It was in my last posting in Colombia where a rift developed between my boss and I, one that I did not manage well. To make it short, I was accused of something I did not do, and it turns out I was stabbed in the back by my own boss."

"*Hijo,* why are you telling us this?"

"Because, Papá, I have just confirmed my suspicions about what happened back in 2004 and must travel back to my past and make things right. Tomorrow I am leaving on a most dangerous trip, one that I may not come back from but, Papá, one that I must do for me and for my friend Pepe."

Sonia interrupted him and asked, "Pepe is that air force general that was taken hostage back then, isn't he, Carlos?"

"And my best friend, Sonia, one that has been held captive for three plus years. To go through life without solving this riddle is not worth living in my book. So I hope you all forgive me and try to understand why I must go away for a short time."

His father stood from the table and said, "Understand, no, please don't ask me to understand, Carlos. But if you feel that you must do this, who are we to try to stop you. *Vaya con Dios hombre,* and come back soon to your family."

Carlos stood also, and they embraced. After a few seconds, all four were next to each other in a tight embrace.

Friday, August 31, 2007, 0130 hrs.

Pepe had crossed the creek and was moving as fast as he could in the deep brush of the jungle while never losing sight of the creek to his right. It was a difficult and dangerous journey. He knew the three people guarding him that night very well. So he knew that neither Juana nor the other two guards could swim. The only way for them to catch him was following the same track he was on because the creek at times was too deep to walk on.

This area of Colombia is characterized by patches of deep jungle interspaced by areas of relatively little cover, the result of clear-cutting by farmers and cattlemen. There are few roads, so the best means of transportation is either by foot or on the navigable rivers.

The FARC has lived in the area for many years and have cut roads in the jungle underneath the foliage. But there are no maps for these roads, and Pepe had no clue where to look for them. So his best bet was to find a clear area and look for guidance from the sun or stars at night.

He decided to travel by night, avoid contact with the locals since they were mostly guerrillas or sympathizers, and head west as best as he could. West were the mountains, and Pepe's best bet to find a friendly face.

Through it all, he kept thinking of Ana and the kids. *My daughter, she is probably a lieutenant by now. Wonder if she went to pilot training. Junior should be a senior this year, ready to take the world by storm. And Ana, dear Ana, have you kept the faith?* Pepe drove deeper into the jungle, oblivious of the thorns and bugs that laid in waiting on every bush. He drove on to freedom!

Carlos checked in for his flight to San Juan, Puerto Rico, under his new alias and passed without problems through security using his new passport. *Well, they pass their first test,* thought Carlos. *Plus Rosario said I had a business-class reservation.*

He did not notice any of his CEID friends on board, so he decided to relax and catch up on whatever movie was offered during the all-night flight. The scheduled arrival for the seven-hour flight was 9:30 AM, so a little shut-eye wouldn't hurt.

Every once in a while, no matter what he was doing, Carlos would come back to the same thought pattern. *She was so detached, no warmth! I wonder, dear Rosario, have you forgotten how wonderful our weekend really was back in 1991. Will it ever return? I know it has not left my heart. But how do I show it? How do . . .*

CHAPTER FIFTEEN

Six days later in Old San Juan, Carlos sat relaxed, tanned, and fit in a restaurant he had found by accident. El Patio was its name, and the locals said the restaurant was *mas viejo que el frio*—"older than old man winter." This was a curious saying for a land with no noticeable change in temperature throughout the year. Most days it was either 85°F if warm, or 92°F if hot.

Carlos had settled down to his secret-agent routine as if he had never left the Agency. He had his new alias down pat. To some in the hotel and areas he frequented, his name was Jose; to others, he had introduced himself as Paco. A nickname he preferred rather than using his own brother's name. He knew by now the head bartender every afternoon; he went by the name of Edgar.

The waiter, Aníbal, was a nice gentleman and already recognized him by name. He served today a local delicacy, *mofongo with lobster*. Carlos was drinking a *mojito* and was enjoying more and more the local food and drink immensely. *No wonder Pepe loved this land, everyone here appears to be in a constant good mood. I should come more to this island.*

Carlos was seated with a perfect view to all access points inside the restaurant. He noticed immediately as Luis Vigo entered the front door and walked directly to where Carlos was seated. Recognizing the familiarity between the two, the bartender waved at Luis and went back to his duties behind the bar.

Luis sat down as Carlos continued to enjoy his delicious meal. They exchanged pleasantries and ordered another pair of *mojitos* and some food for Luis. He chose an octopus salad, and much later, they ordered dessert and an afternoon coffee.

When the coffee came, they finally talked business. The restaurant was empty except for the workers and a lunch customer at the bar that had too much to drink. Luis spoke first as he passed an envelope.

"Jose, this evening, you will move to El San Juan Hotel. There is a key inside for a cabana by the pool that is under your name. Mrs. Hernandez will arrive tomorrow morning at the international airport and will be staying in the adjoining room. She is traveling with our mark in his airplane from Suriname. They are en route here to receive the missiles and exchange payment for them."

"When are the missiles arriving, Luis?"

"They are already here. Tomorrow afternoon, you will proceed as a group to the east side of the international airport to a company called Piezas Borinquén International. From there, you will proceed by plane to Colombia."

The name of the parts company stuck in Carlos's mind. *Boy, Puerto Ricans are a strange lot. On one end, they seem happy and full of life, but on the other end, they act as confused as that company's name is. A company with words in three languages—with Borinquén, the given native Indian name to the island of Puerto Rico—that and politics as dysfunctional as any I have seen before!*

Luis continued to reveal details of the plan that Carlos had not heard before. When he was finished, Carlos asked just one question. "Tell me, Luis, who is Mrs. Hernandez?"

"The boss took this one on herself, Jose. Her reputation is on the line, and she is personally making sure it does not fail."

"But after Al Kassar is out of the picture, why is the mission continuing? Haven't you met all your goals by then?" Carlos asked.

"That, my dear friend, you have to ask directly to her."

"But, Luis, I know you are an Agency informant. Back in 2004, I read your detailed reports on ongoing operations, and you can trust me to keep that and any other secrets quiet. So please tell me why."

"What I did in 2004, I did with the full backing of my superiors. They all knew of the reports, and they backed my actions. It was one such report that sealed Johanna's fate, and for that, I will never forgive myself. It was because of the reports that we initially thought you were the informant that double-crossed Johanna. We now know the answer to that question."

"Who, Luis?" Carlos asked expectantly, momentarily forgetting his previous question.

"A man named Warren Westback. He was an Agency operative who did business with Al Kassar. It was him—well, his treason—who killed Johanna," Luis said these last few words with noticeable anger.

Warren Westback, so that was it! That son of a bitch is going to hear from me. "How do you know, Luis?"

"It took time, Carlos"—momentarily forgetting to use the alias here—"I'm sorry, Jose. We investigated you, we investigated our own embassy personnel, and we even investigated ourselves all to dead ends. It was finally a release of information by your National Security Agency that cracked the case. It seems the conversation between this Warren Westback and Abdul Al Kassar on the night of July 2, 2004, was recorded by one of your secret satellites monitoring for drug traffic information on the airwaves. We got the requested tapes late last year, and a crack group of analysts went to work on the tapes in January of this year."

"I see, have you told the Agency?"

"No, we are taking care of this problem ourselves. Your Mr. Westback is too high up in the food chain to trust your guys."

"I would be happy to do this job for you, Luis."

"No, Jose, you worry about your end. I will take care of Mr. Westback."

"So we are back to the original question, Luis. Why not stop the operation tomorrow after the transfer of missiles and the arrest of Al Kassar?"

"Ask Mrs. Hernandez about that." With that last statement, Luis stood up and offered his hand to Carlos. "I have to go, sir. I have a plane to catch, but I did not want to go without asking you to be very careful and bring you and Mrs. Hernandez back safely."

Moncho Rivera, aka León, met with his senior commanders in his jungle hideout. Their ranks had been decimated in the last three years. In addition to El Jefe, the CRAF had lost two other leaders and three deputies. As a result, two of them were very inexperienced and had little combat between them. The purpose of the meeting was to get an update of the search for the general and make plans for the reception of the Strela missiles.

León spoke first, "Luis, please give us an update on the search for General Ramirez."

Luis Montes replied, "My wife reports that over 150 of our members are actively searching for the general. If he heads west, like we believe he will, he will be captured. If he takes a wrong turn in this jungle, he may never come out of it. His chances of survival are grim. In fact, his best chance for survival is if we capture him and bring him back."

"After how many days did we capture him last time, Luis?"

"Only two, sir, he did not get far."

"This time he's been gone one week. Do we have to put more people on the search?"

"No, the places he can go for help are few and far between. We have those places

guarded. He won't get far."

"If he is alive, Luis."

"Yes, sir, if he is alive."

"Now, Manuel"—León looked at El Jefe's old assistant—"please give us an update on the missiles, when are they arriving, what help do you need, etc."

"The missiles arrive tomorrow evening at Calamar airport. Abdul is sending them with the two missile experts that will do the training."

"Do we really need trainers? Don't we have an Ecuadorian here that can do it? I thought we hired him four years ago."

"Yes, sir, we do, however, these missiles are advanced Russian versions. Our man trained in Israeli missiles ten years ago. He will monitor and learn the training and continue it after the Nicaraguans are gone."

"Who are the Nicaraguans, Manuel?"

"All I know is that a husband-and-wife team is coming. She is a high-ranking member of the Sandinista party and her husband took care of over one thousand Strela missiles for them."

"Aren't the Sandinistas in power again in Nicaragua?"

"Affirmative, they won the last elections by a wide margin. President Ortega played the population perfectly with wide support from President Hugo Chavez of Venezuela."

"Maybe we should do the same in Colombia," said León. He was the only one of the group that was allowed to make a statement like that. Such political ideas were reserved for the leadership and not for the rank and file.

"After they arrive, we have arranged for a two-week training program. The strangers will be flown out after that by the padre," Manuel continued.

"When will we use the missiles for the first time, Manolo?" León asked, looking at his deputy.

"The first opportunity is of our own making. We have released information in the right places that you are having a meeting such as this on the southern flank of the Macarena Mountains. The enemy will know of this meeting and mount an impressive attack. We will lie in wait for the attack and shoot down as many of the aircraft participating as possible. In short, the attackers will be the surprised."

"And when is this meeting scheduled for?"

"In three weeks, *jefe*."

"El Jefe was someone else," alluding to their fallen leader. "Please call me León."

Thursday, September 7, 2007; Suriname

María Elena Borbón sat down with Al Kassar at a local hotel in Paramaribo. They were scheduled to fly out to Puerto Rico that morning. She had not taken any chances this time. Surrounding her were four undercover Spanish agents, and with her, another agent was pretending to be her bodyguard.

Al Kassar got comfortable in his chair and felt safe. After all, Paramaribo was as safe a town as he could buy. He talked first, "I am perplexed, why are you here with a hired gun, Mrs. Hernandez. Paramaribo is the safest capital city in the world."

"It may be safe for you, sir, for a woman, no city is safe. Do you have the money?"

"Relax, enjoy the weather. The money will be with us in the aircraft." Al Kassar seemed too relaxed and friendly, but his face betrayed him.

María Elena interrupted him and demanded, "Your personnel in Puerto Rico have seen the merchandise. I have delivered, now Enrique here will count and take the money in a separate airplane to Nicaragua. I am not entering a U.S. territory with that much cash. Five hundred thousand dollars is a lot of money to bet on a two-bit merchant like you."

Upon the insult, Al Kassar perked up. *Who is this woman to talk to me like that? I will let it pass this time, but she will be back for more candy, more missile deliveries. Next time she will not get away with insulting me!*

Al Kassar got up and said, "I will give you the damn money at the airport. Let's go." He stood to make a handsome profit from this sale; after all, he was a businessman and wanted to make more business like this. Strela missiles were hard to get; in fact, he had more than one failure in the past three years trying to acquire the missiles. *At least this whore delivered,* he thought.

Carlos was in his room packing for the trip to the Colombian jungle. Another person would be apprehensive; however, Carlos was not. He had received training from the best Colombian military jungle experts. The Junglas, Spanish for "jungle people," were an elite group of Special Forces presently commanded by Carlos's best Colombian friend from his years at the embassy.

He decided to make one more phone call and went to his computer to retrieve the phone number. He was going to call Ana Luisa, Pepe's wife. Three years ago, he would talk to her once a month, but as time passed, the calls were less frequent. The last time they had been in contact was the day of the anniversary of his capture.

When he looked at his screen, he noticed a new message had arrived. It was from the only link that remained from his years at the Agency. He opened the message and read,

FR: Barnstormer@yahoo.com

TO: Rockone@yahoo.com

Subject: Update

Credible arrival of vodka bottles, enough for several parties. Vodka is best quality. Will practice for two weeks, planning for a big bash in three.

Nico's in charge of practice. I will shadow Nico's.

Rico arrived my location in June but now has left the house, unsure his location. Orion is still pretty.

Barnstormer

My god! The message could not have arrived at a better time. It confirmed that he was going to a place in Colombia where Pepe had been seen. *But where is he?* Juan Miranda, his Ecuadorian plant, only sent him messages every six months, and to reply to this message would be a breach of security. *At least I know Juan is there, and Orion is working.*

Carlos made a decision to go back in his word to Rosario. He would have to contact someone that could help. *The Spaniards were good, but this was Pepe now in the mix. I must act.*

He opened the bag he was leaving behind and pulled out his cell phone. It took just seconds to find the telephone number for his friend in Colombia. He dialed it and soon was hearing the soft voice of recently promoted Colonel Francisco Gomez, commander of the Junglas battalion.

"Hola."

"Francisco, perdón, Coronel Gomez."

"Carlos, is that you? I can recognize your voice even when you call me from afar. Please stop the formalities and call me Cisco."

For a moment, they talked about the good times, back when they were both just role players in the fight. Now one was a responsible field commander and the other a disgraced agent. Carlos was the first one to get right to the point.

"Cisco, I call you because I need your help."

"Just let me know and it's done!"

"Careful, my friend, you do not know what I am going to ask."

"Ask anyway, Carlos, I could always say no."

"I need you to help an old friend out with a reconnaissance mission, one that could escalate into an assault on an enemy camp."

"Interesting, keep going."

"I would like you to place a UHF direction finder at our old base back in 2003. Two days from today I will start transmitting my position for five minutes straight starting at 1:00 PM."

"You will, Carlos?" The colonel sounded incredulous.

"Yes, I will, and I don't think I have to explain to you what this means."

"No, Carlos, I know this has to be all about—"

Carlos interrupted him in midsentence, "No names, Cisco, just in case someone is listening. If you receive a signal on 243.0 that lasts five minutes, I would like for you to place a recce team in the vicinity of the signal."

"Go on, Carlos." The colonel sounded interested.

Carlos continued, "If the signal lasts ten minutes, that is confirmation I have found my mark. I don't know what you are empowered to do, Cisco, but I ask you to make an all-out midnight assault on the position the same night the signal is received for fifteen minutes straight. The entire process should take no more than two weeks. And, by the way, all friendlies except for the hostages will be wearing reflective tapes that night, make sure you wear your goggles!"

"And you want me to do this without my superiors' knowledge, I presume?"

"Cisco, you know that the fewer people that know, the best chance of success we'll have. And another thing, Cisco, if we pull this off, my nation will be most grateful."

Carlos was not entirely sure of his last statement; he was most confident in the friendship he had formed with the colonel. In fact, he trusted him entirely; however, here he was asking for him to put his career on the line. And there was nothing Carlos could promise in return. He was taking a chance.

"*Bueno*, Carlos, I will do this. My nation's indebted to yours, and my personnel are professionals, thanks to the training you have given us. How could I say no?"

"Thank you, my dear friend, you will not hear from me again until the operation is complete. I ask you to trust me, to put your troops in harm's way with very little notice. I owe you one."

"Don't worry, Carlos, if the truth were known that I normally start operations with about the same amount of information. In your case, Carlos, that information you have given me is to be trusted. You would not lead me down the wrong path."

They said a few other pleasantries and finally hung up the phone. Carlos still had to make one more call. He dialed Ana Luisa's cell phone in Miami.

"Hello," the sweet voice of Pepe's wife answered the phone.

"Hello, Ana, it's Carlos."

"Carlos I miss your calls, what's up?"

Carlos hated to darken her obvious sunny disposition but had no choice. He said in a somber voice, "Ana, I have to ask you the one thing we have discussed before about Pepe's rescue."

"Oh my god, Carlos, you found him?"

"Ana, I don't know if I have, what I need is for you to give me permission to effect a rescue."

Both of them knew the standing hostage rules of engagement of the FARC. They normally would treat their captives with basic human dignity but demanded that the government not try to rescue the hostages. If they tried, the guards were supposed to kill the hostages in retribution.

Ana replied seriously, "Carlos, Pepe and I understand the rules. We even discussed this when Pepe went to war. He would not want it any other way. If there is a chance, rescue him."

"I will not say anything else, Ana. Please do not tell anyone, not even your children."

"Nothing needs to be said, Carlos, I know Pepe trusts you. *Vaya con Dios!*"

CHAPTER SIXTEEN

Warren Westback arrived at the San Juan International Airport on a direct flight from Washington DC. The United Airbus A-320 was cramped and uncomfortable. This flight had no first class, and Warren had to sit between two overweight men.

Ah, to be away from Ophelia and that damn family of hers. Al Kassar called just in time. His invitation for a wild weekend in the islands was too good to pass up. I can't wait.

Al Kassar told Warren to meet him in San Juan since he was there on a small business matter. He had promised to be in the air to Venezuela by the early afternoon. *I hope this Margarita Island is beautiful and the girls likewise.*

Warren was now posted in Washington DC on a desk job he hated. The promotion was arranged by his father-in-law as a reward for the investigation into Carlos Cortes's botched operation with the Spanish CEID. The CIA had a black eye from Johanna Valenz's murder, and a scapegoat had to be found quickly. Carlos had fit the bill and was now gone and forgotten from the Agency.

After he had claimed his luggage, Warren was picked up outside the baggage claim area by one of Al Kassar's men. They then proceeded to the warehouse where the missiles were stored and from where the aircraft would depart later that afternoon.

Warren was perturbed that Al Kassar was not there to meet him. But soon after he got to the hangar at the east end of the international airport and he eyed the Puerto Rican receptionist, carefully examined her finely tuned body, he decided that waiting for Al Kassar was not that bad after all.

A knock at the door, must be Rosario. Carlos opened the door and was surprised to see a man standing by her.

María Elena took over immediately in what probably was her preferred mode of operation on the field, a take-charge attitude. She quickly kissed Carlos on the cheek and said, "José, my dear, I want you to meet Mr. Abdul Al Kassar. He wanted to meet you, and I presume he wants to check your knowledge out. Isn't that so, Mr. Al Kassar?"

Taken by surprise at this woman's openness, Abdul fumbled for an answer and was about to talk when she interrupted, "Come on, José, tell the man everything you know about the Strela. And please excuse me, I'm going out for a swim." With that she took the side door to the adjoining room where her luggage was waiting.

Carlos spent the next few minutes talking to Al Kassar and answering his questions. He was a quick study; in a few short days, Carlos had memorized all he had researched of the missiles.

The conversation ended when they heard María Elena shout from the other room that she was going out to the pool. Carlos was finishing the last question. "And these Strela-10 missiles that we have acquired are the best available in the market. If it senses an aircraft's jet exhaust, it will find it, and if it does, it will destroy everything in its path."

Carlos arranged a departure time for the airport with Al Kassar and excused himself. "I hope I have answered all your questions to your satisfaction, sir."

"Yes, you have, I believe you have a great knowledge of the system. My personnel will pick both of you up at three o'clock. And do me a favor and control your wife in my presence, she is an embarrassment to you, Mr. Hernandez."

Carlos felt like strangling the man right then and there. However, sanity prevailed, and after a vague promise, he closed the door and changed into his swimsuit quickly.

Carlos walked out of his room right into the pool area. It was expansive and beautiful. The vegetation, the style of construction, the sunken bar, all gave you the impression that you were in a remote tropical island.

He did not have to look far to find María Elena. She was in the middle of the pool taking long strokes while moving through the water effortlessly. He picked a spot in the pool where he could watch her and ordered a rum and cola from a waitress. *I believe they still call these Cuba Libres in reference to the sister island still embroiled in communism some forty-seven years after Fidel Castro took over the island. When will that end?*

When María Elena got out of the pool, she glanced at him and waved. *That is the same wave she did when we met in Madrid at Barrajas Airport back in 1991. Boy, how much have I missed this woman!*

She walked toward him while drying her body with a long blue towel. She was resplendent; a finely tuned body that nearing forty years of age was still desired by any man watching her. She came over to the table and sat down.

"Hello, José, missed me?"

Well, that was a mixture of professionalism by using my alias and the same coyness that characterized her back in the nineties. Carlos stayed quiet.

She continued, "All kidding aside, let's go back to the room and talk, it will be safe there."

They sat down in Carlos's side of the double room. María Elena still dressed only on her elegant bikini. She noted, however, that as she gave Carlos details of the plan, he was only looking at her face. *No wandering eyes, he is truly paying attention to what I say.*

When María Elena got to the details of the plan that Carlos had not heard, she purposely slowed down her speech pattern. "The key to this plan is the rescue of any hostages we find in that camp. We will exfiltrate by helicopter leased by the French Special Forces. They have committed to this counting that we may find Mrs. Betancourt." She was referring to Ingrid Betancourt, once an ex-candidate for the presidency of Colombia and now the key hostage of the FARC.

That's when Carlos asked his question. "María Elena, why are you doing this? Why not call the FBI and have Al Kassar and his men arrested here and get this over? And why me, why am I involved?

"Carlos, three years ago, I started an investigation into Johanna's murder and totally destroyed the career of an agent at the CIA. I am doing this to tie loose ends, to effect revenge, and mostly to make up to my mistakes from long ago. I hope that after this you forgive me, and I truly hope that we can find your friend Pepe."

Carlos lowered his head and confided with her, "Thank you for your honesty and concern for me. I must confess to you that I have not kept entirely my word. In short, I have asked a very trustworthy friend in the Colombian armed forces to lay a reconnaissance party down near the site of the FARC camp. I have a concealed transmitter that will emit our position to him, one which is easily triangulated and fixed. Have you heard before of the Junglas battalion?"

You could see the sudden discomfort in María Elena's body language; her stare fixed on Carlos eyes as she said, "Can we ever trust each other? The entire success of this plan rests on its secrecy, and you trust a friend in the Colombian forces well enough to put this plan in jeopardy?"

"The same as you trust the French, María Elena."

María Elena got up off her chair and said as she retired to her room, "Carlos, do me a favor and trust my judgment." She stopped at the door connecting the rooms and continued, "Can we make a deal and only use the Colombians if my part of the plan fails?"

Still sitting, Carlos replied, "You have my word, María Elena."

"We leave at three, be ready," María Elena said as she closed the door.

The east side of Luis Muñoz Marín Airport in San Juan is reserved for the Air National Guard, a C-130 unit, and a varied collection of fly-by-night cargo outfits flying all types of rusting and aging aircraft. The only two modern aircraft parked in the ramp on that side of the airport belonged to Al Kassar. Buying the influence of government personnel was Al Kassar's forte, so the transport craft taking the missiles and the instructors was already loaded and ready for flight.

As they approached the building, all passengers in the van were invited for a final get-together in the only office of the hangar belonging to Piezas Borinquén International. When they dismounted, everyone let María Elena get off first, and she characteristically entered the hangar without waiting for the rest.

The hangar was about one hundred feet wide and large enough to fit two small multiengine cargo carriers. The aircraft with the missiles was on the side of the hangar, too large to fit inside without crowding the other aircraft there out. When María Elena walked inside, she saw three men waiting for the group on the second floor balcony. *The office must be upstairs,* she thought.

Then she recognized him. *Warren Westback is here!* His file picture betrayed him; CEID had file pictures on all known CIA agents, but Warren was special. Since he was identified as the traitor that caused Johanna's death, a special effort was taken by María Elena's group to track and photograph him at every opportunity. *That is him, I must warn Carlos.*

She did not waste any time; at any moment, Carlos would enter the hangar and be recognized. The whole operation was in jeopardy.

María Elena turned around abruptly and headed back outside as if she had forgotten something.

At the door, she ran into Al Kassar and Carlos just moments before they entered the hangar. She looked at Carlos and said, "Jose, I want you to go straight to the aircraft and inspect those missiles. Turn around, go there, and make sure nothing is missing. Once I say good-bye to Mr. Al Kassar, I want to be in the air and fly away to Colombia. Please be my little astronaut and do this for me, dear."

Her demanding manner was in line with her persona. Al Kassar found her request believable and, at the same time, felt pity for this man who had to go through life under the fingers of this woman. *In my country, I would have her stoned to death,* he thought.

Carlos got the message immediately. *How could Warren be here? Is that what she meant by using his code name Astronaut? Better not ask any questions, we can always talk about this later.*

Once that was resolved, the group minus Carlos went up to the office and made final arrangements for subsequent missile purchases from the Nicaraguans. The parting words between the groups wished for growing profits for the newfound alliance. As they left the office, Warren thanked María Elena in broken Spanish for the weekend playboy getaway she had arranged for them in Venezuela. "Mrs. Hernandez, thank you for this invite to Margarita Island. I have always wanted to visit that lovely place. Of course, if you were coming, it would be even better."

"Without my husband," replied María Elena coyly.

"Of course without." Warren felt safe; after all, he was the big Agency contact for the group. *What woman would pass up the opportunity to spend a night of pleasure with me,* he thought.

"Mr. Westback, your participation today and for the weekend party was unexpected but welcomed. *Espero que tenga un fin de semana explosivo,*" María Elena added in Spanish.

An explosive weekend indeed, she thought as she smiled on the way out. Both aircraft were soon airborne on their missions. One would meet a catastrophic end.

As Al Kassar's aircraft approached Del Caribe International Airport in the island of Margarita, Venezuela, Luis Vigo was standing in the bow of a twenty-four-foot fast cruiser going through the final preparations for his mission. In his shoulder rested a cylindrical object with ends open at both sides. It looked like an oversized rifle. He went through a mental checklist.

Bueno, *no other aircraft is due into the airport for forty minutes. The aircraft checked in five minutes ago with the exact call sign as the one that took off from San Juan. We have visual contact with the aircraft and can confirm it is the same type as our target.* He then said loud enough for the two other members of his crew to hear, "Toma esto hijos de puta, esto es por Johanna," as he pressed the trigger of the cylinder he was carrying.

Juan and his team were in a rented boat two miles off the pier at Bahía de Pampatar, Venezuela. The aircraft was on final approach to the west runway of the airport at one thousand feet altitude and exactly three miles from the end of the runway.

Inside Al Kassar's aircraft, the four passengers had just sat down for landing and were looking forward with anticipation for the nonstop weekend party set up by María Elena for the group. *The girls were from Europe, Mrs. Hernandez said, an unexpected benefit of my relationship with Al Kassar,* Warren thought.

The Strela-10 missile was completely untraceable; it left its launcher with ease and, after a loud explosion, lit up and left a corkscrew pattern of smoke as it climbed toward its target. It soon acquired the heat signature of the G-2 aircraft in its path.

Looking out of a window, Abdul Al Kassar saw the missile launch and instantly recognized its smoke pattern. He cried in Arabic, "Look out!"

For all aboard, the warning came too late; the missile found its mark easily and exploded as it sensed the proximity to the heat signature it was tracking. In an instant, thousands of molten metal pieces hit the aircraft with incredible force. Most of the impact was taken by the port engine that immediately exploded in a ball of fire. So violent was the explosion that the engine came off its support bracket and hung, in a twisted fashion, from only one bolt. The aircraft began an immediate veer to the left that culminated seconds later in an unrecoverable aircraft spin.

By the time this happened, Warren Westback was already dead. One of the melted pieces of metal had entered through an aircraft window and hit Warren in his left temple, a kind end for such an evil man.

Abdul Al Kassar was not as fortunate; he and his four accomplices rode the aircraft spin all the way down until the aircraft hit the water. When an aircraft hits the water at an awkward angle, the water acts as a hard cement wall, and damage from such a hit is catastrophic. The aircraft hit on the water's edge at 120 mph still spinning. The impact killed all on board instantly.

Luis smiled with a raised fist. He and his group started their engines and motored out to sea. Six miles out, a Spanish Armada ship, the *Mar Caribe*, picked them up, and they scuttled the boat they were riding in.

CHAPTER SEVENTEEN

How many days? Pepe was beginning to lose count since his escape. *At least a week,* he thought. In the seven days since his escape, he had slowly moved west toward civilization, toward freedom. The jungle transit had not been easy. Pepe was tired, hungry, and soiled from head to toe.

He had survived by drinking water from the plentiful streams and by eating all kinds of plants and bugs he could recognize and tolerate. Yet he was tired, his system was queasy, probably the result of untreated water. Only reason for his stamina was the shape his body was at the moment of the escape, but this too would not last long.

He had only found three clear areas where he could find his bearings. This kept him on a fairly straight westerly course, and now he was facing a river with strong currents and a width of approximately forty feet. He had traveled south on the bank of this river and now had found an area where Pepe was sure he had the strength available to swim across.

I must cross here, civilization in this part of Colombia mostly lives in the west side of navigable rivers. I should find Colombian military forces on that side, he thought. *Too bad the rainy season is in full force, this river was probably a calm stream two months ago!*

Pepe looked at the crossing and inspected the banks. At the moment, he was more interested in finding any hungry crocodiles first and not enemy guerrillas. He took his first step into the water and immediately felt a strong undertow. *I've come too far to stop now,* he said to himself. Pepe jumped into the river.

From experience, Pepe knew that he did not have to worry about any other predators in the water. His wound had healed, and there was no reason to believe that the pirañas that frequented these waters would find him a tasty morsel.

His first and only concern immediately became the current; it was strong. Pepe swam with all his remaining strength toward the other side of the river. At first his stamina was good, and he quickly moved downstream but made good progress toward the other bank.

It was halfway across that the trouble began; as he tired, the river took an increasing amount of control over his body and moved him about with ease. That's when he hit a rock that lied just beneath the surface. The pain of the hit was almost unbearable; his right knee was throbbing and further restricting his swimming strokes. Yet Pepe found the strength to continue. As he swam, he saw another large boulder approaching. He had not seen this boulder, probably the result of moving downstream too fast. He lunged to the other side of the boulder with one last stroke but still hit the rock with brute force.

This time he lost consciousness momentarily when his back took the brunt of the collision. Fortunately the encounter with the boulder shoved him into a part of the river where the water stagnated due to the protecting rocks. Still groggy, suffering from the aftereffects of a concussion and a knee injury, he reached the other side of the river and mustered the strength necessary to get out of the water, and then Pepe collapsed.

At the command post of the U.S. Southern Command, the lieutenant commander in charge of the evening shift was settling down for the beginning of another lackluster weekend tour of duty.

She was a naval reservist doing reserve days and making some extra money. Lieutenant Commander Linda Ortiz had experience in two wars and was calm in stressful situations. The call that put her into action came in from the national command post deep inside the Pentagon.

"Commander Ortiz, can I help you?"

"Commander, this is Colonel Hoyt at the NMCC, we have reports that an aircraft has crashed approaching an airport in Margarita Island, Venezuela. Now get this, the tower there reported that a missile was seen hitting the aircraft as it approached the airport."

"A missile, did they say what type, Colonel?"

"No, but the tower reported a fast-moving boat departing the area right after the crash. If this is true, Commander, we need to alert the authorities ASAP!"

"We have no way to confirm that from this end, Colonel, as you should know the relationships with the Venezuelan government are not the best they could be." She was hoping the colonel knew about Hugo Chavez and the problems that existed between our countries since he took power. "I will call the director of operations and the commander. Is the secretary available?" She was referring to the secretary of defense for whom General Strange worked directly.

"Yes, the secretary is in his residence tonight, and he has not been advised of the situation. I am trying to get more information before I call him."

"May I suggest that you call the FAA at Miami Center, Colonel. They have contacts throughout Latin America, and they may have more details about the crash in Venezuela. As for Venezuela, at least they must talk to each other daily as they transfer flights between the two systems."

"Good idea, Commander, let me call you again in about fifteen minutes, meanwhile I suggest you call your superiors."

"Oh, I am dialing already, Colonel, good-bye."

Brigadier General John James, the director of operations since General Ramirez's abduction, and General Strange were still at the headquarters that evening. In fact, Lieutenant Commander Ortiz reached them both in the same office. General Strange answered the phone and got the preliminary information on the crash. When she was finished, the commander ordered in a voice loud enough for his operations director to hear, "Commander, get the ball rolling to fully man the command post this weekend. We are going to twenty-four-hour operations until we know what happened."

The flight into Colombia was full of dangers, but the pilots Al Kassar hired were very experienced and knew the terrain well. The first three and a half hours of the flight were normal; the pilots talked to air traffic control first with Miami Center and, halfway into the Caribbean Sea, with controllers in Venezuela and then Colombia. As soon as the airplane entered Colombian territory, the plan began to develop; the pilots never intended to land in their filed destination, Bogotá.

As the aircraft approached the last chain of mountains prior to the Cundinamarca valley where Bogotá was located, the pilots killed their automatic position reporting system and dropped below radar coverage. They then proceeded south to their intended destination, Calamar.

The plan was to land in Calamar, unload the passengers and the cargo, and then head northeast into Venezuela before daylight and the danger of an intercept by Colombian aircraft. *It had worked before, and it will work again,* thought the captain.

Controllers in Bogotá thought the flight was legal since it had departed from a U.S. territory. This was the first time in a few years that an aircraft from the United States had gone missing. The controllers had no option, even if they suspected the flight was an illegal cargo drop; they had to notify Colombian and U.S. authorities. The alarm went out.

The approach and landing at twilight was uneventful for the group. Once on the ground, the aircraft proceeded to the southern end of the runway where a large group of people were gathered. When the aircraft stopped and the door and stairs were lowered, María Elena was characteristically the first off her seat and out the entry door.

She was met at the bottom of the stairs by Luis Montes. He seemed to be comparing a piece of paper he held to her face. *I guess that they have a fax machine or computer in the jungle? He must have received my picture from Al Kassar,* thought María Elena.

"Hola, patriota," said Luis as she approached him.

"Hola, soy la Señora Hernández y mi esposo, José, me acompaña," signaling to Carlos.

They were met and greeted by two groups of guerrillas. One group took the two visitors to the main camp, and the larger group transported the missiles to the storage camp, one that was specially built for their arrival.

Luis sent his deputy commander with the precious cargo and escorted the visitors himself. Carlos carried a duffel bag and backpack, and María Elena carried a backpack. They were told the trip would take a day and a half with a thirty-minute rest periods every five hours. They were ready; both agents had been in the Colombian jungle before, and both had prepared well for this.

With luck, we will arrive at the camp at midday Sunday, thought Carlos. *I really hope Pepe is there.*

Saturday, September 8, 2007

"Levántate cabrón, antes que te coma el caimán!"

Pepe was being brought back from his slumber by a man in military clothing. His uniform identified him as a member of the

Colombian Army, and the lack of rank meant that he was a conscript, a two-year draftee with little responsibility and very meager pay.

The soldier was not lying; floating calmly in the water no more than four meters away was a large crocodile looking in their direction.

At first, Pepe did not recognize the uniform, but little by little, he regained consciousness and was elated to recognize the man as a member of the Colombian military. *I'm safe,* was his first conscious thought.

The man helped Pepe to his feet and away from the menacing croc. He was elated to find out that he had rescued a U.S. military officer and one that spoke Spanish as well. The man told Pepe that their camp was a few miles north of their location and asked him if he could walk.

"Por cierto," replied Pepe.

They did not walk at a fast pace. The soldier made sure his rescued hostage did not tire and took extensive rest periods during the day. Pepe did not know that the man was keeping a schedule. He had to be at a certain place on time, and he meant to accomplish that with a tired but healthy companion.

Finally, well into sunset, they reached a small river crossing that seemed to be their destination. At the crossing, there was a group of men in fatigues. Pepe quickened the pace to greet the highest-ranking person of the group while the soldier next to him held back somewhat. As Pepe approached the group, he seemed to recognize the fatigue patterns and told himself the men were not military. Then he recognized Juana in the middle of the group.

Pepe turned quickly around and saw the soldier was pointing his gun at him. "Vamos." The soldier ordered Pepe to continue toward the other group. He had no choice.

The 1830 hours (6:30 PM) meeting started right on schedule at the command center of the U.S. Southern Command. As Napoleonic era traditions dictate, the meeting started with an intelligence update. The briefer was a young air force captain.

"Sir, I am Captain Honoré of current intelligence. I have two updates received this afternoon. First topic was reported by embassy personnel in Venezuela. They have confirmed that the aircraft destroyed yesterday in Margarita Island was a G-2 model and that a missile was seen tracking the aircraft just prior to impact. The aircraft had departed from San Juan International and was owned by a Surinamese cargo company."

General John Strange interrupted the briefer as was his custom, "Tell me, Captain, how sure are they? I mean, how have they confirmed the missile?"

"Several eyewitnesses, sir, with the most trusted, a military controller at the Margarita airport tower. Now what is even more interesting, General, is that the other update I have for you also concerns an aircraft from the same cargo company in Suriname."

"And that is, Captain?"

"The other incident happened in Bogotá, Colombia, sir. An aircraft that had departed from San Juan at approximately the same time was reported missing over central Colombia yesterday. We have seen mysterious disappearances like this before, and they normally are cash or arms shipments to the FARC. The missing airplane was a small cargo aircraft that could have landed anywhere in Eastern Colombia."

"An arms shipment from a U.S. territory, Captain Honoré?"

"Yes, sir," replied the captain.

"Go back to the first incident, Captain, how many souls on board, have they recovered the victims, etc.?"

General James, the director of operations, interrupted the young briefer, "Sir, the reported number of casualties is six, but the search continues for more bodies. There was an American citizen on board, a gentleman whose passport identified him with the name of Warren Westback. No next of kin has identified his place of residence yet, and the body carried no other identification except for his passport."

General James was himself interrupted by a voice from the rear of the briefing room. The person talking was the current CIA agent assigned as liaison to the command. "Sir, this is highly unusual, that name corresponds to our current deputy director of clandestine operations at Langley. I have not received word that he is missing, but the name matches."

General Strange stood up; the room normally buzzing in excitement and low-volume small talk went deathly quiet. "I have heard enough, continue the briefing, but I have a few calls to make. Please brief me if any other information is received at any time tonight, General James." He then pointed at the director of intelligence and the CIA liaison and said, "Both of you follow me, this is going to be a long night."

In Fairfax Station, Virginia, the deputy director of operations of the Agency was sitting in front of his television preparing to watch a rented movie with his wife when the phone rang, a hotline to the Agency. On the other end of the line was Shirley Miller, the duty officer.

"Director Higgins?"

"Yes, speaking."

"Sir, this is Shirley Miller, I have on another line my husband, John."

Instantly, Marc Higgins began to get annoyed. *Why was the duty officer calling late on Saturday night, and why was she holding her husband on the other end of the line?* As much as the director could remember, John Miller was a very weak agent that was sent down to Miami on assignment to Southern Command for his incompetence at headquarters.

"Do you want me to talk to John, Shirley?"

"Yes, sir, it's important. I will monitor the conversation."

"Well, go ahead," now even more annoyed.

He heard a click, and then John Miller began speaking excitedly, "Director, I am in the office of General John Strange. We have unconfirmed reports that an American citizen called Warren Westback was a passenger on the aircraft that crashed in Venezuela yesterday. Sir, I know the name is similar, please tell me that your son-in-law is home safe."

There was a momentary silence from the other end of the line. Marc Higgins's face was ashen; he slowly asked his wife, "Honey, call Ophelia and find out if Warren's there."

She almost did not let him finish. "Why, you should know, Marc, Warren is on company business in Puerto Rico. You sent him there for a meeting, all weekend I think."

"Who said that?"

"Why, Ophelia, honey, I talked to her this afternoon."

Higgins then talked to John Miller. "John, let me get back with you. Shirley, can you confirm Mr. Westback's whereabouts?"

"Sir, I have checked already, he is signed out for the weekend on leave, no destination. I have further bad news, the U.S. passport recovered in the crash in Venezuela has the number that corresponds to his own passport. I have his number on file and am trying to get a fax from Venezuela of the picture in the document."

"This is the same aircraft that was reported shot down by a missile, Shirley?"

"The one and only, sir," replied John from SOUTHCOM.

"Call an emergency meeting for tomorrow at eight, Shirley. I want the entire staff there to include you, John. Now I have to get off the phone, my wife has put two and two together at this end." His wife had fainted.

CHAPTER EIGHTEEN

The final part of the travel to the FARC camp was in the dead of night, and very little light came through the canopy, yet the guerrillas taking Carlos and María Elena there were progressing at a fast pace. Carlos noticed the point man was wearing a very modern-looking night vision goggle that permitted her to find the well-traveled paths of the region. They were now in a mature rain forest with tops of the trees at over 150 feet. Carlos had made a mental note this afternoon for it told him the direction they were traveling.

At the five-hour point, the group arrived at a river crossing for a thirty-minute rest. Carlos noticed a second group was already there and noticed how Luis eagerly met a female guerrilla in the other group. Luis approached the Carlos with the woman at his side and told them, "We will rest here for thirty minutes, I would like to introduce you my wife and life partner Juana."

As they shook hands and introduced themselves, Carlos noted what a magnificent-looking woman Juana was. Small in stature but with a wonderful flesh tone and curved physique that was evident even in the poor lighting surrounding the river crossing, Juana was simply beautiful.

Luis added after the introductions, "I will let her group cross the river first. Juana is carrying an important prisoner that was just recaptured after an attempted escape."

Carlos was going to ask, but María Elena added first, "What kind of prisoner, Juana?" digging for more information.

"Un jódio gringo," she replied, motioning over to the group of guerrillas that were just boarding the raft that would take them to the other side.

With that she said her farewells and promised to look them up in the morning at the camp.

At the first mention of "gringo," Carlos snapped his head and looked in the direction of the boarding party. There in poor light, he saw that they were carrying a man of medium height. *Did I find you, Pepe?* But lighting was not enough to make out the group, and Carlos decided not to approach them.

Juana said good-bye and asked her husband to walk her to the raft. When they were by the dock, she asked her husband, "Impressive pair, Luis, did you notice that after a day of a hard march in the jungle, they are not even winded, Luis?"

Luis replied that he had not noticed but told his wife the pair had been recommended by their best and most reliable arms provider and dismissed her obvious concerns.

"Well, keep an eye on them, Luis, I particularly don't like the lady."

"You would not be envious, Juana? You are far more beautiful than her."

"No, *bobo*, I'm concerned about the strangers, that's all."

"Don't worry, honey, their safety and care are in my hands, be careful and see you in the morning. Congratulations are in order for the general's recapture. Where did you find him?"

"I did not, one of the Colombian soldiers that inform us of army activities found him for me. I had ten such conscripts looking for him. I paid him *cincuentamil* pesos ($25) for his trouble."

As Juana shipped off with her first group of five guerrillas and the prisoner, Carlos noticed that one of them used a large cane to cut down the prisoner's legs so that he would kneel in the raft while two others held him in place.

Hold on, man, help is coming, Carlos thought.

Lieutenant Commander Linda Ortiz was now the second in command at the U.S. Southern Command emergency operations center and was put in charge of relaying hot information back to the Pentagon. The center was now fully manned and working two twelve-hour shifts. The report she was relaying was the result of a preliminary inspection by a U.S. team of experts in crash investigations. They were invited in by the same Venezuelan government that was busy blaming the United States for the catastrophe. Such inconsistencies were common from the budding autocracy of the Venezuelan leader and his followers.

"Colonel Hoyt, I have another hot one, sir."

"Go ahead, Commander."

"I am reading a paragraph classified Secret/NOFORN, Colonel. The away team at the crash site reports,'Confirm the cause of the crash was explosive detonation of ground-to-air missile in mid-flight. Missile preliminary identification is Strela-10. This was confirmed by testing of explosive residue inside aircraft. Aircraft is partly submerged, and remains suggest the aircraft was in a flat spin at impact. Venezuelan government is not aware of these facts, and they have no forensic experts on site.' That's it, Colonel. I will call you later with more updates."

The news of a Strela-10 attack in the Western Hemisphere went through the building in seconds. The Joint Chiefs of Staff and the secretary of defense were called at home to inform them. The secretary then called his counterpart at Homeland Security while the NMCC was advising the FBI and other concerned agencies in government.

Five minutes later, the office of the secretary connected Mark Higgins, General Strange, and the secretary in a conference call. The secretary started the conversation. "Mark, let me begin by giving you my condolences on the loss of your son-in-law. I pledge that the department will do everything in their power to find out who did this."

"Thank you, Mr. Secretary, my personnel are also on alert and will investigate this fully. I will keep the lines of communication open so that we can investigate this thoroughly," replied Mr. Higgins.

General Strange also promised full cooperation and informed the pair that his deployed forces in Colombia were also investigating the disappearance of the second aircraft that had departed San Juan the same day. "There must be a link between these events," added the general.

At the end of the conversation, Mark Higgins added, "Mr. Secretary, I don't know if any of this is related, but I would like to inform both of you that my office is investigating the hatching of an apparent second rescue attempt by French forces of Mrs. Betancourt in Colombia. The last time this happened, the forces were based in Brazil, I believe that this time they are in Peru."

"We cannot leave any stone unturned," replied the secretary. "General, have your forces investigate this too. Call me tomorrow morning at the office."

To which the general replied, "Ten sharp, sir."

The conversation ended, but one of them was holding information back ignoring the pledge made of total disclosure. Just hours before, Mark Higgins called his contact in the Colombian government to inform him about the location of the French Special Forces team in Peru and possible intentions. He had experienced failure in finding the four American hostages in the jungle and was not going to be beat to a rescue by the French team. *No way!* he thought.

Sunday, September 9, 2007

As dawn approached, the team led by Luis Montes arrived at the FARC camp where the Cucho Ramos Armed Front had their headquarters. Carlos noticed very few guards on the way in. *Sign of a confident group. Not much to worry them here,* Carlos said to himself.

The camp setting was in a double-canopy thicket that would not qualify as a jungle due to the ease of travel underneath the foliage. Carlos noticed the huts were all made out of wood with varying roof structures. Some of them had metal roofs, and some had thatch-like palm and brush tops.

At that moment, he felt his arm taken and was surprised to see María Elena holding on to him as if needing some for support. It felt good to feel her this way; he remembered the last time they held similarly was trekking in the mountains of northern Spain.

"Carlos, hold me strong and kiss me," she whispered.

Carlos complied giving her a short kiss in the forehead, and then he noticed why she was behaving like that. Coming to meet them was Juana, and María Elena was putting on a face for her, the face of the weaker sex, the vulnerable look. *I hope to have more moments like this,* thought Carlos and continued holding on even when Juana passed them by to hug her husband.

The camp was expansive; Carlos counted fifteen structures arranged loosely around a center courtyard. Even though trees were fewer in the courtyard, only the smaller trees and the brush was cleared, leaving the cover of the 150-foot trees and keeping the camp safe from overhead surveillance.

Carlos also noticed an odd structure in the middle of the yard. The hut was no more than two-by-two feet and was made of corrugated metal. *Wonder what they keep in there.*

It seemed like María Elena was reading his mind when she said, "I bet the gringo captive is inside that hut, dear."

Why, yes, a solitary confinement cell, he said to himself. He whispered back to María Elena, "I hope that you are wrong." That's when Carlos heard it; coming out of the cell, a very weak but easily recognizable voice was heard saying, "No matter what you do to me, Juana, it is my duty as a military officer to escape. I'll try again."

It was almost a loud Spanish groan; since Carlos recognized Pepe's voice, it was easy for him to understand the words that others may have found undecipherable. *Hang on tight,* hermano, *I'm here for you.*

They slowly passed by the cell and stopped near the largest-looking structure where an obvious welcoming party was assembled. There, a group of ten guerrillas had gathered to welcome the Nicaraguan couple.

A man, middle-aged and looking smug and overconfident, welcomed them. "*Hola, patriotas,* we welcome you to our humble home. I hope your stay here is profitable and short."

María Elena replied first, "Thank you, señor, I also hope our stay is two week's short." She said this while cleaning her forehead of visible perspiration and slowly letting go of Carlos's embrace.

"My name is Moncho Rivera, I am the commander of the Cucho Ramos Front, and you are our guests. Make yourself at home until we meet for dinner later this evening."

Carlos wanted to ask him about the man in the shack, about the chances of survival in such a place in the oppressive heat of the jungle, and many other questions, but he held back. *Not my place to talk now,* he said to himself.

There was an emergency meeting at the Colombian minister of defense office this Sunday morning. The meeting with the military commanders was called by the minister after receiving an early morning call from the president. Minister Pereira was relaying the president's order directly to his military commanders.

He looked directly to the army commander and continued, "I want you to call Colonel Gomez in Leticia and have him travel to Iquitos and stop this French aggression once and for all. Tell the commander there that any mission into our sovereign country will be met by failure and that we will treat any survivors of the excursion as common criminals."

General Huber called from his office at the U.S. embassy in Colombia to the operations directorate at SOUTHCOM. He was connected directly to Brigadier General James who was preparing for the morning call to the secretary of defense by his commander. General James spoke first, "Sir, I bet both of us could be in a better situation on a Sunday morning."

General Huber, an avid golfer, understood the comment immediately. "Not many places in Bogotá to play golf, and today, it would be difficult to get a tee time in any of them. Now, John, explain to me why the general wants me to go to Leticia."

They were speaking on a classified telephone, but neither had pressed the selection for secure conversation. "Sure, sir, let me press the button to go secure, give me a moment please." A series of noises were heard at both ends; seconds passed and finally the terminals at both ends clearly spelled the word "secret" in the screen.

General James continued, "Sir, we have reports that a secret French operation based out of Iquitos, Peru, is taking shape in an effort to rescue a French citizen kidnapped by the FARC."

"You mean Ingrid Betancourt, don't you, John?"

"Yes, sir, the ex-presidential candidate. This was reported to us by the Agency, and since then, the ambassador there has found out that the Colombian government also got word of the operation. It seems everyone knew except us."

"That does not surprise me, now what do you want me to do?"

"First, the ambassador wants you to travel to Leticia and speak to the officer that was tasked to stare down the French. If possible, the ambassador wants you to accompany the officer into Peru and deliver the message in tandem to the French. The Peruvians are okay with this, they believe the purpose of the trip is to discuss cross-border operations."

"Okay, that sounds simple enough, I imagine that the French don't know we are coming. How about country clearance, do I have it?"

"My command post is working on it as we speak."

"John, you know Peru takes thirty days to grant one."

"Not this one, General, we have a slightly higher priority for this mission. You should get it today. Just call it that the Peruvians owe us one, and we cashed in. One more complication, General, the Agency has reported that an ex-agent may be involved in this operation. The name is Carlos Cortes, and he has extensive experience in Colombia. The Agency found cause to let him go three years ago and now has confirmed his involvement in this new attempt to rescue hostages."

"That can't be good, John, we know the FARC has stated numerous times that any attempt to rescue hostages will cause their termination. We can't have blood on our hands, eventually the press will blame us for any failed attempt no matter who did the action.

"Where is this Carlos fellow?"

"They don't know, sir. He was living in Los Angeles when last seen, and the Agency there routinely followed his life from a distance. They had bugged his house and car but lost track of him over a week ago."

"Why are they so concerned about one man's disappearance then?"

"All they told me is that he is a disgraced former agent and a very good friend of Major General Ramirez. He once vowed to rescue Pepe from his captors but ran afoul of the authorities."

"So they put two and two together and have implicated him in this affair."

"That's the way it looks to me."

"Okay, John, I will be on the lookout for this fellow and have my personnel try to find his whereabouts if he has entered the country. Can you send me a picture of him?"

"I will have my personnel fax you a picture as soon as we get one from the Agency. I will send more information on your trip and the country clearance later today. Adios, amigo."

As this conversation ended, a parallel conversation had started between the secretary of defense and General Strange.

The secretary was speaking, "John, the president was briefed today that there appears to be a chain of events that would imply the arrival of Strela-10 missiles into the hands of the FARC. The facts are that the key passenger in the aircraft that was shot down was Abdul Al Kassar, a known arms merchant."

"Yes, sir, based in Suriname, if I am not mistaken."

"That makes him, not Warren Westback, the reason for the missile strike. Furthermore, the other aircraft that departed Puerto Rico at the same time was probably carrying the missiles to the FARC. We lost track of the aircraft twice, once as it was approaching Bogotá, and the second time was four hours later when an unidentified aircraft crossed the border between Colombia and Venezuela and was lost into that no-man's-land."

"Then why do you suppose that Al Kassar's aircraft was shot down?"

"Greed, the Agency briefed that someone in the organization wanted the profit from the new missile deliveries all to himself. The best way to gain this customer and the considerable amount of money the FARC paid for the missiles was to get rid of the boss. So they used one of the missiles on the provider."

"I guess the loss of that revenue was sacrificed for future profit, right, sir?"

"That's the way I saw it."

"Any instructions that came out of that meeting or any others you may want to pass on now, sir?"

"The president was noncommittal, he gave no specific orders other than he requested the intelligence apparatus to redouble their efforts in searching for these missiles. The agency figures the total amount is nine."

"Nine, sir, how do they figure this number?"

"I don't know anything about airplanes, John, but it seems that the type of airplane missing over Colombia is rated to carry only a certain amount of cargo load. That equates to ten Strela missiles and the related maintenance package."

"I see, and ten minus one equals nine."

"Exactly, John."

"Okay, sir, meanwhile my personnel are putting the finishing touches of my request for forces. We will request the deployment of surveillance assets, more intelligence analysts, and a buildup of General Huber's staff in Colombia."

"And the objective will be to find the missiles, John?"

"Yes, sir."

"I'm serious here, John, the president has not authorized any military actions in Colombia. What we do in the future will be coordinated through the National Security staff and the Colombian government. I doubt if he will grant you permission to use unilateral military actions to destroy these missiles."

"Yes, sir." With these final words, the conversation was ended, and the general once again felt like a very long rope kept his arms tied in Miami all the way from Washington DC.

At 5:30 PM that afternoon, a briefing was organized for Marc Higgins at CIA headquarters. Briefing him was a tall young man that had that fresh-out-of-school look common at the Agency. *Probably a Yale man*, the thought passed through the director's mind after seeing this man for seemingly the first time.

The briefing was organized by John Miller, SOUTHCOM liaison, and the director noted only him and his wife, Shirley, were present for the update. *Wonder what they have to tell me that did not merit a larger audience.*

The young agent named Scott started, "Sir, this briefing is an update of the investigation into the crash of aircraft T600S in Margarita Island, Venezuela. The investigating team reports that the recovery process is complete and that all passengers have been recovered and accounted for. Sir, I am sad to report that the initial cause of death of Mr. Westback is reported as head trauma caused by the crash. If it is any consolation, death was immediate."

The agent paused here and got an immediate reaction from the director. "Go on," said Director Higgins impatiently.

"Sorry, the team reports that the other four victims were carrying Surinamese passports and that the owner of the company, Abdul Al Kassar, was one of the victims."

Shirley Miller interrupted the briefer and said, "Sir, the next part of the update is disturbing, and I would like to summarize it for your benefit. The team has worked tirelessly since yesterday; with full agreement from your daughter, we have borrowed Mr. Westback's personal laptop, personal papers at home, and studied his career since 1992. The team has discovered the following:

- That Mr. Westback has known Al Kassar since his first assignment to Albania in 1994. It seems that Al Kassar provided arms and ammunition to the Agency's effort to arm Albanian freedom fighters for Kosovo.

- The Agency's links to Al Kassar were cut in 1998, and all contact by our personnel apparently ceased then.

- There are some e-mails in Mr. Westback's private Gmail account that were addressed recently to an AK at the dot-com address for the Puerto Rican company implicated in the whole incident."

After this interruption, the room became very quiet, and the briefer continued when there was no reaction from the director. "Sir, the last e-mail in the laptop is brief, it reads, 'Looking forward to spending a great weekend in the Caribbean, signed Spike.'"

Warren's first tactical call sign! This is all unbelievable but true. Marc's thoughts momentarily drifted away from the briefing as he considered the implications to his own career and to his family. His focus came back when he heard the briefer utter another name from the past.

"Sir, we are also trying to find the whereabouts of an ex-agent named Carlos Cortes."

"What!" Higgins said, almost jumping out of his chair. "Why are you doing that, don't tell me that he is involved?"

After this outburst, Shirley Miller again interrupted the briefer and said, "Sir, please forgive me, but the facts as we know them merited that we check in with Mr. Westback's all known enemies. I checked with our Los Angeles office, and they report that Carlos is not in his apartment and that he received a leave of absence from the university where he works. We have checked for his use of a passport with ICE, any of his credit cards or bank accounts to no avail."

"And you think he is involved in Warren's murder?"

Shirley disregarded her boss's accusatory tone and continued, "I ordered a review of the telephone records of his family in Los Angeles and found nothing, however then we checked the telephone records of General Ramirez's wife in Miami and noted that she received a call from a Puerto Rican hotel that same day. It is well-known that Carlos still contacts her every few months."

"Very flimsy evidence, Shirley," said the director. "You know the lady is from Puerto Rico, it could be her family."

"No, sir, we did not stop there, please roll the clip, Agent."

Scott clicked an icon in his computer, and seconds later, a small screen popped up in the briefing room screen. The movie started, and all present could see that it was from a security camera in a hotel front desk area. Standing in front of the hotel clerk was none other than Carlos Cortes; the three senior CIA agents instantly recognized him.

"As you can see, Mr. Carlos Cortes checked in under an assumed name to the El San Juan Hotel on Friday afternoon and checked out the next day. It was that room that called Mrs. Ramirez."

"Where is he now, Shirley?"

"Roll the second clip, Scott."

Scott complied, and the screen showed a recording from a different camera. This was obviously an exterior security camera in the hotel entrance. Carlos could be seen leaving the hotel and heading for a waiting car. With Carlos and clutching his hand was a beautiful tall woman. The recording was stopped, and a blowup of the woman's face was shown on the screen.

"The woman with Carlos has been identified as María Elena Borbón, goes by the alias of Rosario and is a covert agent of the Spanish CEID."

"Same organization that implied Carlos was involved in their agent's murder three years ago?"

"Yes, sir, same one, even the same agent. I would bet that both Ms. Borbón and Carlos boarded that second aircraft and are now somewhere in Colombia."

"And their mission is?" asked Higgins.

"We don't know, but I am willing to bet that it has something to do with General Ramirez," said Shirley.

"Okay, let's find out. Check all possible contacts and get me the phone number of the operations director at the CEID. I want to talk to him." Marc Higgins got up and walked to the door. At the door, he turned around and said, "Thank you for keeping this quiet. John, you head back to SOUTHCOM and find out what they know."

The heat of the day seemed to sap every ounce of strength from Pepe's body. It was late afternoon, and Pepe could not tell in his cell what time it was. He was completely disoriented, beaten, and brokenhearted. *I was so close, was he a real soldier, and was that Carlos I saw or a mirage? I must stay strong, I must stay awake.*

He was lying in a pool of excrement that had not been cleaned in quite a while. His cell was a two-foot-square-by-eight-feet-tall corrugated steel hut, but the bottom had broken off long ago, and his only support came three feet deep at the bottom of the old latrine.

Although Juana had not ordered it, her men had mercilessly beaten Pepe since the moment they had recaptured him. Just a poke here and a shove at the right time had slowly sapped Pepe's strength. His knees were throbbing from countless hits by stiff reeds to his legs.

How long will they keep me here, how long did they keep me last time? Pepe simply could not remember. Once again, he began to lose consciousness, and his mind began to drift.

At that moment, a small door midway on the cell's door opened, and the increased light startled Pepe.

"General," Juana Montes's voice was soft and maternal, "I am truly sorry for what is happening to you, but you asked for it. Here is a water bottle, I will bring you some food tonight." She closed the small door and returned to her hut.

Pepe opened up the bottle and drank the contents immediately; his body needed it. He was lucky; the last hostage that had been recaptured was put in the cell and was pulled out dead three days later. The Colombian hostage was a middle-aged man; it seemed that everyone had forgotten that he was in the cell until an unscheduled visit by Father Frank had discovered the body after he had asked to see the prisoner. Juana was not going to let that happen again.

In the early evening, María Elena and Carlos retired to their small hut that would serve as their sleeping quarters for the next two weeks. In it, there were two small cots, a writing table with a small lamp, and two wooden chairs that had seen their best day. Everything else they carried into the camp would have to rest on the floor.

Once they entered the hut, neither spoke. Their training took over, and instinctively, they both canvassed the room for any signs of a microphone or any other recording device. They looked everywhere, under the table, chairs, and closely examining the cots. They found nothing.

They did not notice how nervous they were, not for the mission they had launched, but because this was the first time in sixteen years they would be sharing a room by themselves.

When the search had finished, Carlos said in a whisper, "Seems clear to me only the thin walls can double-cross us."

"I agree," María Elena whispered back. She continued her ritual by unpacking a few things from her pack. She took out a picture frame and placed it on the table, then sat in one of the cots to take out some of the clothes she had carefully packed before.

Carlos was curious and took a look at the picture. It was of a young man in a soccer uniform. He was tall and appeared to be in his late teens.

María Elena noticed this and said unemotionally, "That is our son, Ricky, he is fifteen. We need to maintain a good story line if asked."

Carlos whispered back, "I know, you picked a good picture. He could pass for my son any day. My father keeps a picture of me from high school where I stand on the same pose. The only difference between the pictures is that I am wearing a baseball uniform."

For the moment, María Elena showed no emotion. Of course the picture was of Charlie, their son. There was too much time between their relationship in the nineties and this day. There was too much danger for both of them for her to spring any surprises on the relationship. *Another day, another hour,* María Elena thought as she held her composure. Carlos did not notice the small tear that formed in her right eye.

CHAPTER NINETEEN

Monday, September 10, 2007, 0230 hours

The French Special Forces have many unique units. The French Air Force has a helicopter unit to support operations of these forces flying the Aerospatiale SA-330B Puma. Tonight, one of those helicopters was heading north over the Colombian jungle carrying two members of the elite Premier Regiment Parachutiste d'Infanterie de Marine of the Army Special Forces.

They had left Iquitos, Peru, at sundown, and after a required fuel stop at the Peru-Colombia border, they were now approaching their drop zone. It was a grueling 640 nautical miles round-trip, but it was the type of mission the crew of the helicopter had practiced many times.

They were approaching their drop zone downwind of their focus area. They had to avoid the area where the beacon signals had stopped by at least seven miles so as to prevent the helicopter noise from alarming the enemy.

The third crew member was at the door reading the rescue hoist; this was a special design capable of lifting ten fully armed men from

214

the ground to safety. Today, its task was to drop the two soldiers through the jungle canopy to the ground.

The two men were elite members of the regiment that specialized in deep-cover surveillance of target areas. Their job was to approach the hostage camp without being seen, discover the hostage location, and observe the best avenues of entry for the eventual rescue mission. They were both volunteers.

The three people in the rear of the helicopter did not need a signal; since the helicopter was traveling at nearly eighty miles per hour for the last two and a half hours, the sudden decrease of forward velocity was signal enough they were nearing the target zone. When the helicopter slowed to near hover speed, the third crew member opened the door and readied the hoist.

In the cockpit, the pilots were both wearing night vision goggles and were receiving uninterrupted GPS signals from space. They were heading for coordinates provided by an upper high frequency beacon that pinpointed the travel progress of María Elena Borbón in the jungle. The beacon's reception was not consistent, but enough data had been received to pinpoint a general area of about two miles square.

As they approached the drop zone, they were looking for a river just east of their intended target. As soon as they saw the river, they slowed the helicopter and lit the green signal, clearing the operation of the electrical hoist just west of the river. In less than two minutes, their human cargo was safely on the ground, and the hoist was secured. They turned due south and returned to Peru.

On the ground, the soldiers inventoried their equipment and made sure that all of it was secure for travel using the buddy system. They both pulled out night vision goggles and turned them on. The lead scout then pulled out a PDA and attached it to his left wrist. He turned it on and began walking; there was no time to waste since in three short hours, it would be daylight, and they would have to stop forward progress then.

The PDA was a marvelous invention for the Special Forces. What started as a gadget for geeks had matured into a mapping system that could be adapted for their type of special operations easily. For example, they were traveling under thick foliage and normally the GPS signals would be lost in such a scenario. However, this PDA had a forward motion sensor developed for runners and hikers coupled to a compass that provided very accurate navigation when the GPS failed to update.

Tonight, slowed by thick jungle areas and very few cleared out areas, they would only travel four of the seven miles to their intended target.

As the cool morning breezes began to wane and the limited daylight trickled through holes in the canopy to ground level, Carlos arose, quickly changed, and went outside to find a place where he could exercise. He was finding excuses for not spending any more time alone with the beautiful woman sleeping in the cot beside him. A woman who, for the time being, was off-limits.

The night before, Carlos had gone to bed first and watched in the darkness how María Elena had carefully undressed and changed to a cotton nightshirt that covered her to her knees. The darkness only allowed him to see shadows and motion, but what he saw was a delicate rite of preparation for bed he had first noticed sixteen years ago.

Carlos walked to the center of the compound and instinctively walked right to the cell where the hostage was being kept. Pretending he was looking for a latrine, he tried to open the door but found that it was bolted. Yet he pulled on the door and made enough noise to wake whoever was inside the cell.

"That is not what you are thinking, Mr. Hernandez," Juana Montes said as she approached him from behind.

The voice startled him, and he swung around to see who was speaking. "No es una letrina?" Carlos asked in return.

"*No, no es.* It's a cell, and inside is a hostage that tried to escape. He is an important prisoner, so I would request that in the future, you do not come this way. As for your necessities, here we go in the jungle and bury any residue to prevent the odor of humanity to give our location away."

Carlos sensed her uneasiness and tried to sooth her instincts further, "Can you also tell me where I can exercise? I am getting older, and no longer do I have the resistance of one thousand camels."

"Some *patriotas* are playing *fútbol* on a small field one hundred yards that way," Juana said pointing in the direction of Carlos's own hut.

"Gracias," Carlos replied and quickly went away.

Inside the cell, Pepe was indeed awake. If there was any doubt in his mind about who was talking outside his cell, the last comment, the one about one thousand camels, gave Carlos away. It was always the same excuse; every time Pepe mercilessly beat Carlos in the racquetball courts, he would utter the words. Blaming Pepe's endurance, not his skill, as the deciding factor for the losses on the court. *Bless you, my friend, please be careful and tread carefully with this woman*, Pepe said to himself as he prepared to greet Juana after only one full day in hell. *This time is different, my savior is here. I will survive. I will see Ana and the kids again*, he kept repeating to himself.

Carlos headed in the direction of the soccer field and stopped momentarily to relieve himself on a bush about three feet from the jungle path leading there.

Once again, he was startled from behind but by a different woman. "Men do have it easy, I for instance have to find a much more secluded place." María Elena was standing behind him.

He finished peeing and turned around slightly blushing. He noticed she was dressed exactly as the day prior but was sporting a different hair clip to keep her lustrous long hair tightly wound. "What, you have a different hair clip for every day?"

María Elena got closer to him and pretended to kiss him in the cheek. When she was closest to him, she whispered, "Batteries only last for so long."

As she approached, Carlos held her by both forearms and looked deep into her eyes. "So there is where your transmitter is, clever?" he whispered back but failed to release her arms when the conversation was seemingly over. Instead he looked at her face intently and, without provocation or invitation, kissed her deeply in the lips.

María Elena was startled, but found herself not fighting him and returning the kiss with vigor and excitement.

"Excuse me." Luis Montes's remark startled the pair. "I heard you were looking for a good game of *fútbol*."

They were surprised and blushing, so deep was their attention to each other that they had both let their guard down, and neither heard Luis approaching. *Can't let this happen again,* María Elena made a mental note.

"Oh yes," she replied. "Carlos wants to play, and I want to watch." Certainly the soccer field would provide a further opportunity for her beacon to send a good signal to the French team.

"Good," Luis replied. "Today will be a great day since my parents are bringing our son to the field where you will do the training, and Juana and I can enjoy our child. We had to move our son to the safety of the nearest town after the attacks we suffered last month."

Carlos, not knowing who was Luis's father said, "Excellent, let's go play."

Walking to the field, Luis noticed the pair holding hands even in the close confinement of a jungle trail. *That's odd, they act more like lovers than husband and wife.*

Major General Huber had decided against traveling to Leticia to meet with the Junglas commander and ordered his airplane to take him directly to Iquitos, Peru. He traveled by army C-12 aircraft, and the flight took him three hours.

He had flown part of the time although when it was time to land, he let the flight's copilot back in his seat. During the flight, he had benefited from clear skies, giving them a rare look over the Amazon jungle. The terrain consisted of miles and miles of flat green foliage only interrupted by the occasional river. As they approached Iquitos, the first large town east of the Andes, Huber was surprised by the width of the Amazon River. *Must be at least a mile wide,* he thought.

Since it was an official visit, General Huber was in full marine uniform and was met at the airport by the Peruvian Army local commander. Brigadier General Francisco Manrique was in charge of Amazon operations for the army. This was a vast region with few roads, three border areas, and large navigable branches of the Amazon River.

They shook hands and headed for the terminal building and the VIP lounge inside. The building was not large, but General Huber noted how it could easily handle at least four flights simultaneously.

Inside the building, the generals exchanged some pleasantries before the start of the scheduled tour of military facilities that had been hastily arranged for the American.

General Huber interrupted an aide to General Manrique who was giving a review of the tour ahead to ask, "Can we stop by the helicopter operation on the north side of the ramp? I flew Puma helicopters in a previous assignment and would like to see the one there."

Manrique replied, "Sure, General, they belong to a French oil exploration firm, but I am sure they won't mind a short visit."

With that, Huber stood up and waited for General Manrique to lead the way. They walked on the aircraft ramp directly to a lone hangar where a Puma helicopter was parked. The maintenance effort around the craft was similar to efforts to recondition the helicopter for flight after a mission.

Huber noticed a second helicopter was parked inside the hangar with both side doors covered by a tarp. To the casual observer, it looked as if the helicopter was undergoing maintenance. To Huber's trained eye, it looked as if someone was trying to hide something sticking out of the helicopter doors.

As they approached the hangar, they were met by a tall Frenchman who was smiling and extending a hand to greet them. He identified himself in perfect Spanish as Monsieur Richard, the leader of the exploration team, and asked what he could do for the pair.

General Huber asked for a tour of the Puma in English and mentioned he only wanted a nostalgia look at a helicopter he first flew back in 1988. General Manrique excused himself and walked back to his car telling the visiting general to take as much time as he needed.

When the Frenchman escorted General Huber to the Puma, they both climbed in the cockpit and sat in the pilot seats. Once there, Huber stopped all pretentions and said in perfect unaccented French, "Monsieur Richard, I know who you are, and I know why you are here."

"Oui," the man said, attentive but surprised.

Huber continued, "In fact, I recognize this same helicopter. I flew this tail number back in France when, as a marine exchange officer, I was assigned to the RESCO [combat search and rescue] unit of the special helicopter squadron in support of your Special Forces."

The Frenchman was about to rebut, but Huber did not let him and continued, "My government has sent me here to tell you that you must stop operations and return to France immediately, or we will have to let your secret out. Not only will we tell the Peruvians the reason why you are here, but we will also tell the world community, and they will certainly be enraged by your actions. Our State Department is sending the same message to your foreign minister as we speak. As a prior pilot for RESCO, I felt obliged to bring you the message in person. I warn you, if you fly north out of Iquitos, we will stop you. That is all."

The officer, who obviously held no more rank than lieutenant colonel, was speechless. General Huber exited the helicopter, offered his hand, and said, "Thank you for the tour, Monsieur Richard, you helped me remember the good old days." He then turned around without waiting or expecting a reply and walked to the waiting car of General Manrique.

As this happened, Huber's aide was calling SOUTHCOM headquarters in his satellite phone to pass the following: "Message delivered in person, French have been advised."

After a vigorous twenty minutes of soccer, Luis and Carlos accompanied María Elena to the center of the camp where they met with Juana and the rest of the team of trainees. They would be instructed by Carlos in the fine art of missile targeting and launch operations.

Juana was only going to spend some time with her son, Pepe Luis. The two-year-old was growing quickly, and it pained Juana greatly not to take care of him daily.

The team had to travel on a jungle path to a major vehicle-capable road about three miles away. The road was carved in the jungle by man and was capable of providing safe travel to the few all-wheel drive vehicles the front possessed. It was the last vehicle that carried the box where the training-only Strela missiles could be safely carried. The team got into the vehicles with Carlos and María Elena boarding the last car.

Nobody else got in the car with them, and except for the driver, the couple was alone with their training missile. Soon they were driving west at no more than ten miles per hour.

Carlos asked the driver for his name and was very surprised when the answer came back. "Sir, my name is Juan Miranda, and I am going to be the chief training officer for the missiles once you have trained me. It is a pleasure to meet you."

Carlos was taken aback. *Barnstormer right here with me, and he does not know who I am. Can I trust him?* He answered the driver in Spanish, "Well, Mr. Miranda, you have a lot to learn, tell me, have you ever fired a missile like this?" Carlos knew the answer.

"No, señor, I trained on them in Ecuador. And it was a different Israeli version that we never fired in anger."

That confirmed it; Carlos's next words were in English. "Barnstormer, I know who you are, and I am here to help you."

Juan Miranda swerved his car momentarily in surprise and looked in the direction of Carlos. He said in broken English, "Sir, I am at your service."

The deputy commander of U.S. Southern Command and two other generals were meeting with General Strange in his office. The three, including the directors of operations and intelligence, consisted what the general called his "very small group" of confidants. What was said in this type of group meeting never left the confines of the general's office.

"Guys," Strange was speaking, "we are caught between a rock and a hard place. We are convinced that a rescue operation is being planned by the French deep into the Colombian jungle. Several steps have been taken to stop this plan in its tracks. Neither we nor the Colombians have any plans that we know of to rescue hostages there. So what do we do, where do we go from here?"

Everyone in the room stayed silent. The general continued, "I have spoken to the secretary of defense who spoke with the president, and they are both unanimous in their decision. The bottom line is that they have given me the power to decide where we go from here. I am asking for your advice."

Once again, silence. The deputy commander was a very young navy three-star admiral who they knew would not sacrifice his career by making tough decisions. He would take days on decisions that other officers would make after examining the facts once. The director of intelligence abhorred risk taking and would not brief his findings to the general unless his personnel could confirm them three times. Only General James stood out in the group as an action man. But the director of operations was a cautious planner. He knew that Washington would never approve a plan of action that had a high risk of failure and especially in a foreign country like Colombia.

"Now, gentlemen, I'm waiting." The general was losing his patience.

General James said, "Sir, I ask you to consider that any attempt to a rescue with limited planning would lead to failure. I have been involved in this type of planning before, and it would take weeks if not months of preparation to make a successful attempt."

General Strange looked at his officers; the three-star was nodding nervously the previous comments, and his chief of intelligence was writing furiously on his notepad. Both were avoiding eye contact. *Pitiful!* Then he said, "Okay, gentlemen, what do we do if the French continue their plans or, worse yet, if this guy Cortes tries to rescue General Ramirez single-handedly?"

When the chief of intelligence heard Carlos's name, he perked up and said, "Sir, let's not mistake Mr. Cortes for a washed-up hack. He was quite famous in Iraq back in 2003. I can't remember exactly, but they had a nickname for him, something like the 'Lion of the Desert.' Equally, the lady with him is very well-known as an outstanding agent and merciless pursuer of arms merchants."

"Not Lion of the Desert, Carlos was known as the Secret Angel of Western Iraq," General James corrected him.

"Now that's what I call news, we should not then misjudge these two," said Strange. Then the general looked directly at his director of operations and said, "James, plan a rescue attempt. Consider all barriers, and let's prepare a Request for Forces immediately to make sure that General Huber has the right personnel for it. We will meet again in twelve hours, I want an update from all of you then. You are dismissed."

At one in the afternoon, the group training on the Strela missiles took an afternoon break. They were slightly exposed in the southeast corner of a small field. The vehicles were all carefully camouflaged underneath the trees.

Most of the morning was spent on preparations for the first lesson scheduled to start during the afternoon period. Carlos had spent the morning with Luis and Juan Miranda while María Elena had given a basic English lesson to the other trainees. It was ironic that the Russian missile's export version came with markings in knobs and panels in the English language.

Juana Montes had spent the morning with María Elena's group. *A little English would not hurt,* she thought. She had learned some basics from Pepe who had routinely tried to introduce her to the language that he introduced as the international language of commerce. But Juana was very nervous throughout the morning. It had been two weeks since she last put her eyes on the beautiful Pepe Luis. Her two-year-old was growing quickly, and any time away from him was very troubling to Juana.

At last, it was 1:30 PM when Juana noticed her little son being held by the arm by her mother-in-law in an obvious effort to show his parents that he could walk quite well. Juana shouted Luis's name and ran to the opposite side of the field. When she reached the pair, she quickly lifted Pepe Luis up in her arms and cried with joy. An instant later, Luis joined his wife, and all three embraced in the field.

They were joined by María Elena and Carlos, and quick introductions were made by Luis. "Mamá, these are José and María Hernandez from Nicaragua. They are here to help us defeat the enemy."

Mrs. Muñiz greeted them and was impressed by the tall white couple. *Too white to be mestizos,* she thought. *This man, I have seen him somewhere before but can't remember where.*

After the short introduction, Carlos took María Elena in the direction of the training area and asked her if she remembered the last name used in the conversation. "Did she say Muñiz or Montes?"

To which María Elena replied, "No doubt Muñiz, Pedro and Evelyn if I remember right, why do you ask, Carlos?"

"This is all starting to make sense, María Elena, and if I am right, I cannot meet Mr. Muñiz when he comes tomorrow."

"Why do you say that?"

"María Elena, when Pepe was captured and the colonel was killed, there was one body missing from the car crash. It was the body of the driver, a man I knew and respected. His name was Pedro Muñiz, and his body was never found."

"So you are saying—"

"That the only body in that car when it went down the embankment was Colonel Platford. That Mr. Muñiz planned and executed the mission for his son, Luis."

"It makes sense. Could Mrs. Muñiz identify you?"

"I don't think I ever met her, plus I did not see any reaction in her face when we were introduced."

At the other end of the field, Mrs. Muñiz was saying to her son and daughter-in-law, "*Hijo,* that man Jose gave me goose bumps. Be careful with that couple." She did not mention that she had once met Carlos Cortes in an embassy Christmas party because she simply could not remember that.

"*Gracias,* Mama, Juana, why don't you assign Roberto to guard them. We need to be sure that they are a clean couple if we are going to trust them further."

"You don't have to ask me twice, *cariño*. I already made up my mind that they are not to be trusted."

The pair of French Special Forces had advanced well this evening. They had noticed that paths cut in the jungle were better traveled. If the coordinates they had received were good, they were only half a mile from their target. The last transmission they were able to receive had been at noon and only momentarily. Even though María Elena was in the clear, they were not, and the antenna they had extended gave them a very weak signal. Yet the direction finder had confirmed they were still heading to their original destination or close to it.

At this point, they parted ways with the senior scout staying behind to communicate with the home station while his junior partner would try to get as close as possible to the enemy camp. Pair would communicate using a UHF radio with frequency-hopping technology; it was untraceable by the FARC. The next half mile would probably take him the rest of the evening since he could not risk detection.

Soldiers trained in the art of reconnaissance move slow, breathe softly, and take deliberate steps in order to avoid making unnecessary sounds. They can move within yards of another human while avoiding detection. They even wear the scent of the jungle to prevent animals from detecting their position.

It was four thirty in the morning when the scout saw his first human. A local was walking down a two-foot-wide path carrying an AK-47 rifle. *He is obviously a sentry walking his beat and fighting the urge to sleep. Good man!* The guerrilla passed two feet from the scout who missed detection entirely; so good was the camouflage that the soldier had crafted.

He decided to find the camp structures and dive deeper in the jungle. Even though he had not been seen, the morning would make it harder to hide, and it would demand constant stillness to avoid detection. By 6:00 AM, he had moved another fifty yards but now could see a camp well defined and approximately five structures were visible from his lair. *I hope this is the right camp,* he thought.

CHAPTER TWENTY

Wednesday, September 12, 2007

The flurry of international activity between Spain, France, Colombia, and the United States had steadily increased in intensity the last two days. The president of Colombia, unaware that Spain was involved, had demanded the immediate pullout of French forces from Peruvian soil. The United States, worried that the situation would undermine the improving relations between governments, kindly asked the French to desist in trying to rescue Mrs. Betancourt.

The French, with two soldiers in harm's way and commitments to the government of Spain, began immediate high-level talks with the Spaniards. The election of a new leader in France, who was scheduled to visit Washington DC in a month, made the discovery of the plan an unforeseen and untenable situation.

In the end, the Spaniards relented and asked the French to convey a message to their agent in Colombia prior to pulling out their troops. Basically the message was to wait out the two-week training period and return home with Al Kassar's men.

Carlos and María Elena woke early that morning; he had feigned being sick the previous day and did not attend the training period for the missiles. However, Pedro Muñiz never showed up, and now with no other possible excuse, Carlos was heading for the training field with the possibility of an encounter with Pedro.

All the problems of the last two days had squelched any urge at romance between the couple. In fact, Carlos noticed how María Elena was avoiding his eyes at every opportunity. But he said to himself that these troubles would pass, that the kiss on Monday meant all in the world. All they had to do was survive this mission.

Once they arrived at the field and started their training, Carlos asked Luis in passing about his father. Luis explained that his father had missed the opportunity to visit the previous day, so he expected him near noon today. *I have to act fast,* Carlos thought.

At eleven thirty that morning, Carlos wrapped up his morning session and headed to the clump of trees where María Elena was teaching her English class. There, eleven guerrillas were participating eagerly in the session. Among them was Luis who had been coaxed by Juana to learn some English himself. Juana had stayed behind in the camp to take care of other matters, but her lieutenant Roberto was one of the eleven.

Carlos approached Luis and told him that his upset stomach had returned. He told him that he just needed a longer siesta, and he was heading to the water hole ahead of the group. Roberto, tasked with guarding the pair, noticed this but decided to stay with María Elena in order to keep his real orders secret. *She is the prettiest woman here, I will guard her,* Roberto convinced himself.

Carlos walked the ten minutes to the water hole but continued on the trail to the nearest town for another five minutes. He was following the stream that formed the water hole. When he stopped, Carlos selected an area in the jungle that was especially thick in vegetation close to a rock formation that provided enough elevation for the water to cascade down five feet. It was a beautiful sight in an unforgiving jungle.

Carlos figured that if Mr. Muñiz was coming today, he would take advantage of the noon break to visit his son. That was Mr. Muñiz after all, a man of conviction and tradition. He would not interrupt the very important training periods if he could help it.

Another ten minutes passed and Carlos figured the morning classes were wrapping up soon. He had been waiting patiently by the path with his entire body hidden from view from opposite direction traffic.

Pedro Muñiz was nearing Carlos's lair when he coughed. This gave his position even sooner to Carlos. Mr. Muñiz had almost passed Carlos on the path when he finally noticed him to his right. This startled him; at fifty-five years of age, he still had good vision, and he recognized Carlos immediately.

"Carlos Cortes, what are you doing here?"

Carlos approached the man to within a punch throw before answering, "Better yet, Pedro, what are you doing here?"

"Mr. Cortes, this is highly unusual for an agriculture officer to be in this part of the jungle." Pedro sounded inquisitive, not confused.

Carlos answered, "Come on, Pedro, you know I was in the CIA. Nobody can keep a secret like that in the embassy community. But I ask you"—as he was speaking, Carlos noticed a bulge in Pedro's right pocket, the size and shape of a small caliber gun—"why did you do it, Pedro, why?"

Pedro knew instantly why Carlos was here and what was going to happen next. He decided not to wait and went for the gun in his pocket. That was his last conscious act.

Carlos threw the entire weight of his body into a forward punch to Pedro's nose; the palm heel strike instantly snapped the nose, and it started bleeding profusely. Pedro's eyes swelled, and he had difficulty in seeing his attacker. Instinctively Pedro backed away while still fumbling for the gun.

Carlos knew that the gun would never be used, so he did not worry about it. Instead he moved quickly to grab Pedro from behind and placed his hand forcefully in his mouth.

Pedro, unable to breathe through his nose, held tightly by his left arm and mouth and, with the other hand stuck in his right pocket, began to suffocate. He could not breathe and in two short minutes, he was dead.

Carlos completed the job he had started by taking Pedro's body to the rock formation and dropping it head first to the bottom of the stream. The place he had selected was not visible from the path. When found, the cause of death would most probably be misdiagnosed as caused by the fall.

Carlos then cleaned the blood from his hands and returned to the training field. For now, he was out of danger.

Colonel Gomez received a telephone call from his deployed personnel in the Meta Department. It was to tell him that the first UHF signal had been received at their deployed site. The signal had lasted for ten minutes and had an embedded Morse code message. The message read, "Life Danger Deploy ASAP."

Apparently Carlos had sent this message fearing for his safety or fearing for that of the hostages. Having lasted only ten minutes, the message was not desperate yet, but it was going to take him two full days to deploy an assault force without the knowledge of his superiors. *Hope I'm on time for Carlos,* Cisco thought as he picked up his phone and began giving orders to his executive officer.

It was six in the evening the next time that the French soldier calmly monitoring the rebel camp checked his PDA for messages. He had to conserve battery life, and that meant he could check his messages every twelve hours. He would not get many; the only other PDA within range was the one his partner used.

Jacob, his partner, had a much better setup. His hideout was safely more than six hundred meters away from the camp in a completely isolated area. He had deployed a small black antenna and attached it to a tall tree that dominated the space around his hideout. Having a clear shot to the sky, he was assured very good connectivity with an Iridium satellite facilitating contact with his boss in Peru.

Today, the news received was discouraging. *Come this far and get nowhere!* Jacob was more than discouraged, he was pissed. *How many times are we going to try to rescue this woman,* he kept thinking about the danger he had placed his team in just to cave in at the last moment to American pressure. At least he had only the Americans to blame; little did he know that the governments of Colombia, Canada, and the United States had all requested the French to pull the team out.

So Jacob had written the message to his partner at 4:00 PM that he was sure to read at the appointed hour. *Come back tonight, mission aborted. Jacob.*

His partner read the message at 6:00 PM and began making preparations to pull out. He knew from the mission plan that any pullout once deployed would start at 11:00 PM so as to minimize the amount of coincidental brushes with the enemy.

The cabin was dark by the time Carlos and María Elena returned to their room that night. It had been a long day, and the evening dinner was prolonged by a long planning session with the camp commander. He wanted to make sure his fellow *patriotas* were advancing nicely in their training. After that, they also stayed for the group discussion on Marxist doctrine and even participated with all on a lively review on why the Nicaraguan revolution had given way to democracy back in 1990.

Due to darkness, Carlos fumbled to find the light switch by the table but stumbled on María Elena who was also looking for the switch. *Typical,* he thought. Their legs crossed, and both fell to the floor in a clumsy but safe way.

María Elena was the first to laugh, and Carlos joined her quickly; they were sitting, legs crossed in the wooden slats, tired, and worried about many individual things. But right now, they were only thinking about that kiss two days ago.

Their eyes locked and would not move away from each other. The eyes also did not lie; they were speaking of love although they could not talk. For what seemed to be an eternity, they looked at each other in the darkness. Faint smiles could be noticed, and those smiles also betrayed the love they felt for each other.

Finally María Elena could not wait anymore, and she made the first move. The kiss transported Carlos back to that last day in Spain, back to 1991. It was soft and full of passion. A passion not encouraged by lust but by love. The last sixteen years had not cooled the feelings they had for each other.

They kissed for a while and enjoyed it without moving their hands other than to hold each other and caress their faces. Finally María Elena stopped her kisses for a second and said, "Please make love to me tonight, amor."

Carlos did not need any more orders, but instead of continuing his soft caresses, he stood up quietly to pull the bed covers out of both their cots and laid them together on the floor. As if he had planned it, he then moved the mosquito net frame out of his cot to cover the covers. Then he came to María Elena and extended his hand.

By now María Elena's eyes had adjusted to the dark, and she was watching in amazement how Carlos had prepared their bed. She then extended her arm and let him help her into the newly made enclosure.

Outside the hut, Roberto Suros was standing guard as ordered and stood there hearing the goings-on inside. *Just a couple of married people making love,* he thought, *I would give anything to be there instead of José.*

Lovemaking was soft and coordinated and lasted for quite a while. In the end, both just relaxed with María Elena on top of Carlos where for a moment she fell asleep. They were in love again.

Before he fell asleep, Carlos said a prayer for his victim Pedro Muñiz and for his friend and thought, *Hang on, Pepe, I have not forgotten you.*

CHAPTER TWENTY-ONE

Thursday, September 13, 2007

Pepe was not well this morning. He had not responded to Juana's words when she delivered the morning food and water. Juana summoned two of her men and opened the cell. Inside, covered in filth and slumped to the floor was Pepe. His body lay half-submerged in water and excrements.

She touched his forehead softly and instantly noticed a high temperature; his body also kept shivering continuously. Juana sprang into action. Quickly ordering her men to take Pepe to the hut that acted as infirmary and to change his clothes and clean him up, she also headed in the direction of the hut where the team medic slept. *We cannot lose this man, he is my golden egg*, she thought.

Once they laid Pepe out on a cot, the medic arrived with a small backpack that contained his entire supply of medicines for the camp. He did not have much; that prior month, he had run out of many medications and of the necessary antibiotics to treat several maladies. "Caramba, este hombre se ve mal," the medic said to Juana who was standing by his side.

They started by taking off his filthy clothes and washing his body to remove the dirt and excrements that were attached to his legs, arms, and body. Once they had done that, Juana noticed the pale look of Pepe's body; he had lost his color, making his situation visibly obvious.

He had seen the symptoms many times before; the medic turned to Juana and said, "Este hombre tiene malaria."

Juana knew there was no medication and immediately worried about Pepe's survival. She knew that in his weakened state, they could lose him in less than a week. *I must do something,* she thought and turned around after giving orders to her men to guard him.

Outside she met her husband who was walking to get some breakfast just prior to departing on another very long training day with their guests from Nicaragua.

"Luis, I have bad news, it seems that the general has malaria, and he is in very bad shape."

"What can we do, Juana?"

"The medic is out of medication to treat his sickness, and we have to go get some. The general is too valuable to lose."

"I agree, what do you want me to do?"

"You know how worried you are about your father, why don't you take a break from the training and head to town with one of your men. You can be back by sundown, and that way, you can see your father at home."

"Okay, that's a very good idea. I will give our son a hug for you, dear. What if I don't find medication?"

"That's why you are taking one of your men, silly. Have your man leave no stone unturned until he can find the medication. I will have the medic make a list and give it to you after breakfast."

"Okay, querida, that is a good plan."

"And you are a good man, Luis." With that, they parted not before she gave him a slight kiss in the cheek. Anything more would break camp policies where public shows of attention were strictly forbidden.

The French commander sounded apologetic when he was connected to General Huber. It had taken quite some time to find the right telephone number for the general in Bogotá. It was a French military attaché that finally made the connection possible.

"General Huber," the general always answered the phone in a tone of voice that made lesser people cower.

"General, I hate to call you, but I have a very delicate problem, and I seek your help please. We last spoke in Iquitos, and my country has given me some orders that I cannot complete without your support."

"And that is?" Huber asked in perfect French.

"My country has decided to pull out of the mission you came all the way here to talk to me about. But I have a problem, we have two men deployed to the area, and I have to get them back."

This was an unexpected surprise; the general never thought the French had actually started their mission, and he had not planned for this eventuality. "They are deployed, may I ask where, Monsieur Richard?" He had lowered his tone of voice and was now speaking in a nice way.

"I'm afraid that until last night, we had a member of the team within twenty yards of the rebel camp." Richard had decided to be open and honest with the general even though the classification of his mission prohibited him from discussing the facts with the general. This was the code of the Special Forces, and it was the same throughout the world, safety and security first.

"Twenty yards, scare bleu!" Again the general continued his questioning in a nice way, "Richard, please tell me what you want."

"We attempted to move one of our helicopters forward last night so that we could be ready for their extraction tonight, sir. But they were intercepted in the middle of the night by one of your helicopters. Even though the crew of the other craft spoke Spanish to our crew, we know that neither the Peruvian nor the Colombians have the technology to perform such a difficult intercept in the dead of night."

"And?" General Huber questioned.

"Well, we need your permission to do the entire mission tonight. Our men should be ready for pickup by 0100 hours."

"No, that is not going to happen in my watch, but let me tell you what we can do," the general continued.

By now the guerrillas had gotten used to the long start-up and warm-up process of the training Strela missile that Carlos and María Elena used to teach. What they did not know that that time was used by María Elena to communicate with her CEID team and with the French rescue forces in Peru. Cleverly disguised as one of the missile systems was an Iridium phone transceiver that could transmit text via satellite, and messages received were shown on the device's small LCD.

There was trust in this process since one of their own, Juan Miranda, was learning to boot up the missiles and had performed it successfully once.

Today's message had surprised María Elena, and she showed it to Carlos immediately: "Ángeles Zero, Águilas Diez." The mission to rescue them had cancelled, and they were supposed to abort the mission and return as scheduled once the training class ended.

Carlos wasted no time; even though it was early in the morning, he considered all that had happened and turned on the VHF transmitter continuously. The radio transmitter he had installed was a small emergency beacon that used the missile's power and had a small antenna completely concealed in the simulator. He had the capability to type a Morse code message, so he did, adding the message:

.——, —., ..., .-., .- [1 G SAR]

To pass the message for the rescue of one general.

Now we sit back and wait, hopefully the rescue will happen in the next two days. I hope that Pepe can hang on, I also hope that Luis does not find his father today, Carlos thought.

By noon, Luis and one of the female members of his group arrived in the town of Calamar. Luis wasted no time and headed straight to his parents' house. His mother met him at the door.

"Mama, what happened? Papá never made it to the training field on Tuesday?"

"Oh my god," she responded, "I thought he was with you all this time."

At that moment, his son ran up to Luis, and for a second, his father was not in his thoughts. He hugged his son hard and told him how much he missed him. He then slowly returned to his original state of mind and began to worry about his father's fate again. He again looked at his mother and said, "Please do not worry, I will search for Papá and will not rest until we find him."

"Yes, son, I am deeply troubled, you know he is all I've got."

"I worry about that, you take care of Pepe Luis and let him not get into trouble."

With that, Luis turned around and gave orders to his female companion. He gave her the list of medications and told her not to fail in this task. With that, he departed and headed toward his training area. *He had to follow that path,* he thought. *I hope that Papá did not stray into a land mine area.*

General Huber's executive officer came in with a report from a noncommissioned officer stationed with a technical assistance training team in Leticia, Colombia. The report was classified confidential and, at first glance, looked like a regular periodic report except for what it said in the last line.

The sergeant had finished his comments by stating, "I believe that a major operation against a high-value target is being planned and executed without our knowledge. This is very unusual, since I've been here, we are usually trusted and counted on our counsel for all operations the battalion is tasked with. I believe they are on a rouge mission without even the approval of their commanders."

When he finished reading the report, General Huber called his assistant back and asked him to contact the Junglas battalion commander.

This was a highly unusual move for an American in a foreign country. To do this correctly, the general had to contact his counterpart in the Colombian armed forces and request permission to talk directly with Colonel Gomez after explaining carefully the reason why that was necessary. But General Huber thought this was a special moment and that he could not wait for the bureaucracy to catch up with the events.

To his credit, Colonel Gomez also was not worried to break the established procedures. Once the phone call was placed, he answered his own phone and asked the general how he could help him.

"Colonel Gomez, I have reports that several of your helicopters are moving north from Leticia, and we have no notice at the embassy that you would be undertaking such a large operation today."

239

"Beg your pardon, General, but I am under the impression that I don't have to ask for your permission to fly my helicopters."

General Huber saw immediately that his strategy to call directly was not working, so he decided to change the direction of his line of questioning. "Quite so, Colonel Gomez, but we are undertaking missions of our own in the area and would hate to have an accident with your helicopters."

"At the altitudes we fly and the ones you fly, there should not be a problem, General. Why, we are probably separated by over twenty thousand feet."

Of course Colonel Gomez did not know of the agreement that General Huber had reached with the French forces on the other side of the border. In order to relocate the two men caught behind the lines, Huber had agreed to send in his own rescue team to pluck out of the jungle the Frenchmen. Assigned to that mission was a Special Forces helicopter team in country for a training assignment.

They spoke for another five minutes, but Huber never got any information from the Colombian. In the end, they said some parting pleasantries and hung up the phone.

In Bogotá, Huber was more than ever convinced that a mission of some sort was underway. He would have to get information on it from someone else.

In Leticia, Cisco called his aide and asked to be in the manifest for the next helicopter leaving on the rescue mission. *I trust the Americans with my life,* he thought, *but Carlos told me to trust no one. That is a promise I will keep.*

Driving back to the guerrilla camp that evening, María Elena, Juan Miranda, and Carlos were discussing the chain of events that the Junglas battalion would probably follow in an effort to rescue them. Carlos led the discussion by stating what he knew of the unit and its leader and predicting that the rescue would take place either tomorrow night or the day after.

In preparation for the rescue, Carlos had to ask Juan to do one more dangerous task for him. When the car stopped to drop them near the guerrilla camp, he turned to Juan and said, "Juan, I have one last dangerous mission for you. Tomorrow as you drive away from here, I want you to ditch the Bronco and head back by foot to the training area."

"In order to cover your tracks, you must make it look like you were attacked and injured, even possibly taken prisoner by some Colombian patrol that had a chance encounter with you. Instead you will carry the UHF radio back to the training area and turn it on continuously. Let the Junglas find you and then lead them to our camp.

"At most, it will be two days before they find you. When they do, you can lead them on a path to the camp free of the minefields you know so well. Understand, compadre?"

"*Si, jefe*, a very dangerous mission, but I will do it."

At that moment, the truck carrying Luis Montes and his party arrived at the drop-off point. Carlos finished talking to Juan and went to greet Luis.

"*Hola*, Luis, I hope you found your father in good health," he said this in a very serious tone, one that did not betray any sign that Carlos knew his father's fate.

"No, I am afraid not, José, my father is missing, and I pray that he is all right."

"So do we, my friend," he said this as María Elena joined them for the trek back to camp.

By now Carlos had noticed that Roberto Suros was tasked with tailing them, and he suspected that he was staying close to their hut at night. So that evening, Carlos purposely left the hut after they had retired for the night. Outside and just a few feet from the front door was Roberto resting upright against a palm tree.

"*Hola,* Roberto, what are you doing here?" Carlos asked.

"Señor, I am here for your safety. We don't want our guests to be in danger," Roberto said these words as if he did not believe them, automatically giving a clue as to the real reason he was there even though he did not voice them.

This man is dangerous, I will have to take care of him first when the attack comes, Carlos thought. "I suggest you don't follow me, Roberto, for what I am going to do is not too pleasant to smell."

"I will guard your wife, señor, go in peace."

Heading away from hut, Carlos decided to take a few minutes and delay his return. So instead of walking to the soccer field, he turned toward the center of camp and decided to enter the camp infirmary that still had its lights on. Inside he found three cots occupied and two additional persons inside. One he assumed was the medic, and of course, he instantly recognized Juana.

"José, what a surprise to see you here," Juana said.

"I could not sleep immediately and decided to take a late-night walk, Juana. Seeing the infirmary open, I got curious about the camp's health status and decided to walk in."

"Well, I am glad you are interested in our health," Juana said in reply, wondering to herself what the real reason was for the late-night visit. On instinct, she asked, "Do you need any medication, José, we have little to offer."

"No, Juana, I was just wondering why the need for the two guards outside if the prisoner is delirious with fever and nearly moribund. And how about these two soldiers, what do they have?"

"If you need to know, the two soldiers have a mild case of leishmaniasis, a sickness of the skin, and of course, the captive has malaria."

"How is he doing?" Carlos asked superficially.

"Bad, real bad, if we don't find medication for treatment soon, he could die."

Carlos made a mental note to send out a different message tomorrow. *'Malaria' in Morse code, that should suffice,* he thought.

Carlos then turned his attention to the young soldier next to Pepe in order to show his interest with all those in sick bay. "And he, he looks too young to be disfigured like that." The boy looked no more than fourteen, and his face and arms were marked with grotesque growths.

The medic went into a minute-long explanation of the cause and effects of leishmaniasis. Sores, bizarre at times, were the visible signs of this sickness that attacked equally both sides in this conflict. It was possible to cure with medication, but then again, they had none in camp.

They were startled by a voice coming from the direction of Pepe. "Cah—los." It was Pepe who had opened his eyes and was stretching an arm in their direction. The speech pattern was broken and nearly incomprehensible, but Carlos new immediately that he had made a mistake by coming over to visit a very sick man. He ignored him and turned his back to Pepe to continue discussing the boy's fate with the medic while Juana went to take care of her captive.

After another few minutes of chitchat, Carlos bid farewell and walked back to his hut. Juana followed him outside and, noticing Roberto Suros was not near, made a mental note to put Roberto's brother on assignment also. *I could swear that Pepe was calling José just now, Carlos, is that what I heard?*

CHAPTER TWENTY-TWO

Friday, September 14, 2007

Colonel Gomez had made the decision to deploy with his troops. So at one in the morning, he was still up making plans with his staff. Two of his personnel had already deployed forward and, with any luck, would be in position near the camp by morning. They were equipped with similar equipment to the French Special Forces but with an American slant to them. Gone were the PDAs that the French used for communication, and in their place, they had low-power radios to communicate with each other.

Deployed forward were Sergeants Rubio and Suarez. Rubio would be the point man while Suarez would have the most dangerous mission. Not having state-of-the-art high-power radios, Sergeant Suarez would have to move nightly to a place where he could reach his command post. Moving in the dark, in an alien zone, was extremely dangerous; but the sergeant was ready for this task.

Tonight they had reached the clearing where the daily missile training was performed. Unsure of where the rebel camp was, they sent a report back to Colonel Gomez from the clearing and decided to wait until the next night before they traveled any farther. They found a part of the surrounding jungle that provided good cover and separated themselves by thirty feet. Now the real monotonous part of their watch would start.

General Huber called his boss in Miami early the next morning. He reported what had transpired the last two days and suggested that a rogue rescue operation was imminent. This information General Strange carried with him to the eight thirty morning meeting at SOUTHCOM.

"And General Huber then lost contact with Colonel Gomez at about three thirty in the afternoon when the colonel's office reported him deployed with his troops." The general was finished retelling his staff the main points of his morning conversation with Huber.

Characteristically his staff remained silent when he was finished. Even his ever-proactive director of operations was quiet, eschewing the general's story. He finally made a grunting noise, waited until everyone looked his way, and said, "There are no active clues as to the hostage location, boss. We have none, the Agency has none, and, as far as I know, the Colombians have none."

"Bullshit, Johnny." The general's tone surprised all as they had never heard him curse or refer to one of his generals in a familiar way. "If Mike thinks there is a rescue operation in the works, there is! I trust his judgment, and he has not let me down since we first met while deployed to the Balkans."

The general paused and gave his staff a disapproving look. He then stood up and said to them while turning his head side to side, "I am really disappointed with your work so far. If I am to act on the events in Colombia, I need your best work, so I am expecting a briefing by 1300 hours on the events unfolding in Colombia and your recommendation for the way ahead, that's all. I would start by investigating what those two Frenchmen were doing near Calamar." The general then left the room in a hurry, leaving his entire staff in a trance.

That same morning, Marc Higgins went to brief his boss at the Agency. H. I. "Gus" Grant was named the CIA's acting director as a result of a second wave of reforms since the Office of the Director of

National Intelligence was created. In addition to the director, there was one other person in the room, a uniformed man that Marc did not recognize.

Since his brief was personal to the director, Higgins ignored the other man and began his report on the events unfolding in Colombia. His main points included the fact that the Agency was convinced that Carlos Cortes was in Colombia participating in a rescue attempt of a hostage presumed to be General Ramirez, that the French Special Forces had indeed cancelled their participation leaving the operation in danger of total failure, and that Colombian military forces had deployed in secret to a base near San José del Guaviare to participate in a presumed rescue operation.

As he was talking, he noticed how the uniformed gentleman was taking copious notes. He finally noticed the rank of major general and decided to meet the man when he was finished. He was not given the opportunity to make the first approach.

When he was done with his update, Director Grant asked no questions but said, "Marc, thank you so much for the update. I would like you to meet Major General Omar Vazquez of the U.S. Army. He is our new acting deputy director of operations starting today."

Marc Higgins went speechless; he did not notice that General Vazquez had stood up and was offering his hand as a goodwill gesture. "But, but . . . that is my position," Marc replied.

Grant continued, "Marc, I am sorry, but after you leave the office, you must report to the office of the inspector general. As of today at 9:00 AM, I have ordered a complete investigation on the events surrounding the case against Carlos Cortes, the death of Spanish CEID agent Johanna Valenz in 2004, and the involvement of Warren Westback and your office in these cases. While you are under investigation, you will retain the title of deputy director but will be banned from performing any work for the Agency until you are cleared. General Vazquez knows the way to your office and will have your personal items sent to your home today. That will be all."

Marc Higgins, consummate Washington insider, left the office a ruined man.

Luis had fanned out his troops in three different directions. His main concern was to explore the three avenues of approach to their practice field from the town of Calamar. He took the main path between the two and sent smaller teams to search the two alternate paths. They also had the duty to inspect the two minefields that were laid protecting those paths.

It was two thirty in the afternoon when Luis heard the words he did not want to hear. "Aquí, jefe, lo encontré!"

They were near their water hole, a place they had visited daily while the training was underway. *Here? What could have happened, my father knows this area so well?* Luis racked his brain with questions he could not answer while he climbed a slippery set of rocks on the south side of the pond. When he got to the top, he could see his man next to what appeared to be his father some thirty feet down a steep embankment.

He hurried down to them, and reaching his father, he held his lifeless body in his arms.

"It looks like he slipped on the rocks, señor," his man said, trying to comfort his feelings and explain the reason for the accident.

"Déjame," Luis said in reply while in obvious pain!

That same man came to the practice field with the news. Juana, in charge for the day, took the news hard and stopped training. She assembled all and told them that they were returning to camp and that Luis was taking Pedro's body back to his mother. She could not hide the tears that moistened her face as she spoke.

Carlos felt a bit of remorse as these were human beings; he had killed one of them and was preparing to instill even more casualties in their ranks. Yet he surmised, *They kidnapped Pepe and deserve what they have coming.*

María Elena was more aware; she had sensed the change in Juana and her attitude toward them. It was growing more detached daily, and this last bit of news would not help. *I don't like her stare when she looks at Carlos. I must talk to him as she suspects something.*

When they drove back to camp, the Suros brothers insisted that they ride back with them. They did not say they were ordered by Juana. This eventuality prevented Carlos from making any last-minute plans with Juan Miranda. *I will have to trust his judgment,* Carlos thought.

They had stayed behind to pack up their gear and were ten minutes behind the rest of the group. As they left the field, Rubio and Suarez compared notes via wireless. "That tall man doing the training must be Mr. Cortes, what do you think?"

"Must be," replied Sergeant Suarez. "His only message today is weird, what do you think he meant by 'malaria'?"

"Well, the urgency is still there, he transmitted for fifteen minutes on time. The word 'malaria' may be in reference to the hostage, I think." He seemed unsure of what he had just said.

"Okay, I will report to the colonel the situation and recommend he deploy an attack force forward to at least our location. We should attack by tomorrow night at the latest, or our friends could be in trouble."

"Hey, *mano,* you see the woman that is with Mr. Cortes. What a beauty."

"You kidding, I trained my binoculars on her most of the day." Suarez was lying of course. He was a true professional and had meticulously studied the situation confronting them in close detail; but being a Jungla, he could not let his machismo be challenged.

General James was briefing his commander standing up. "Sir, General Huber is on the way to San José del Guaviare right now. He will supervise the extraction of the French soldiers and take the opportunity to confront Colonel Gomez as you ordered. All the Colombians know is that he is visiting our deployed troops at the airport."

It was seven thirty at night, and General Strange could care less what the Colombians thought. He was under a tight schedule to brief the secretary who in turn was under orders to keep the president up to date on events unfolding in Colombia. The idea was to offer Colonel Gomez directly American support for a rescue operation, an operation that by design would be meticulously planned and carefully executed. And one that would be approved by the presidents of both countries. General James estimated that the plan would take at least two weeks to execute.

They were discussing the plan in detail when the executive officer for General Strange walked in the room and gave a note to the general. He read it and looked up at his director of operations. "Huber reports that Colonel Gomez and his troops are not in the airport in San José and that all his helicopters have gone. Damn, I want you to find Colonel Gomez now. Where is Colonel Gomez?" General Strange shouted at the group.

Juan Miranda had just dropped off all four of his passengers and was driving the five miles to the storage area where the CRAF kept their ammunition and supplies. It was a secondary camp to their main headquarters. He drove a mile down the road and suddenly veered off the road and rammed his truck into a small tree. He got out of the truck and then carefully placed a hand grenade near the windshield of the passenger side. When he was satisfied with the location, he pulled the arming ring and ran away.

The explosion caved in the truck's windshield and caused other damage to the body. The sound of the explosion was muffled by the jungle, and it did not travel far. Immediately following the blast, Juan grabbed a piece of glass from the truck and, sitting in the driver's seat, cut his arm slightly. He bled immediately and used the blood to smear the immediate area surrounding his seat.

Satisfied that the accident looked like a government ambush, Juan cleaned his wound and bandaged it and set out with a few supplies back to the missile training area he had just left. It was a five-mile walk, and it would take him two hours if he did not encounter any other fellow guerrillas.

It was already dark when he approached the area. Juan walked to the center of the field and sat down unfolding a white flag he was carrying in a backpack. He decided to wait for contact.

At the other end of the field, Sergeant Rubio was alone when he noticed a lone figure walk to the middle of the field. He trained his night vision goggles on the man and noticed with clarity how the man calmly sat down and then unfurled what to him looked like a white flag and draped it over his head. *I'll wait for Suarez to get back before I do something stupid,* Rubio thought.

At the rebel camp, Juana was visiting with their leader León. Also in the room were Luis and Manuel Alonso, the second in command. Juana had waited until Luis had returned to camp and was now stating her concerns to her boss.

"So I am very worried with the events that have transpired in the last two months. I don't know, boss, we have lost thirty fighters in clashes with the government, another twelve have escaped into the jungle, and now we have strangers living with us, plus Luis's father is dead." She looked at her husband and put her arm in his shoulder.

"Why are you linking the Nicaraguans to this, Juana? Didn't they provide us with a modern weapon, and now they are training us how to use it? Is the training acceptable?" He looked at Luis who was in charge of the training.

Luis, feeling beaten and sad, replied, "I guess so, León. I mean, Juan seems to be learning a lot. He tells me these missiles are going to be lethal when employed." He turned to see Juana's reaction to his reply and noticed instantly her displeasure.

"I know we needed these missiles, and I am thankful to the couple, but my instinct tells me there is something wrong here. Please don't ask for specifics, I just don't like José Hernandez. Why, just last night he came walking into the infirmary and asked about the general's status."

"So what have you done, Juana, I mean, in response to your instincts which I respect?" León asked.

"I have the Suros brothers guarding them 24/7."

"Well, I think that is enough for now. I can't think of a more ruthless pair of *patriotas*. If the couple gives you any trouble, have the brothers take care of them. I would hate to lose the opportunity to do more business with María though. We have attempted to get the missiles many times before, and only this couple has been able to satisfy us. And they promise a steady supply."

The meeting was adjourned, but before she retired for the night, Juana went to visit the Suros brothers and gave them explicit instructions to follow the couple always and most importantly gave them permission to shoot to kill if any of them made a false move.

She went back to her hut thinking about the general. His condition had worsened today, and the medic had lost confidence on his recovery without the needed medicines. Luis had brought back news from his personnel in Calamar. Padre Chico was flying back the medicines in two days. *Hope he is in time*, thought Juana as she went in her hut to try to console Luis further.

Meanwhile María Elena and Carlos had just finished making love. They had dressed again and packed their belongings. They were ready to bolt immediately if an attack came.

Just before she finished packing her only backpack, María Elena, holding something in her arms, turned to Carlos and whispered, "Carlos, I have to confess something, I lied."

"Que, cariño?" Carlos whispered back.

She was slow and deliberate; she unfolded her arms and gave him the picture sitting on their table, the one with the teenager in the soccer uniform. Then she said, "This is no pretend child, Carlos, his name is Charlie, I gave this sweet fifteen-year-old his name in honor of his American father whom I love very much."

The fact that she was talking in the present tense did not go unnoticed. Carlos wanted to shout, his eyes moistened, and he embraced María Elena for a long time. When he finally let go, he noticed María Elena was crying, and he said, "Now I have two more reasons why this rescue must succeed. I came here for Pepe, but now I am doing this for the three of you. There is no way I am leaving this earth without first laying eyes on Charlie. Come, my dear, let us rest, for this is going to be a very long night."

CHAPTER TWENTY-THREE

Saturday, September 15, 2007, 12:01 AM

Colonel Gomez had made all the decisions up to now. However, the Junglas' main forces were now in place at the training area and had now interviewed Juan Miranda and accepted his support in the rescue attempt that was to follow. So Gomez had ceded control to Captain Octavio Páez, his most experienced and capable officer.

They had decided that the best course of action was for Juan and Captain Páez to lead a small group of men down the road and path to the rebel camp. The main group of men would follow them a minute later, and all would be moving at a fast pace. Five minutes after leaving the road and entering the narrow path to the camp, they were expecting to meet the outside ring of security, and Juan was trusted to help in neutralizing the guards.

Following that, they were to approach the camp covertly. Juan represented a treasure trove of information. He could pinpoint the key places in the camp that they had to identify. That included the cell where the hostage was being kept and Carlos's location. If everything went according to plan, they would be finished with the rescue by sunrise.

Colonel Gomez could not stay behind, so he assumed the role of a line soldier. As they left the training area toward their objective, he thought, *Captain Páez is a good man, he knows that nothing ever goes as planned. I pray to God that when that happens, he is ready for this task.*

12:15 AM

General Strange was on the phone with the commander of the Colombian armed forces. He was a good friend ever since they had attended Army War College during the 1996-97 school year. Being a marine, Strange made quick friends with the international officers at school that year including General Crespo who was a straight shooter. Tonight, Crespo was not mincing words when he had at first told the general that he knew nothing about an impending rescue.

Crespo had returned to his office from an evening reception and had ordered his staff to inquire further on Strange's inquiries. After some menacing words from his deputy, the second in command in Leticia had acknowledged that Colonel Gomez was deployed on a real operation and had taken his best squad of men with him.

Then General Crespo had personally called on secure phone the leader of the helicopter squad now deployed with Gomez. That was the way that Crespo did business; he got his hands dirty at every opportunity and got the truth out of his personnel. The end result was complete trust in him by all his subordinates.

The helicopter commander had confirmed that Colonel Gomez was somewhere east of the town of Calamar where they had dropped the entire squad off; however, he did not know the coordinates of the rebel camp or where he was supposed to pick up the team after the attack. He did not tell his commander that two helicopter gunships had already deployed forward and were on call, waiting for Colonel Gomez to order them into the fight.

"General, my personnel are deployed as you said, but I cannot confirm what their mission is. If what you say is true, then I have the best men available for the mission already there. I hope you trust us to complete this mission successfully."

The two generals talked for a couple more minutes, but at the end, they did not accomplish anything more. When he hung up, General Strange called his aide-de-camp and said, "Call Army-South and tell them to get their hostage recovery team together. I want the best doctors they have at Brooks Army Medical Center on an airplane to Colombia ASAP!" When the aide was about to leave, the general added, "Oh, and alert my airplane's crew. We are going to Bogotá in the morning."

1:00 AM

Juan, Octavio, and two other men were approaching the site where the outside perimeter guards spent the night. Juan was expecting the guards to be wide awake. The events of the last three months had everyone on edge; throughout the region, a government attack was expected at any time. And recently a guard caught sleeping on the job was executed by León himself the next morning.

They had slowed down their trot to a slow walk. As expected, when they neared the guards, they were asked for identification immediately. Juan answered the query, "Soy yo, Juan y tres mas."

The guard came out of the tree and said, "But I see only two of you, Juan, who is with you?"

The guard did not recognize the second man who was dressed similarly as they were. He kept looking at the face, but he could not see much in the dark. As they got closer, he repeated, "But where are the other two?"

That was the last thing the man ever said. As he got closer to Captain Páez, he distinguished a gleaming blade being carried by the captain. Before he could react, Páez lunged at him with the knife and stabbed him right in the heart.

The other guards fared no better since the two other Junglas had circled around them and had equally dispatched them silently. When they were finished, the group waited for the main force and began to divide into different strike packages.

They could not be discovered now. Any misstep would jeopardize the mission and cost Carlos and General Ramirez their lives. So they sent three personnel with radios and Colonel Gomez to the soccer field east of the camp. Another team stayed behind at the guard post to stop anyone from surprising them. The main team headed by the captain and Juan headed to form a semicircle around the southwestern edge of the camp. Even with their modern communication radios, great training, and night vision goggles, it would take them almost two hours to get in position.

2:15 AM

General Strange had reached his home for what was going to be, if he got any sleep at all, a very short night. He could go for months just taking short naps at night; it was the way of life of a marine officer, but he was not proud of it. He truly liked to sleep.

In his home office, he was arranging papers when his secure phone rang. It was the command post who had a conference call with the secretary of defense. The call was connected to his phone, and Strange soon found out the new deputy director of operations at the CIA was also online.

"Mr. Secretary, I am truly concerned because all clues point out that tonight a rescue operation deep in the Colombian jungle is underway. In addition, there is an ex-CIA agent in the mix, one that was close friends with General Ramirez and has vowed to rescue him in the past."

"I tend to agree with the general," Omar Vazquez interrupted the two powerful leaders. "At the Agency, we have confirmed that Carlos Cortes was in contact with a group of Spanish CEID agents in Puerto Rico and that the same group took off toward Colombia the same day of the aircraft shoot down in Venezuela. We believe the sale of surface-to-air missiles was just a ruse to get the team in and rescue high-value hostages."

"And that same group was in cahoots with the French?" asked the secretary.

"Yes, sir," stated Vazquez. "And to think we thought the rescue operation was averted when we forced them out of the fight."

"Explain yourself."

"Let me try," General Strange now butted in. "It seems that Mr. Cortes had an ace up his sleeve, Mr. Secretary. When he was an agent in Colombia, Cortes made friends with the colonel that is now leading the rescue operation. I believe that Colonel Gomez represented the escape clause in the event that things went bad."

"So what is wrong with all of this, General?"

General Strange remembered that the secretary did not have a military past. So he carefully replied as if he was talking to a layman, "Sir, in an operation such as this, preparation is the key to success. Any operation put up on a shoestring is bound for failure. Look at our fiasco back in 1980 at Desert One in Iran."

"But the time for preparation has come and gone, General. What are you recommending we do now?"

"Sir, Colonel Gomez is a very competent man, and he leads the best battalion in the Colombian armed forces. At this moment, all we can do is provide forces in support and wish for the best. I have ordered that the army's hostage recovery team deploy immediately to Colombia and the two helicopters rescuing the French soldiers stuck in the jungle to stand by in support of the Colombians. I have also ordered fighter aircraft to take off and be on call if needed, and finally, I am personally going to be there early this morning to report the events as they unfold."

"Very well, General, I will report this to the National Command Authority [NCA] and directly to the White House. Keep me informed. And that goes to you too, General Vazquez, please let us know the moment you have an update from Agency contacts."

"General Vazquez, do me a favor, and don't hang up," General Strange added.

"I'm still here," Omar Vazquez answered. He had never met the SOUTHCOM commander and was wondering why Strange still wanted to talk to him.

"General, what are your people telling you of this Carlos Cortes? I am very worried that our fortunes rest in the hands of a rogue agent and a Colombian renegade officer."

"Sir"—the new DDO at the Agency still wore a uniform and respected the rank difference between them—"I have only limited information on Mr. Cortes, however, his background is impressive, first in his class, an impressive performer back in 2003 during the Western Iraq desert operations, and a competent clandestine service resume. We have opened up an internal investigation on what transpired in Colombia back in 2004, and everything points at a summary execution by a jealous peer."

"So you think we are in good hands here?"

"No, I am not saying that. Who knows what actually happened to him after his dismissal from the Agency. One thing I can add, General, is the fact that some of my agents in the headquarters are still ardent supporters of Mr. Cortes. He seems to have a group of admirers that comes from his competence as an agent for over ten years."

"Thank you, General, for an honest appraisal," General Strange added in closing. "Like the secretary said, keep us informed please."

"I will, sir," Omar Vazquez said from his Langley office. *Another sleepless night, Omar,* he thought as he hung up the phone.

3:30 AM

Carlos left his hut at the precise time he had briefed Juan Miranda he would. The idea was to confirm to Carlos that the attack was being executed that night. If he had no contact with Juan, he would return to his hut and wait for the next night.

Outside his hut, Carlos noticed Papo Suros stirring from a lookout position. Carlos walked right to him and said, "I cannot sleep and am going out for a walk."

"I am under orders to follow you, José. We don't want you to stray into a minefield by mistake," Papo Suros lied for his last time.

"Then let's go, Papo." Carlos strode away in the direction of the soccer field. Papo grabbed his AK-47 and followed.

Behind them, Roberto Suros was watching what transpired with suspicion. He also grabbed his gun and became more alert. *If his woman tries to leave also, I am first going to rape her and then kill her slowly.* Roberto decided to wait as he considered his options.

Two degrees north of the equator and fifty miles out in open waters, the USS *Ronald Reagan*, CVN-76, was coming to life at approximately the same time. A nuclear aircraft carrier and a new addition to the U.S. arsenal, it was sailing the waters just off the west coast of Colombia in support of a Southern Command initiative called "Partnership of the Americas."

The internal preparations of the carrier had started three hours earlier. On orders from the NCA, crews had been briefed, aircraft had been loaded and readied, and the takeoff sequence had started on board.

The first to take off were the rescue helicopters that were always airborne when flying operations were underway. Next in line at the catapults was a solitary E-2C radar plane now waiting for clearance for takeoff with its engines revved up at full power.

The carrier's ramp was a beehive of activity. Personnel wearing distinctive colored shirts were doing their duties amid the noise and winds that accompanied flight operations from such a moving platform. Overseeing all, personnel in white shirts were performing safety duties that ensured safety among the participants.

A loud clang that shook the entire ship signaled the release of the radar plane from its catapult. In moments, the airplane had accelerated to over one hundred knots of speed and was slowly lifting up to his assigned holding point for the night's activities.

At the opposite side of the bow, two F/A-18Es were sitting on the starboard catapults. All the checks had been made on them, weapons' safety pins had been pulled, catapult connections were checked and approved, and the pilots had advanced power to maximum afterburner waiting for their release. Exactly fifteen seconds after the E-2C had taken off, the first of two fighters was released, followed seconds later by his wingman.

Another eight aircraft waited patiently in line. Four were in-flight refuelers and the other four additional F/A-18 fighters fully loaded with precision weapons.

The carrier had not sailed with its full assortment of combat aircraft. Only half of a normal carrier air wing was on board since the objectives of their current operations included coalition training and goodwill and not combat operations. But a carrier never sailed unarmed, and the weapons selected for the mission were probably the best the weapons officer could provide tonight.

3:40 AM

Carlos and Papo were nearing the clearing of the soccer field when Papo noticed another man walking toward them. He instantly raised his weapon in alarm and asked the man walking toward them for identification.

Juan Miranda responded, "It's Juan, Papo, don't be alarmed."

Hearing this, Papo Suros relaxed a little bit while wondering why Juan was there, away from his assigned camp and late in the evening. But his attention was focused on the newcomer, and that was his fatal mistake. He had not noticed how Carlos had stayed slightly behind him but within arm's reach.

As they approached, Juan Miranda offered a hand to Papo in a greeting, and in response, he transferred his weapon to his left hand.

This was the best opportunity for Carlos to prevent alarm. He moved quickly, grabbing Suros by the head and shoulder and violently twisting both in opposite directions. The spinal cord fractured at the neck, and Papo Suros took his last breath soon thereafter.

They were joined quickly by two others. The taller man spoke first, "Rock, my friend, it is good to see you."

"Cisco, what are you doing here?" Carlos could not believe his friend had deployed with his troops.

"Don't worry, I am not in charge, Captain Páez here is. Listen to his briefing on our plan of attack."

3:50 AM

María Elena left her hut at the prescribed time; she was ready for action. Carlos had told her that the mission was on if he had not returned in twenty minutes. She carried a long knife carefully held against her clothes. Her plan was to get close to whichever Suros brother was outside her hut and kill him when he least expected it.

She looked in the direction where she expected to see him watching out for them but did not discern anything in the dark. She walked toward the tallest tree standing guard over their front door and began to see the shape of a man as she got closer. The man was lying prone seemingly asleep. The available light was insufficient to tell features, but what María Elena saw when she was two feet away made her gasp. Roberto Suros's throat had been slashed.

Suddenly, out of the shadows, three silhouettes appeared where there was once darkness. María Elena tensed and raised her knife up in self-defense. She then heard one of the three speak.

"Señora, *no se mueva,* you are safe now," the whisper was soft and reassuring.

At that same instant, Carlos was now in position with the main assault force near the center of the rebel camp. They were attacking from the direction of Calamar or from the southeast. They were waiting for a flanking element that was approaching the camp from the north end in order to surprise the two guards in front of the infirmary. From his vantage point, Carlos could notice that they were still awake. *Juana runs a tough group of guerrillas,* he thought.

At the soccer field, Colonel Gomez had ordered his two helicopter gunships airborne. Their time over target was at exactly 4:00 AM. Armed with two .50-caliber machine guns and one 7.62 mm mini-gun each, they would bring to bear a great amount of lead to a small area in support of ground operations. They were flying with night vision goggles, and the mini-gun was equipped with an infrared receiver capable of detecting men underneath the foliage.

Following Carlos's instructions, he had also sent a message on an HF radio "in the blind," or transmitting without getting a response back. The message read, "Barnstormer reports Orion operational at site of ten Strela SAMs and other stockpiled ammunition. No innocent lives at stake. End of message." He gave the report three times at one-minute intervals.

The message was received at a top secret communications site in Maryland, and the code words were decoded. Twenty minutes later, the message reached the desk of Shirley Miller at the CIA command post; she had not slept for thirty-six hours.

3:55 AM

An explosion shook the camp! The loud retort was sure to wake everyone in camp.

Shit. What was that? Carlos thought.

Back in the path to the training site, a rebel group of ten was coming back to the main camp to report Juan Miranda's disappearance and the discovery of his blown-out truck. They were coming to receive instructions from León.

They had stumbled on what was the last of a string of trip wire detonated mines that the Junglas had rigged in the area to surprise any combatants escaping tonight's attack.

Since they were coming from the opposite direction, they tripped the last and largest of the mines, an antitank mine that one of the Junglas had proudly carried in his back. "To make a big bang," he had joked to his friends.

Sitting next to Carlos, Captain Páez instantly recognized that his plan was shot. He went to his mike and transmitted to all his troops, "Abort, abort, abort, follow my commands, men. Lieutenants Garriga and Guevara, fall back to soccer field with your men and female companion. My group will recover the hostage. That's all for now."

Back in the soccer field, hearing the abort order, Colonel Gomez ordered the rest of his helicopters airborne.

At the camp, the rebel forces began to stir instantly. It was standard procedure for Juana to move General Ramirez to a safe area the moment that any attack was suspected. Her personnel knew their orders well and reacted with the precision of a well-oiled machine.

Luis also reacted alertly. His mission was to protect his newly acquired missiles and to protect the lives of their visiting instructors. He and his men would move the Nicaraguans to safety.

Before they parted ways at exactly 3:56 AM, Juana told her husband to watch out. Her instinct had quickly told her that the detonation they had heard was much louder than those heard when one of their antipersonnel mines went off. Not a rare occurrence in a jungle inhabited by very large jaguars and monkeys of all sizes. "Te quiero, Luis," were her last words.

From the other side of the clearing and totally hidden from view by the foliage, Carlos and Octavio were studying the situation. "What do you think they'll do now?" asked the captain.

"I don't know," Carlos replied.

"I know." Now Juan Miranda was talking. "They will split up into two groups. One, led by León, will be heading north to the secondary camp where the ammunition is stored. The second group will be led by Juana who has the responsibility for the hostage. She will head by the hostage holding area and proceed east to a stream located a two-hour walk from here."

"Okay, one thing I know is that we cannot stay right here." Captain Páez continued, "I have to move my cell to be in a position to rescue the hostage." He next spoke into his mike and told his personnel that they were moving south and then east in order to try to intercept Juana's group.

Carlos overheard him and was still studying the situation unfolding in front of him. He said, "Captain, trust me and get your men to follow me. I have a better plan." He had considered the southern route but had noticed how men were also heading in that direction led by Luis. "Tell Colonel Gomez and your lieutenants that a force of men is heading toward them, they are probably looking for María Elena and me."

"What's your plan, Carlos?"

"It's very dark out there, and people are busy forming up. If we walk straight out of here and head through the open area and to the left of the latrine there, they will probably think we are part of Juana's men. Tell your men to keep to the left of Juan and me."

Captain Páez understood immediately that this plan was solid with excellent chances of success. He replied, "Give me thirty seconds to brief my men and go. Juan, you lead the way."

4:00 AM

The helicopters arrived at precisely their prebriefed time. On the hour, they broke radio silence and spoke to Colonel Gomez for the first time that night. They were coming in from the direction of Calamar and were at two hundred feet and hovering at the south end of the soccer field.

Colonel Gomez welcomed them on his secure radio. "Good morning, men, I have a target for you. There are reports of men heading our direction from the main camp. The camp is located one mile northeast of our location. Lieutenant Guevara is heading toward us with a force of ten men. Locate him and watch for any other groups pursuing the lieutenant in your infrared scope. You are cleared hot on any individuals more than halfway here from the main camp. Be aware that friendlies are still in the vicinity of the camp, and you are to refrain from flying in that direction, understood?"

"Yes, sir," was the reply. The two helicopters gunned their engines and flew over Colonel Gomez in the direction of the main camp.

Back in the main camp, Luis had reached the location of Carlos's hut. He was dismayed to find Roberto Suros dead and the Hernandez couple missing. He was thinking what next step to take when he heard helicopter noise in the distance. *Juana,* he thought, *they are coming for the general.*

His next move was a mistake; instead of heading back and either following León to the alternate camp or following his wife to give her added protection, he led his men in the direction of the helicopter noise. Luis kept revolving in his mind the warnings Juana had voiced. *Juana was right, the couple of traitors must have led the helicopters to our camp. I wish I can catch them before they get to the safety of the helicopters. They must be at the soccer field.*

Lieutenant Guevara was speaking to the helicopter pilots. They had reached his retreating troops and were now hovering and searching northwest of that position. "All my troops are safe, and I have the female companion of the American with me. Captain Páez and the remaining troops are near the main camp. If you see any other people heading this way, they are the enemy."

Once again, the reply was "Yes, sir."

While Guevara led his troops back to the field, the attack helicopters started moving forward at slow speed while scanning the area ahead of them with their infrared camera. One pilot was on night vision goggles, safely flying the helicopter forward and maintaining his separation on the other helicopter. The other pilot had removed his goggles and was searching for people with the camera.

The flight leader was the first to find the men in Luis's unit. He calmly positioned his hand on the Gatling gun's pipper that was slewed to the infrared picture and pressed the trigger; the guns came alive. The second helicopter started firing four seconds later.

It was raining bullets. The area where Luis now had his men was covered by foliage, but the cover provided by the trees was not heavy enough to stop the bullets. He had seen two of his men fall and was unable to determine their status because he kept running forward. He was now running at full speed. Rosita, a young lady and a good fighter, was running next to him on the path, and he saw her fall next. Her face had just exploded when a bullet, traveling at supersonic speed, tore through her face. *Can't stop now, they're escaping.*

Luis thought he had made it. He and one of his men were letting the noise of the helicopters fade behind them. That's when one of the M60 machine guns opened up from the side of helicopter number 2. The sergeant manning the gun was on night vision goggles and had a perfect view of the path below him. The .50-caliber bullets from the machine gun tore into Luis's chest and killed him instantly. The other man was luckier; he was hit by a bullet and fell to the ground bleeding from his leg. There were now six dead and five wounded guerrillas.

The helicopter commander saw his duty done and ordered them back to the soccer field to wait for other instructions. It was now four ten in the morning, and the transport helicopters would be on station in ten minutes. Colonel Gomez had made the decision to leave Captain Páez behind and return for him when he called for a pickup. Such was the trust that commander and subordinate had for each other.

4:15 AM

Carlos had led the group of soldiers across the clearing at the camp and was now following Juan on a path that led to the empty hostage internment camp. Juan knew that Juana would follow the evacuation plan precisely and continue to the east of the hostage camp. They were moving quickly, trying to make up for the lost time they forfeited while evading others.

When they arrived at the camp, Captain Páez took over the chase. He told Carlos and Juan to stay in the rear and placed his best tracker as the point man. He guessed they were no more than five minutes behind the escaping guerrillas and that the group would be moving slowly due to the litter that carried the hostage.

The group left in pursuit immediately but was careful not to miss any trip wires the guerillas may have left behind as they escaped. The going was slow and laborious. Carlos and Juan did not have night vision goggles, so they had to stay pretty close to the last man in the line. It would be sunrise before they made contact with Juana's group.

5:00 AM

Aboard the E-2C, the aircraft commander was requesting a status from his crew. They had just established an orbit at twenty thousand feet over the eastern slopes of the Andes Mountains. They were about one hundred miles from the area of interest they had been targeted against.

The fighters were reaching the target area at thirty-five thousand feet. They belonged to VFA-14 out of Naval Air Station Lemoore, California. Their effective combat range was extended tonight by in-flight refueling. The "Tophatters," as they were affectionately called, were trained and ready. Tonight they were carrying five-hundred-pound JDAM precision guided munitions.

The refuelers, S-3 Vikings, were headed back to the *Reagan*. Other tankers had just taken off the carrier to replace them.

The E-2C aircraft commander called the fighters on the secure radio and told them there were no further orders, to hold in place until replaced or told to return to ship.

At CIA headquarters, Shirley Miller was briefing her new boss on the intercepted communications from Colombia. "Sir, the communication has been checked twice for a correct interpretation. The code word 'Barnstormer' was established four years ago to identify an Agency mole in the FARC. He was given a beacon with the code word 'Orion' for use if ever he saw the FARC acquire modern surface-to-air missiles. I can confirm that Orion is turned on and is operational now at coordinates deep in the Colombian jungle. Sir, there are no towns in the vicinity, and the possibility of innocent casualties is minimal.

"So you are suggesting we bomb the area?" General Vazquez asked.

"Yes, sir, that is what our book on standard procedures suggests."

When Shirley left his office, Omar Vazquez started a long chain of events that led all the way up to the president. At 7:00 AM, the president was briefed by his National Security advisor, and at 7:05 AM, he gave permission for the strike. Concurrently the U.S. ambassador was told to call the president of Colombia and request his permission. There was no provision for a last-minute cancellation of the strike if the president of Colombia said no.

7:20 AM

Moncho Rivera, aka León, was briefing his remaining troops on the day's activities. He knew that the government was close behind, so he was planning that for the time being, they were going to pack up his secondary camp and retreat to a safe area.

Unaware of Luis Montes's fate and unsure of Juana Montes's status, he decided to break radio silence and receive a direct update from them. Sunrise had occurred at 6:14 AM, and the day was cloudy above the foliage.

His initial query on the radio went unanswered. Thirty seconds later, he repeated his query and requested both Juana and Luis to report. Juana Montes was the only reply; she proceeded to give him an update of her situation.

Fox 10, the flight lead of the eight-ship fighter formation, called final and hot at fifteen thousand feet and sixty seconds from target. Each aircraft in his formation had received clearance to strike and the exact coordinates of the Orion beacon.

The last thing he had said to his Madhatters formation was "Let's do it, boys."

To which the flight lead of the second four-ship flight, Fox 20, immediately responded, "And girl, boss." Lieutenant Commander Allison Denton reminded her male equal of her status.

Sixty seconds later, Fox 10 let go of his two JDAMs, and in the next two minutes, another fourteen bombs would be released.

On the ground, León was carefully listening on a poor connection of his HF radio as Juana was detailing the status of her troops and the health of her captive.

His conversation was interrupted by a hissing sound that he could not immediately recognize. Seconds later, his quiet was shattered by the loud explosion of two five-hundred-pound bombs. He was not close to the weapons storage area, so the concussion from the bombs only rattled him a second later as he fell prone to the ground.

The bombs had hit exactly on target, and now they were cooking off the weapons stored in the crude armory of the CRAF. After what seemed to be a hundred explosions, Leon was feeling confident that he was going to survive the attack. However, one of the two bombs of Fox 24, the last F/A-18E in the formation, had slight damage to its guiding vanes and fell short by 250 meters. The bomb fell ten feet away from the CRAF commander and, in a split second, incinerated his body. Moncho Rivera was dead.

7:25 AM

Juana's conversation with León was interrupted for unknown reasons. She had rested her group concealed under a light clump of trees and within sight of a medium-sized stream. If León recalled correctly, this was the exact place she should have evacuated the general in case of trouble.

A minute after the conversation was cut, she heard the explosions. *Oh my god,* she thought. *Now what?*

Meanwhile Captain Páez had moved his men into position. The closest his troops were to the guerrillas was five meters; he could not get them any closer without being noticed.

He had posted his two best troops on the other side of the stream to catch in the cross fire any of the rebels that chose to run instead of fighting. Next to him was Carlos now armed with a 9 mm handgun that Páez had given him.

It was eight against nine; however, Páez was not counting on Juan to be a good soldier, so he kept him to the rear and under orders not to move.

Juana had made up her mind. Upstream from them was a small town, and she new that it was a town of sympathizers. She got up and told her men to get ready to go. As the men stood and began to move, the jungle came alive with gunfire. Men began to drop everywhere.

Juana instinctively went down to the floor and headed in the direction of her captive. Pepe was lying in the open about the stream's edge where the medic was caring for him. As she dragged her body closer, her mind was made up. If she was going to die here, the general was also meeting the same fate; she was going to kill him.

As she approached the pair, she noticed how fire was also coming from the other side of the stream; they were surrounded! Next the medic fell; a bullet had pierced his left temple, and he slumped dead immediately. Now she saw a man running upright in her direction; he was coming from her right and had a handgun in his hand.

"Drop your gun, Juana, and live!" Carlos shouted.

Juana did not move; she rested lying prone on her chest with her left hand clutching her Beretta Tomcat .32-caliber handgun. She said, "Esta bien, me rindo."

Upon hearing this, Carlos did not relax his grip but was going to let Juana live if she gave up. He stopped feet short of her position.

As she got up, Juana kept her gun hidden from view; she even kept her balance as a grenade exploded just thirty feet to her left.

With the commotion, Pepe had opened his eyes and gained momentary consciousness when he saw his best friend Carlos and Juana together in front of him. He called out, "Carlos," loud enough for all to hear.

Carlos made a grave mistake; he looked Pepe's way.

Juana immediately moved to uncover her weapon and, with the left hand, opened fire on Carlos. Quickly three bullets entered his chest.

Juana never got to fire the other four bullets in her magazine. By this time, Captain Páez had reached their position and fired at point-blank range into her. Four bullets later, Juana Montes, hero of the guerrilla movement, laid dead.

Now all of the rebels were accounted for, and it was time to call for air support. The captain called Colonel Gomez with the sad news that his friend Carlos Cortes was gravely wounded in the firefight. However, he also had great news; General Ramirez had been rescued alive.

EPILOGUE

Four Days Later,
Wednesday, September 19, 2007

The beds at the Brooks Army Medical Center (BAMC) in San Antonio, Texas, seemed new. The walls and floors were clean, and the personnel were cheerful and helpful at the same time. Ana Luisa Mendoza and her family were caring for their loving husband and father. She had arrived directly with Pepe in a medical evacuation airplane, and their son and daughter had joined them there.

The room was in the intensive care section of the hospital. Even though there was little room available, two unusual objects were displayed. One was a large bowl of yellow roses sent by the president himself. The other was a large poster that sported two large blue stars and the words, "Welcome Back, Major General Ramirez."

Ana Luisa had retold the story of the reunion with Pepe a thousand times. Yet family, friends, and press kept calling, and she kept answering the phone. Although she cheerfully described the improving situation with her husband, there was still tension in the room.

The tension emanated from the intensive care ward next to theirs. There Carlos Cortes, a dear friend of the family, was fighting for his life. Even though Carlos had no military background, the CIA had requested that the embassy transport him back to the States in the general's air ambulance. General Strange had taken care of the rest by requesting from the secretary of defense an exception to policy. Immediately, the request was granted, and Carlos was admitted to BAMC.

Sitting with Carlos in his room were his father, Carlos Manuel, and María Elena. Even though there was a strict "one family member per room" rule in intensive care, the hospital had waved this rule for these two heroes of the day.

Ana Luisa and María Elena seldom left the ICU, but they had to eat. At midday they were walking together to the hospital's cafeteria and updating each other on the status of their loved ones.

When it was María Elena's turn, she immediately started to cry. Not common for such a strong woman, the tears were flowing off her eyes uncontrollably. Ana Luisa noticed and wrapped her hands around her in a tight embrace. She finally said, "Ana, I don't know what I will do if I lose him again. I met him when I was young and adventurous and fell for him. Now, after sixteen years, I have found him again and vowed not to lose him, but it seems that the good Lord in not going to let me keep him. Even worse, I don't know if he is ever going to see his son, Charlie."

"Please, María Elena, be calm, I know how hard it is to lose the one you love. I had my moments of despair when Pepe was kidnapped and taken hostage, but I always kept informed and never thought he would not come back. Every moment, every second, I kept waiting for the front doorbell to ring and expected to see my Pepe in his uniform smiling broadly. I want you to keep your hopes up and think positively. Will you do that for me please?"

Still sobbing, María Elena said, "I . . . can try, Ana. Look at me, I am supposed to be the rock. Aren't we the strong sex?"

"Most of the time we are," replied Ana Luisa. "I have noticed you are not eating much, and Carlos Senior told me you had thrown up. That is not good for you with all the stress of Carlos's injuries. You need to perk up, my dear. Let's go have a good soup. I hear it is chicken tortilla soup today."

At that instant, their calm was shaken by the hospital's public address system. It announced, "María Elena Borbón, please report to intensive care unit immediately."

Friday, July 4, 2008

María Elena was sitting on a bench overlooking the Pacific Ocean. Her head was down, and her posture seemed as that of a person in deep contemplation. That is unless you noticed that her attention was focused on another person.

Lying down below her in a hand-carried crib was a beautiful one-month-old baby girl. She had a pink outfit on that was purchased in Mexico by her aunt, Sonia Cortes. Her name was Carmen Eugenia and was affectionately called "Genie" by all. María Elena checked the baby to see if she was uncomfortable and moved the crib so that the sun would not hit her beautiful blue eyes.

It was the Fourth of July weekend, and the beach was Bellows Beach in Oahu, Hawaii. They were invited to Hawaii by the new vice commander of the Pacific Air Forces, Lieutenant General Jose Luis Ramirez and his wife, Ana.

A cool breeze was blowing, and the sun was still fairly high in the sky. She was planning in her head a feast in celebration that night of paella and sangria. Not necessarily Fourth of July fare, but Ana Luisa had encouraged the idea since the paella sounded a lot better than hamburgers and hot dogs.

She had volunteered to cook early tonight and complete dinner before the fireworks started. The baby stirred and made a slow move to her side. "*Calma, niña,* you are like your father, very impatient." She wondered aloud, "Twice I spent wonderful moments with your father and twice I got pregnant. And I confess, my dear, both times were the most wonderful times of my life."

She looked up and saw in the distance three men jogging toward her. They were unmistakable, one was young and over six feet tall, and the other two were middle-aged but still very athletic-looking. The two older men, one tall and one short, were the best of friends.

As they approached her bench, they started sprinting, and the young man easily beat them to her side. When he arrived, Charlie

Cortes said, "Look, Mamá, these two old men cannot keep up with me."

She nervously fingered her wedding ring in her left hand and said, "That your father and Pepe are here at all is a miracle, son. Enjoy his company while you can since you are soon to be a man and will move away, marry, and succeed in life."

Carlos and Pepe arrived next. Carlos looked fit, and only the three scars in his chest reminded all of the long six months of intensive care he had received. "How's my little princess," Carlos said as he sat down next to María Elena.

She did not answer but grabbed him and kissed him passionately in front of all.

The End